GAME CHANGER

LAS VEGAS VIPERS BOOK ONE

STACEY LYNN

Game Changer

Las Vegas Vipers Series

Book One

Stacey Lynn

Content Editing: My Brother's Editor

Proofreading: Virginia Tesi Carey

Cover Design: Shanoff Designs

1

LIZZIE

"**Y**ou need to call him."

I closed Instagram, my new obsession when it came to Garrett Dubiak, goalie for the Las Vegas Vipers, also one of my best friends, and dropped my head back. My mom stood behind the couch in her living room, giving me a soft smile full of pity and sadness and worry.

"I know I do." I reopened the app and showed my mom the picture. "I'm just scared. He looks happy."

My chest burned, and it had nothing to do with my recent bout of heartburn that came and went with no rhyme or reason and on a sporadic timeline. My mom's hand curled around my shoulder. I lifted my other hand off my stomach and placed it over hers. She was warm, kind and tender, and she loved me more than anything.

"Maybe he is. But he still has a right to know. You know that."

Three months ago, Garrett and I met up in North Carolina for our friend's baby christening a few days before Christmas. We hadn't spoken for a year, due to a massive miscommunication on both our parts. We spent one night together. One night where I was sure we were *finally* on the same page and then Garrett dropped the news in my lap that he'd been traded from Chicago to Las Vegas where he was now the starting goalie for the leading team in professional hockey.

The next morning, uncertain of where we'd go from there, I'd left before the emotional goodbye we'd have, the arguments, and I asked for some time to figure things out.

Twenty-four hours later, I came down with a nasty sinus infection that required antibiotics, which must have affected my pills because I was now pregnant—

With Garrett's baby. My best friend. My lover. The only man I'd ever loved.

He'd called. At first, I was too sick to talk. Then I was too fearful he'd want answers to questions I didn't have.

Start a long-distance relationship? Give away everything I'd ever known for a chance with him in Las Vegas?

I was born and bred in Chicago. Outside of my three years in graduate school at Oxford University in England, I'd never lived anywhere else and never wanted to. My family was here. I loved my life here, the career I'd built, the success I had and all my friends and family and knowing Chicago better than I knew the back of my own hand. Could I walk away from all of that for him?

As soon as I found out I was pregnant, I had my answer.

Yes. Yes, I absolutely could.

And then I saw him on Instagram.

Nadia Belchinova.

Russian. Long legged, big boobed, and with striking features, I'd been about ready to book my ticket to Vegas and tell him everything, tell him I wanted this baby and I wanted it with him when the first picture of the two of them popped up on his Instagram feed. The first non-professional marketing photo he'd posted in over three years.

That was six weeks ago. Since then, I'd become obsessed with not only following his hockey career, but the pictures online of both of them, individually and together. She was the sister to a teammate, his back-up goalie. The comments of pictures they posted were filled with congratulations from teammates, old and current, along with fire flame emojis and others that made me want to throw my phone across the room.

I'd left him, hadn't been brave enough to talk to him. Had I waited too long? Had I lost him? The unknown kept me from reaching out to him, even though my mom was right.

Garrett had a right to know.

"What if he loves her?" I asked, brushing my thumb over his face, thick beard he always grew once it came close to playoff season, and stared into his rich blue eyes. He was the best man I'd ever met, and I knew he not only wanted to have children, but how badly he wanted to be a dad.

"He might," my mom said, squeezing my shoulder. "But he loved you at one time, too. You know the right thing to do with this. And I caution you, the longer you continue to put it off, the harder it's going to be. On both of you."

"I know." I forced myself to close down Instagram and pulled up my text string with my best friend Katie.

She'd been my roommate in college and now married to Jude Taylor. I'd met Garrett back in college the same night Katie met Jude. Now, Jude played down in North Carolina for the Carolina Ice Kings hockey team. Katie and Jude were now married, the reason Garrett and I went to North Carolina in December, and it was Katie's text that made my chest squeeze.

They're at the Lantham Hotel. Please, go fix whatever you broke. And then someday, tell me why it's taken you so long?

Outside my parents, I hadn't told anyone I was pregnant except my boss. Shawna knew but that was because she saw the ginger ale I started drinking and suspected. I couldn't tell Katie. I couldn't ask her to keep it from her husband, who was Garrett's best friend. I couldn't ask her to lie to her husband or to Garrett.

Because this time, our brokenness didn't come from a miscommunication. It was totally one hundred percent my fault, and I had no idea how to fix anything. I knew what Garrett wanted that night, but we were drunk, and while it was a lousy excuse, I'd replayed that night in my mind a hundred times. Would I still have slept with him, knowing it'd probably be the last time?

It was too late for shoulda-woulda-coulda's. The baby in my stomach who started making his or her appearance known with morning sickness that lasted for half the day made that obvious.

Now, I needed to pick myself up by the bootstraps and do the most terrifying thing in the world.

Tell Garrett Dubiak I loved him. That I was having his baby. And I wanted to be a family.

THE LAS VEGAS Vipers were in Chicago for a three-game series. They'd already won the first, and I watched them win the second two doors down from the Lantham Hotel at a bar, sipping ginger ale and slowly eating a steak dinner with asparagus and a baked potato. I was slowly coming out of the phase where everything made me want to puke.

What I could manage to eat stayed down, but my diet had massively changed. I should thank the baby bean for making me healthy. Gone were my days of fried foods, onion rings, french fries, and chicken—in any form—in mass quantities. Now, I craved red meat and vegetables. For the first time in my life, I not only willingly ate broccoli, but thought it tasted like the best food in God's creation.

I'd been to enough of Garrett's games over the years to know the drill. They'd head back to the locker room, shower and change, and have a quick post-game wrap-up depending on how they played.

Then they'd hop on the bus. The hotel was five miles from the arena where they played which meant it could be either a ten-minute drive or forty-two. Chicago traffic was finicky like that.

Fortunately, based on my traffic app, traffic was moving relatively quick, so after I waited long enough, I paid my bill and slid off my stool.

It was nearing late March, which meant Chicagoans were equally prepared for the quick burst of spring during the days along with the lingering, blustery chill of winter. It'd snowed last weekend and for the last few days, the weather had been warm enough to melt the snow, but now there was slush, grayed from the roads and the curbs and mixed with the salt and sand mixture the plows used. I trudged over the wet and freezing sidewalks carefully to not slip in my black boots.

When I imagined seeing Garrett again, I'd hoped I could *wow* him with a slinky black dress. Hell, maybe the heels he'd so carefully stripped off my legs the last time we saw each other. Instead, I was dressed in Ugg boots, a knee-length North Face fluffy coat. My scarf was wrapped around my throat and all of it still barely stopped the chill from the lake effect wind.

Nerves assailed me as I stepped into the lobby of the hotel. It was gorgeous, modern, and one of the nicest hotels in Chicago. I'd been there before for work conferences, the occasional after work drink or dinner meeting when other managing financial advisers came from out of town.

Tonight, I barely took in the elegance of the lobby as I tore off my mittens and stuffed them into my coat pockets. I scooted around tourists and men and women dressed like they were preparing for a late night, black-tie event until I reached the hotel's lobby restaurant.

Lit only by chandeliers and tabletop candles, the room cast a soothing and sensual glow over its modern, straight-lined furniture. I moved to one of the booths there, stripping out of my coat and tucking it next to me on the bench. Once settled, I pulled out my phone.

I'd debated whether to have the front desk call up to his room, but there was always the chance they'd refuse, or wouldn't admit the team was staying there. The benefit would be if he chose not to come talk to me, I wouldn't have to hear the rejection.

Pull on your big girl panties and just do it.

Before I could talk myself out of it and catch the El back to my condo a few miles away, I pulled up his contact. With a trembling finger, I tapped his name and brought the phone to my ear.

The steak I ate earlier threatened to revolt as I waited for the phone to connect, or for him to ignore it.

It rang three times and I whispered a *"thank you"* to the server who delivered a glass of water and menu in front of me.

And then Garrett's voice, rich and low as always,

rumbled through the phone. "I didn't expect to hear from you."

As far as hellos went, it wasn't great. "It's been a while. Good game tonight."

"You watched?"

I tapped my fingers on the table. This was awkward and Garrett and I were never awkward. "You're playing great. Vegas is lucky to have you."

"Yeah." He cleared his throat and pain slashed my chest in a breath. "That's what your note said. Listen, Lizzie... I'm not sure why you're calling, but I don't know if it's smart."

"I'm downstairs." I powered through tears and the rattling in my chest. I'd expected distance. I hadn't expected the space between us through a phone call to feel like we were on opposite sides of Lake Michigan. "I'd like to see you. To talk."

Seconds passed. Long enough I imagined him scraping his fingers with his beard. Run a hand through his hair. He might be pacing. It was long enough I could take a long drink of my ice-cold water.

"You're a pain in my ass, you know that?" He said it with a chuckle. My nerves released like a valve, making it easier to breathe.

He'd said the same words to me last time I saw him. He'd gotten a seat next to me in first class for our flight to North Carolina. I not only hated flying but usually ending up throwing up while I did it, so even though we hadn't spoken in over a year, I was focused on trying not to lose my mimosas all over his lap. Even then, pissed at me, he'd helped me.

"I know. Please?"

"Give me ten. We just checked in."

"Thank you." My voice wobbled and I hung up before he could tell.

Now, I had to wait.

Ten more minutes until I threw Garrett's life into a tailspin.

2

GARRETT

I didn't need ten minutes. I'd already spent the last twenty pacing our small hotel room that my teammate, André, was threatening to kick me out of the room. Pacing because I'd had my phone in my hand, debating whether or not I was going to call Lizzie.

Three months ago, after one crazy weekend and one incredible, unforgettable night, she asked me for space in a note, sneaking out before I woke up and catching a different flight back to Chicago. Since what I'd asked for was a lot, and I knew she needed time, I waited a few days to reach out. By then it was the day after Christmas and I was moved into my new home in Las Vegas.

She never called back. Never answered a text I sent.

A guy could only take so much rejection before he moved on. I hadn't expected the brutal silence from Lizzie, not with how we'd left things, not with the night we spent together, but I'd told myself maybe she'd made the right choice. If she wasn't going to give us a shot at being together the way I knew we both wanted, perhaps a clean break was better than small slices over a handful of years.

A pillow flew through the air and smacked me in the face. "Get the hell out of here and go see her."

I grabbed it before it could fall and tossed it back toward André, our backup goalie and all-around decent guy. He was on the bed, back against the headboard, feet crossed at the ankles, scrolling through TikTok on his phone. Probably trying to find the most inappropriate TikTok to send to the team at three in the morning because he was an asshole like that.

"I don't know what to say to her."

He gave me two arched brows in response, followed by an eye roll. "You could start with letting her know there's nothing going on with you and my sister in case she's seen the pictures. Then you could throw yourself on your knees and beg her for one more chance. Or better yet, be a caveman and throw her over your shoulder and haul her ass back up here." He pointed a finger at me. "Warning, if that's your decision, I can't guarantee I'm leaving."

"Fuck off," I muttered. Suddenly, I was a thirteen-year-old with zits and their first crush at an eighth-grade dance terrified to go get the girl I wanted. Not that I was speaking from personal experience on that one.

Lizzie had the power to shred my heart into useless pieces and she hadn't exactly sounded *happy* when she called.

"Fine. But if I crawl into your bed and cry on your shoulder and need lots of cuddles, you can't say you weren't warned."

"Call Nadia for the cuddles."

"Asshole."

André was the only one on the team who knew there was nothing going on between us. Nadia needed help getting a jealous, clueless ex-boyfriend out of her life. I needed someone to accompany me to my first fundraising event in Vegas. I didn't want to go alone or be the third wheel with all my new teammates and their wives or girl-friends. André told me to take her. She and I got to talking. I told her straight-up we'd only ever be friends, mostly because I was in love with Lizzie, but I'd told her I'd help her out if she needed it. Nadia agreed, hoping it'd reinforce what she was trying to get across to Toby—they were over.

So far, it hadn't worked.

"I'll be back." I grabbed our room key and slid both it and my phone into my pocket. "Don't forget I warned you about the cuddles."

The door slammed shut behind me. On the way down-stairs, I was a mess. Lizzie could be here for a multitude of reasons. Only one would be what I wanted, for her to come to me, say she'd had the space she needed and wanted to try something.

But even then... it'd been three months and not a single call or text. I was already torn between wanting to give her everything she wanted and anger she'd screwed up our friendship. We'd never been so complicated, but that didn't mean her silence didn't gut me.

In the elevator, I checked my outfit. I'd thrown on jeans and a flannel shirt in case I'd gathered the balls to call her first and she was willing to see me. Now, I looked like a lumberjack, and I undid the buttons at the wrists. Rolled them to my elbows. Unrolled them. Rerolled them.

Lizzie sent me into a tailspin every time we were together.

Settling on the rolled up to just beneath my elbows look, I swiped my palms down my beard. It was currently a dark, puffy mess and itched like hell. I grew it out every year during the end of the season but shaving it as soon as playoffs were over was the best sensation. I scratched at my neck as the doors opened and stepped into the lobby. I'd had enough nerves returning to Chicago to face my old team that I'd spent all week trying to concentrate on playing well against them and not on the woman who drove me crazy.

But now all I had were thoughts of Lizzie. Memories. Desires. By the time I reached the hotel's restaurant and bar, I was an equal mixture of so damn happy to see her I could kiss her and so damn pissed at her I wanted to throttle her.

Which, in all honesty, were typical reactions I had when it came to her.

I finally spied her, her blonde hair poking out over one of the booths. I'd know her anywhere, even in the smallest glimpse. It helped the bar was mostly filled with couples dressed to the nines in sparkling cocktail dresses and bespoke suits.

I took a moment to settle myself.

What in the hell did I want from this meeting? Were we any closer to being on the same page? Or were we still reading two different books?

SHE WAS as gorgeous as ever. Her blonde hair was wavy, hung down past her breasts and her eyes, such a pale but still vivid amber that made me thirsty—and not because they were the color of my favorite whiskey—blinked up at me as I reached the table.

Like every time I first saw her, she stole my breath and shot a jolt of heat straight to my dick. I rocked back on my heels, hands shoved into my jeans pockets to stop from reaching for her.

"Hey."

She blinked, and for a moment I saw a glimpse of fear. My stomach churned before she wiped it away. "Hey. It's good to see you?"

Was it? Because she didn't sound so certain herself.

I didn't ask. That she didn't stand and hug me didn't bode well for what was about to happen.

She rubbed her hands together before gesturing to the other side of the table. "Sit. Please?"

I did, sliding to the center of the booth and dropped my phone on the table.

"You look good, Lizzie," I said. "How are you?"

"Good." She nodded and took a drink from a glass that looked like beer, but Lizzie didn't drink beer. She ignored the water sitting next to it. If there was a drink option on the table, she'd go for anything other than a beer. "I'm good. Work is good. Busy as always and you know... I'm good."

The nerves I'd felt in the elevator spiked. Lizzie didn't ramble, at least, never with me before. I sat back in the booth and draped an arm over the back, tried to get comfortable, but that was impossible. Being around Lizzie turned me into a live wire. One wrong touch and my body could explode.

"You're playing well. I watched your game tonight. How was it? Playing against Chicago?"

It was tough. Mentally and physically. The Storm knew me better than anyone and knew how I moved. I hadn't been able to relax a single second of the games we'd played, but that wasn't why Lizzie called me and just like I couldn't relax playing my former team, I couldn't relax with her.

A server strolled up, a young guy with short, cropped black hair. "Can I get you something to drink?"

"I'll have what she's having." I pointed to her beverage

and watched as she bit her bottom lip. "Looks good. What is it?"

"Um." She rolled her lips together. "Ginger ale."

A faint pink rose on the apples of her cheeks, and she glanced at the waiter. Ginger ale? Fuck that.

Yeah...no. This conversation was going to need more than a soda that tasted like piss.

"Strike that," I told him. "I'll take a lager. Anything light you have on tap." The tension at the table made me wish I could have something stronger, but we weren't supposed to be drinking on away games.

"Will do."

"Thanks."

As soon as he walked away, a heavy silence fell between us. I could have gone first. Could have pushed more. I could have thrown myself on my sword once again, but this was Lizzie's show. I knew her well enough to know that while she sat across from me, nervously rubbing her hands together and tucking hair behind her ears, fiddling with her gold hoop earrings, she'd been practicing some speech of hers long before she called me.

Hell, she'd already been downstairs when she made that call.

So yeah, she was the one who left with a note and didn't return my calls. I could feign contentment while I waited. She took another sip of her ginger ale, and for someone who hated carbonated soda, that alone piqued my curiosity.

She set the glass down, ran her pale pink painted fingertip down the edge, dredging up condensation, and brushed it on the napkin.

Her head tilted to one side and she worried her bottom lip between her teeth. "Are you happy?" A faint pink hue stained her cheeks, and I sat up straighter in the booth. "You know... with..." She paused and cleared her throat. "With Vegas?"

Holy hot damn.

She wasn't asking about the team.

She'd seen the pictures.

If she wanted to know about Nadia, she'd have to ask. She hadn't made things easy for me for years, and while I didn't enjoy being a dick to her, I needed more than this. I needed to know her intent before I opened myself up.

The server returned, slid a circle coaster onto the table and set my beer on top. "Thanks," I told him, and brought it to my mouth.

"I can't complain about Vegas, but I haven't lived through a summer there, either. Winter's nice, though. But that's not why you called and we both know it. Talk to me." When she didn't immediately start, I leaned in. "Why are you here?"

She puffed out a breath through her full, gorgeous pink painted lips, and I steeled myself for whatever she was about to say. A vise gripped my chest and squeezed painfully around my ribs.

"I'm sorry I didn't call when I got home. And I'm sorry I left the way I did. I didn't want... I didn't want the goodbye we would have had that morning to be harder than necessary." She stalled, and I swore I saw a lump in her throat as she struggled for words. The part of me that loved her wanted to leap across the table and hold her, slide my hand through her hair the way she loved and promise her she could tell me anything. The part of me that was so damn hurt by her kept my ass in the booth. "I got sick when I got home. I couldn't talk for days and then... well, I'm sorry."

She blinked at me. Long blonde lashes fluttered across her cheeks and her eyes dimmed. "I'm so sorry for all of it. I knew we needed to talk, but some things happened after I got better and I needed time."

She'd been sick. It explained the first few days like she said. But it'd been months now. "You could have told me that. Or texted me instead of ghosting me."

"I know." She paused to lick her lips, took another sip of her ginger ale. So help me God. If she used that damn soda as a way to procrastinate for another single second, it'd end up smashed all over the carpet. Screw the cleaning bill. "But that's why I'm here. To apologize and explain."

Her hesitation made my pulse kick up. In all the years I'd known Lizzie, I'd never seen her so damn uncertain. "What do you want then? From me? With this visit? Just give it to me straight, Lizzie, because you're killing me here."

She opened her mouth and as she did, my phone lit up, vibrated on the table and she glanced at it. Her cheeks turned white before I looked down. *Fuck.* Nadia's name flashed on the screen as it continued to ring.

I declined the call and blacked my screen. No doubt she wanted to confirm an event we were supposed to attend together next week, and she wanted to remind me to wear my tux. It was pretty much the only conversations we had.

But that wasn't what Lizzie thought, and it was clear in the pain lancing across her face, followed by sadness as she rolled her lips together.

"Don't," I all but growled from across the table. "You don't get to be pissed about this. *You* left *me.*"

"I know." She squeezed her eyes closed and when she opened them, tears swam in her eyes. It *fucking killed me* to stay cemented in my seat. "I know all that, which was why I didn't call you earlier. I want you to be happy, and if it's with her... I'm glad for you."

She didn't mean a single damn word of it. Not based on

the way she blinked back more tears and gripped her ginger ale so hard her knuckles turned white.

Fuck this. Screw Lizzie, whose damn presence could make me want to throw away everything I'd ever worked for and goddamn, I was so pissed she could still baffle me. I needed her to fight for me. For us, and if she couldn't... I needed to figure out a way to move on from her.

It wouldn't be with Nadia, but I needed the woman I loved to show me something that would keep me there.

"Nothing's changed, has it?" My chest burned and my blood sizzled in my veins. Lizzie sat across from me looking like I threw a puppy into oncoming traffic and she still said nothing. "Nothing's changed," I repeated, disgusted I'd hoped, considered this would go different. Thank God I didn't throw myself on my sword and beg her to give us a chance.

How big of a fool would I be?

I stood, grabbing cash from my money clip in my pocket. "I can't do this. Not with you. Not anymore."

I yanked them out. They waved in the air right as Lizzie's chin lifted and her teary, gorgeous, and sad eyes met mine.

"I'm pregnant."

My knees locked. Vaguely, I saw the cash in my hand wafting in the air because I'd frozen as her words rushed through with the force of a thunderstorm.

Her eyes grew as that storm built in my gut, spread through my limbs and rolled to my ears. The entire room tilted and I slapped the cash in my hand down on the table so hard it rattled, my palm flattening. "What?"

She nodded and sounds of the room flooded my system until it was overloaded with the cacophony of chatter and glasses clinking and laughter and forks scraping on plates. I scanned the room, looked to see if anyone else had noticed the fucking rug that had just been pulled out from beneath my feet.

"What'd you say?" I asked and fell to the edge of the bench. There was no way she'd said that.

There was no way she'd *keep* this from me. Not for this long.

"We didn't use a condom that night. I got sick right after, went on antibiotics... birth control must not have worked..."

Holy hot damn shit. She was fucking serious.

"You're having my baby?"

3

LIZZIE

Our table jolted from the force of his collapse into the booth across from me.

I hadn't expected a parade or shouts and whoops of joy. In truth, I'd played this scenario in my head on an endless loop for the last six weeks since I took my first test.

In any of those scenarios, I'd never considered Garrett would stare at me like I'd grown three heads. Or worse, stare at me like he'd never seen me before in his life. Which was exactly how he was gaping at me.

"Yeah," I finally said and damn, it'd grown hot in here. Sweat lined my brow and I brushed my hand over my chest. The intensity of his stare made my nerves spike. I couldn't tell if he was looking like he wanted to throttle me or throw me over his shoulder and whisk me away to his room. "I'm sorry. I didn't mean for it to happen. And I just... I needed time to wrap my head around everything, and I haven't been feeling well."

"Ginger ale," he rasped, his gaze dropping to my glass. "I should have fucking known."

He swallowed and grabbed his beer, draining the rest in one large gulp. My skin itched, too damn tight for the bones it covered on my body. Never, in the history of our friendship, whether we were having sex or not, had a conversation been so difficult, had he felt so far away from me.

"I'm sorry," I said, licking my lips and willing more tears back. Crying wouldn't solve anything.

"Just give me a minute." He leaned to the side and lifted his empty glass, probably trying to get the server's attention, and once he had it, he slipped back into the booth and dropped his forehead into his hand. It trembled as he shoved it through his hair and down the jawline of his beard.

My fingertips burned with nerves and fear. I'd never felt so helpless when it came to us, but helpless had become normal in the last few months. Sure, I could be a single mom. I had the money and a family support system where I could do this on my own. But that wasn't what I wanted, and it wouldn't be what Garrett wanted.

He'd lost his dad when he was little. From everything he told me about his dad prior to his death during a military training mission, he'd been an incredible man, and Garrett wanted a family. Wanted the wife and kids he could love the way he'd been loved.

"I don't know what else to say, except I'm sorry." I croaked it out and our server appeared. He brought another drink for both of us and I grabbed it, thankful for something to soothe the shards of glass lining my throat.

But I also had to be careful. The ginger ale helped my nausea but too much ruined it.

"When are you due?" he finally asked, collapsing back into his seat. His hands fell to his lap and all the color had left his face. His eyes were wide, glassy, almost as if he'd heard the worst news in his entire life.

"September fourteenth."

"Off season." He nodded and reached for his beer. "Good. That's good."

"Is it?" Because while I hadn't expected a parade, I hadn't expected him to appear deadened or sound so cold.

"Fucking hell," he groaned. "You've had what... weeks to process this? Can't I have five minutes?"

"Of course." *Of course* he could. Now that I'd told him, I wanted us to figure out a plan. I had several of them. I had questions. I needed to know what he wanted, how involved he wanted to be. I'd had time to think through all the scenarios.

He'd had sixty seconds.

I waited while he took another sip of his drink and scrubbed his hands down his cheeks, blowing out a breath so hard his chest heaved with it.

He was so damn handsome. Probably not something I should have been thinking about, but I could barely take my eyes off him. He'd worn a simple black and red flannel shirt and jeans, but that shirt molded to the curves of his chest and his broad shoulders like it'd been painted on him.

He stared at the wall next to us like it was the Sistine Chapel, and he wanted to memorize every beautiful stroke before he faced me again.

"I don't... I don't even know what to say or ask right now." He huffed a laugh, but it was cold, full of nerves and he ran his hand through his mop of thick hair again before taking his beer into his hand. He gestured to the ginger ale in front of me with a dip of his chin. "The soda. You said you haven't been feeling well?"

"Yeah." I cleared my throat. My palms were clammy and

cold despite everything else in me feeling like it was about to explode. I hadn't expected it to be this hard. "All day. Not so much now, but I've found things that help, I guess."

"How long have you known?"

Garrett had a wicked switch when it came to his anger. Almost always totally laidback, that trigger could be flipped with no warning when someone he cared about had been hurt or mistreated. I'd seen it happen, with men who wouldn't leave me alone in a club, an ill-timed grab of my ass as I walked by. Never, in the years we'd known each other, had I saw the beginning of that anger directed at me.

Now, his jaw twitched and veins appeared on his forearms as he curled his hands into fists. "How long have you known?"

"Six weeks," I rasped. "I was sick almost as soon as I got off the plane after..."

"North Carolina. When you snuck out on me."

Damn it. Tears blurred. An arrow to my heart couldn't have hurt worse than the accusation. He had every right to be mad at me. Every right to be upset and his body practically vibrated with that anger. And worse, there was disappointment in his eyes as he looked at me.

"Yeah." I cleared my throat. "I was sick for two weeks, the first round of antibiotics didn't work, so I needed to go back and then I figured I didn't have my period from all the stress of that."

I wasn't embarrassed to talk about the female body or cycle. My mom had raised me to be empowered and confident and she'd always shared everything openly and honestly. But I couldn't remember a time when Garrett and I had talked about periods. He gave a slight flinch when I said it, which made nerves that had turned down to a simmer rush back to the surface.

If we couldn't talk about this...

"Anyway. I just figured it'd happen. But then I started getting sick again and was so tired."

"And you didn't call. As soon as you knew, you didn't tell me."

I shrugged. Lame. I knew it. But what was I supposed to say? I'd been scared. Sad. Horrified we were the ages we were and this had still happened. In between bouts of puking almost all day long for a week while I tried to figure out a way to cope, I'd cried so hard my stomach hurt, and it'd taken every ounce of courage to call my parents and tell them.

They loved Garrett. Always had. They loved him still, but they did *not* love hearing we'd shacked up for a night and he'd knocked me up.

Worse, they didn't love I didn't call him right away either.

"I needed time," I admitted. To figure things out. Figure out what I was going to do. Figure out what came next.

And I'd thought I'd done it. I was online preparing to book a flight out to Vegas when that first picture of him and Nadia popped up.

As if I summoned her, his phone lit up again with a phone call, her name bright white, a beacon highlighting my mistakes and regret and I couldn't stop the flinch of pain seeing her name caused.

He grabbed his phone, fisted it, blacking out her name and declining the call, and glared at me.

"I don't know what else you want me to say." My chin wobbled.

Six weeks ago, I could have gone to him and things would have been different.

Now? He was with someone. "I'm sorry," I said again.

"Yeah. So am I." His voice was guttural, cutting me to the core as he shoved out of the booth. He threw down another twenty to add to the cash already on the table and barely glanced at me. "You've had time to process this. I'm asking you to give me that. I can't... I can't sit across from you and think straight. Not right now."

I understood. I totally understood. It didn't stop his words from slicing my heart open and causing me more pain than I'd ever felt.

I bit my tongue to try to stop the tears.

"I'll call you," he finally said. His dark eyes scanned my face and if he saw the pain in my own, if he cared, he didn't show it. "This time, answer it."

Garrett Dubiak, the only man I loved, the father of the baby I was carrying, spun on his heels and walked away from me after looking at me like I was a stranger.

And I was pretty sure he took my heart with him.

4

GARRETT

The game played in front of me. Ice dust flew in the air, skates stopped on a dime. My eyes tracked the puck through the cage of my helmet, but all of it was a blurry whir. I was distracted. Moving slow.

Hell, I was playing so damn poorly, the center for the Chicago Storm, and my old teammate, had paused for a second and asked if I was okay.

It was *that* obvious, and if he could see, my current team could tell too. Based on the clenched jaw of our coach's face every time he glanced my way, he definitely wasn't happy.

How could I be expected to focus?

I'm pregnant pregnant pregnant repeated through my mind. Every swish of the skates danced to the tune bouncing around in my brain.

Pregnant

Pregnant

Pregnant

I was going to be a dad. A father.

By a woman who lived two time zones away from me.

How in the *hell* was I going to be able to be the kind of man and Dad I wanted to be?

Fuck.

The buzzer sounded, signifying the end of the second period, and I skated off the ice as fast as I could in all my gear.

I threw my helmet into the locker in the visiting room. Down the hall was Chicago's locker room. There'd be leather couches, the logo on the middle of the floor. The lockers would be gleaming, filled with the stench of my former teammates' body odor I could recognize them by on scent alone. They'd been my brothers. And if I needed anyone now, it was them.

Not that I didn't like the Vegas guys, but three months didn't compare to seven years.

"What are you going to do?" André asked, taking the seat next to me.

I squeezed my eyes closed and rubbed them until dots speckled my vision. "Not talk about it now."

"Then figure out a way to push through this, G. We need you out there."

Fuck. For a moment, I considered telling Coach to put him in. We were up by one, but I'd only been lucky to save a few shots on me during the first period because my defense kicked serious ass. Dominick Masters and Max Mikolajczyk were behemoths on the ice. And our third line was beastly.

One goal had been called back for interference when the center for Chicago skated into the crease and bumped into me. That was when he'd asked if I was okay. I hadn't even noticed him there and usually I'd shove them right back out.

"I know. I will, it's just, fuck, I can't stop thinking about it."

I got back to the room last night, and because André was

a smartass, he'd opened his arms and asked if I needed those cuddles. I'd surprised the hell out of myself when I'd fallen into them for the most epic man hug in history. I wasn't even embarrassed about it. I needed that connection. The feeling I wasn't alone when I felt like I was living in a swamp.

She was *pregnant*. And she'd waited so damn long to tell me? And in that time, she'd still avoided a couple phone calls. I understood to an extent. Her world had been shaken up, but instead of leaning on me, the guy who'd always been there for her, she'd pushed me away.

Hadn't she known I would have jumped my ass on a plane, games be damned, to be there for her in a heartbeat? What did that mean for our future and her ability to trust me?

On top of the bomb she dropped in my lap, I'd had to call Nadia back.

That conversation was about as fun as poking a beehive with a large stick.

"Oh…. Oh…. *Does this change things? With us?*"

I'd blinked. Because she'd sounded so pained and I was damn tired of that sound coming out of the mouths of women in my life. And *us*? When in the hell had she thought that? When I opened my mouth to tell her, she'd laughed an awkward laugh with her Russian accent. Told me she didn't mean it like that. That we'd see each other for the fundraiser event next week and that'd be that.

"At least it worked out for one of us, yes?"

Yeah. Not really. Not since I had no idea how I was going to do this.

"Dubiak. You good?" Coach Vik stood in front of me, and hell, I hadn't even seen him approach. "Something shaken you? Being around your old team?"

"Nah. It's not that." I leaned back in my chair and grabbed my helmet from the floor where it landed earlier. "I'm good. Just a rocky start."

He assessed me with a glare, slid his gaze to André, who clapped his hand on my shoulder. Without him, I would have had a complete meltdown last night. He was a quiet guy and wouldn't tell anyone what was going on. Some of the guys, most of the younger ones gossiped worse than I'd ever heard my sister and her friends. André was always on the outskirts of it, listening, maybe chuckling, but he didn't spill tea unless he was drinking it. "He is good, Coach. I will whip him into shape."

I rolled my shoulder, throwing off his hand. "Dumbass."

"Good. You know this team better than anyone, so I won't sit here and tell you what they're doing. Just keep stopping them, hear me?"

"Yeah." I held out my gloved hand, and he punched it. "I got it. No worries."

He walked away and I stood. The need to move and maybe punch something making me restless. I had to see Lizzie.

We had to figure this out. And there was no way it was going to be over a phone call, video or otherwise.

"Hey Coach?" I lumbered after him, like an elephant on skates in all my gear. "Actually, can we talk?"

His thick gray brows furrowed together and the harsh lights of the locker room bounced off his bald head, making it shine like a bowling ball. "What is it?"

"We've got a few days off after this once we get home, yeah?"

"Why?" He crossed his arms over his chest. Coach Vik was a great coach. He'd actually played for the Rangers years ago, back with my buddies Joey and Jude Taylor's dad.

He loved this team, I swore, more than he might have loved his own daughters. His wife had certainly thought so, which was why she left him a few years back. "Need to hang with old friends?"

"No." Not in the way he was thinking, anyway. "But I do have a personal issue I need to deal with. Any chance I can talk to the team travel planner and fly back Saturday instead of tonight?"

It was an unusual request. The team had to fly together. Always. No exceptions. Hopefully his need for me as a goalie getting ready to head into playoffs would allow an exception.

"Personal issues?"

I didn't want to tell him. He was not a hearts and flowers kind of guy. Hell, I wasn't always so sure he had a heart. I'd tell the team eventually, at some point it'd come out, anyway. Shit always did. But not until I knew more. Had a plan. Could talk to Lizzie without wanting to yell at her.

"Yeah." I shrugged, the move not visible due to the bulk of all my padding. "Saturday. I can be back then."

His eyes narrowed and his arms uncrossed and his hands settled at his hips. With a single nod, he dipped his chin. "Be back for Sunday skate or you're benched for a week."

Relief pulsed through me. "Thank you, Coach. I appreciate it."

"Just go win us the game, Dubiak. That's all I give a shit about." He took off to talk to the defense and power play coach, leaving me staring at my skates, anticipation thrumming its way up my spine.

That'd give us all of Friday and Saturday. Tonight, if she answered when I called. It still only gave me forty-eight hours. It'd have to be enough. I wasn't leaving Chicago without seeing her, without us figuring out what we were going to do.

She was having my child, and I wasn't going to miss a single damn second of it.

IT WAS late by the time I got to Lizzie's condo. When the team left from the arena straight to the airport, our travel coordinator had already rescheduled my plans. A ride to a hotel three blocks from where Lizzie lived, and a plane ticket back on Saturday afternoon. I didn't go to the hotel, though. I requested the driver to take me to Lizzie's building, a high-rise off the Miracle Mile on Michigan Avenue where she had a view of the lake and Millennial Park. Part of her money came from her parents, or should I say her grandparents who had made a boatload of money decades ago, investing in commercial real estate. Despite growing up financially secure and having her trust fund, Lizzie's success came from her own hard work ethic, drive, and confidence. Three of the sexiest characteristics I didn't know I loved until I'd met her back in college.

I slipped out of the town car and walked into her lobby. The doorman opened the door for me, dressed in a red suit coat with gold filigree at his shoulders and black dress pants. Inside was as opulent as I remembered. She'd bought it after she returned from Oxford with her MBA, using a small amount of her trust fund from her grandparents as the down payment.

Back then, I'd been three years into playing for the Chicago Storm, just getting over the excitement of puck bunnies. The reality of making it to the pro level was wearing off and hockey was, for the first time in my life, becoming a job. The best job in the world, but the haze of the newness of traveling and partying and girls throwing themselves at me was wearing off.

Lizzie had returned with a boyfriend, someone she'd met in Oxford who was from Milwaukee. That relationship lasted only a couple of months, but it was a year after when she and I fell into bed together for the first time since college. That first time hadn't been like this last time though, getting her pregnant aside. We both knew back then we'd be friends first. We'd always hang out. We'd have fun. We'd fall into bed together when we were both available and in the mood, but it would never go farther than that.

She didn't know I loved her back then. Shit, I wasn't even sure if I knew it then.

Things were different now and making this walk to her building's security desk carried a weight no previous trip held.

We didn't have the luxury of having sex and then brushing it off. We wouldn't have the luxury of going three months without talking or seeing each other. From now until eternity, we'd be tied together. Somehow, we had to figure out a way to make it work when we were so far apart. Both spatially, logistically, and I assumed—emotionally, because I still had no idea where we went from here.

"Mr. Dubiak," the security guard manning the desk called as he recognized me.

"Marco." I dipped my chin and shook his hand. He was a Chicago Storm fan, a single dad who'd worked two jobs to put his three kids through college. The last time I saw him two years ago, he'd shown me pictures of his first grandchild, a newborn girl with a red and white bow in her hair and a Chicago Storm jersey on. I'd signed it for him—the jersey, before he gave it to his daughter—not the baby or the picture. "How's it going? Any more babies?"

"No. But Patrice is engaged. Getting married next summer."

Talking to him was a blast. He was a damn good man, and I admired how hard he worked, how kind he was. Out of all the guards I'd met here over the years, he'd always been my favorite. Probably because he treated everyone like he'd treat his kids.

Every time he told me about his kids, every time a teammate got married, I couldn't help but think *I want that. The family. The noise to come home to after a long road trip.*

Tonight, it seemed so close and so far out of my grasp, my head spun.

"Is Lizzie home?" I asked, tapping my hands on the counter. "I just got done with a game and thought I'd swing by and surprise her."

"She's in. Came home an hour ago. How's the new team? Looking good out there tonight, even if I didn't want you to win." He pointed to a small television set behind the counter that was now showing Philadelphia playing in Montreal.

"Can't help I go from a great team to the best." I shrugged and gave him my signature smile.

Marco threw his head back and laughed, teasing me about how Vegas was going to make me soft to the cold weather.

We'd ended up with the win, sweeping the series. Somehow, I'd been able to shove Lizzie into the recesses of my mind for this game. It wasn't my best game, allowing three goals, but fortunately, we'd scored five. Afterward, when the team lined up and punched gloves, my old friends asked me to come get a drink with them.

It'd killed to tell them I couldn't. That I had other plans.

More than one had asked about Lizzie with a smirk twisting their lips.

If they only knew.

While I could usually shoot the shit with Marco for a while, tonight I was anxious.

"Mind if I head up?"

"I gotta call her and let her know."

I figured. At least this way I was already in the building and she couldn't run. I probably should have shown her the respect of a phone call, but given her recent track record, I wasn't too certain she'd answer the phone so soon.

"Sounds good."

He picked up the phone at his desk while I headed toward the elevators and hit the button to Lizzie's floor.

Unlike her, I didn't have a speech planned. I didn't have apologies. I scrubbed a hand through my hair. *What in the hell am I doing? What* did *I want from this?*

There was no way we could clear the air over the last few months, hell, the last year and a half when our friendship had separated due to a miscommunication on both our parts. But I couldn't let more time pass either without us planning the next steps.

Before I knew it, the elevator doors were opening and I found myself gaping at her as she stood in the entrance to her apartment. Her back held the door open, she had her bottom lip between her teeth. She wore no makeup and her hair looked like a family of squirrels had taken up residence on the top of her head. She wore a long, atrocious looking white robe that was tied at her waist and her eyes were half open.

Shit.

"Did I wake you up?" It wasn't quite ten on a Thursday. I hadn't considered she'd be sleeping.

"I had a dinner after work, and I sleep a lot these days." To prove it, she brought her hand to her mouth and yawned. "But it's okay. I'm glad you're here. Come on in."

I towered over her and she was no slouch in height. But for a guy who was six-four, not having to get a crick in my neck every time I looked down at a woman or bent to kiss her had always thrilled me about her. Tonight, looking so tired and worn out, blinking up at me with sleep and hope in her eyes, I realized I only had two questions for her.

Can we do this together?

And did she love me too?

5

LIZZIE

There were two things I learned about pregnancy before I truly believed I was pregnant and bought a copy of *What To Expect When You're Expecting.* One, puking all day sucked. Two, pregnancy makes you tired. Like zombie tired. Like, barely make it through the day without three naps and still fall asleep at eight o'clock tired. Having a limited caffeine intake didn't help.

Tonight I'd had a work dinner. I sipped a hot ginger tea while trying to hide my yawns so I didn't appear disrespectful to our out-of-town clients. The effort it took to be *on* had zapped all my energy. I'd barely made it home, stripped out of my clothes and thrown on sweats before I crashed face-first on my couch, a book in my hand.

When the phone rang with the doorman's alert tone, I figured it'd be my parents. They stopped by frequently with food for me, knowing I was too tired to cook. And after I called my mom last night crying, I didn't doubt at all she'd want to see me.

My parents loved me, still treated me like I was sixteen

but somehow managed to love me as an adult that didn't overstep boundaries at the same time.

When Marco told me Garrett was here to see me, and was on his way up, I'd barely had time to throw on a robe. He'd seen me in all manner of dress from the ritziest dresses to the most casual clothes to nothing at all, but him seeing me in a T-shirt of his I stole from him a few years ago that I still slept in would have been humiliating on a whole other level given where we currently stood.

Which was on the most rocky, unstable ground we'd ever been on.

It also shouldn't have surprised me he'd come. We'd been friends for years. I knew the kind of guy he was. I knew how badly he wanted a family and to be there for his kids. Granted, I'd expected a phone call in a few days, not him showing up after a game trailing his suitcase behind him—

Wait.

Suitcase?

I arched my brows as he wheeled it into my apartment and the door shut behind us.

"Before you ask or say anything," he said, kicking off his shoes. "I talked to my coach and told him I had some personal issues to deal with here. Our travel planner changed my flight so I don't have to be back until Saturday. I want to spend the weekend with you, talking, figuring out how we're going to do this, handle everything, what you want from me. I can go to a hotel if you want me to, but I'd really like to stay in one of your guest rooms."

My... my guest rooms? If he wasn't so vivid in front of me, the scent of his sandalwood-scented body wash wafting gently into the air between us, and if he didn't still look so disappointed in me, I'd assume I was still dreaming.

But...

"Here?" I asked, stupidly because he'd just made his point pretty damn clear.

He rolled his full lips together and scratched his sandy brown beard at the hinge of his jaw. "I've already missed six weeks. Don't know how much more I'll have to, don't take that from me."

The vulnerability in his stormy blue eyes was a stab to my heart. My hand went to my chest to rub away the pain, and as his gaze dropped, I let my hand fall.

He could undo me with a question and a look, and I wasn't nearly coherent enough to deal with this.

"Um. Yeah. Of course."

The first night I'd met Garrett, I'd crashed in his bed. We didn't have sex that night, but instead, we'd stayed up until five in the morning, drunkenly laughing and talking about our families, our friends. We'd talked about his dreams to go pro, my plans after graduation to go to England. Basically, from thirty seconds after we met, we clicked. There'd never been an awkward moment between us until three months ago and now, it was all we had.

I didn't know how to handle it.

"Do you want something to drink? Water? I don't have alcohol..." my voice trailed off as he stripped out of his suit coat and tossed it over the back of the couch.

"I'm good."

My hands knotted the belt at the waist. Without his suit coat on, his scarf opened at his throat, my brain struggled to function correctly. My hands had the instinctual urge to reach for him, settle my hands at his trim hips and rest my head against his chest for comfort.

Now, I fisted the knotted belt at my own waist and tried to hide the lust trickling through me and down my spine.

Garrett had always been all man. Brawnier, bolder, and

bigger than most of the other guys on his team, he'd still grown over the years. And yet he was gentle and kind. His voice was always a quiet rumble that sent sparks of desire to my most private areas, and even now, as we stood on opposite sides of my living room, my nipples hardened beneath his shirt.

I forced my gaze up to meet his and saw the same torment in his eyes that had to be showing in mine.

Garrett swallowed, dragging my gaze to the opening at his throat and then cleared his throat. "You're dead on your feet. Get some sleep and we'll talk tomorrow."

He came toward me, reaching around me at the last second to grab the handle of his suitcase. "Which room do you want me in?"

I had three extra rooms. One I used as an office. He could have either of the first two right off the living room.

"This way," I mumbled. The last time Garrett had spent the night in my home, he'd been in my bed. I wasn't sure he'd ever so much as seen inside my guest rooms. Now he was sleeping in one. It only solidified how far apart we were. I opened both doors and stayed in the hallway as he peeked inside the rooms. Both were plain, simply decorated with a couple small succulent plants and books I enjoyed on shelves and the top of the dressers. They were almost identical with oak headboards and furniture and cream bed coverings. Pops of green from the plants were the only colors.

"You can have either of these."

"Got it."

I stepped backward toward my bedroom, fighting the urge to cry and apologize for the thousandth time. "I, um, have some time off." I'd planned on taking two weeks when I was going to go to Vegas. "I can take tomorrow off. I might have to do some work in the afternoon, but that way we could talk?"

His tongue peeked out at the corner of his mouth and he nodded. "Sounds good. Thanks."

A yawn hit me, and I covered it with my hand. As I did, my hand got tangled in the belt at my waist, undoing it enough that my robe slipped down one shoulder.

Garrett's gaze dropped, eyes narrowed and heated with a fire that singed me to my toes.

He made a sound, half laugh, half choking, and turned toward the door. "Nice shirt. Been wondering what happened to that."

He disappeared into the room, shutting the door before I could say a thing, leaving me standing in the hallway, embarrassed, aroused, and so freaking tired I could fall asleep standing up.

"Good night," I whispered to the empty hallway.

Feeling more alone than ever even though my favorite person in the world was only feet away from me, I turned and trudged back to my room.

He was here. That was a good sign, right?

BEFORE MY EYES opened in the morning, I rolled to my side and slapped my hands to the nightstand. I found the crinkling plastic of saltine crackers I kept there and popped one into my mouth. I'd learned early that if I ate before I ever sat up, I could at least get through my morning routine before my stomach rolled. I chewed slowly, one hand on my stomach, and then my eyes flew open.

Garrett was here.

How could I forget? Last night hit me with the force of a

sudden burst of nausea and I sat up, flinging covers off my lap and threw my legs to the side of the bed. My stomach dipped and flipped and I grabbed another cracker, munching on it as I pushed out of bed and grabbed my cell phone from the charging station.

"Shit," I muttered around my cracker and trudged toward my en suite bathroom. With my eyes barely open, my head pounding and my stomach threatening to revolt, it took me longer than necessary to type out a text to my boss, letting her know I wasn't coming in.

Fortunately for me, Shawna Roberts was a mom of three, understood how difficult working during pregnancy could be, and had been more than supportive when I finally told her I was expecting and when I'd made plans to go to Vegas.

Hell, she might have been more disappointed than I was when I told her it hadn't panned out the way I'd hoped.

But now? I lifted my head from my phone and glanced in the direction of the bedroom where Garrett had slept. Could it now?

No. I shook my head, flipped on my faucet tap and after setting down my phone, splashed my face with cold water and gave it a quick wash and layer of moisturizer.

None of that mattered now. Not with another woman in the picture. Garrett and I had never crossed those lines before and I wasn't about to start now.

Hell, that was assuming it was even an option for me. Pretty ballsy considering how happy they looked together and how I'd treated him as of late.

"Crap on toast," I muttered and dried off my hands. I'd have to see him at some point. We needed to talk, only now, considering how upset he was and how distant we were, I had no way of knowing how it'd go.

The only thing I was certain of was that I would *never* keep Garrett from this baby's life. He'd have as much participation as he wanted and I would always help him make time for the tiny little peanut-sized ball of molecules who already seemed to make it entertaining to drive me crazy all day.

With a yawn, and in desperate need of my one cup of coffee I allowed, I headed back to my room where I threw on a pair of sweatpants and sweatshirt, tucking Garrett's T-shirt I wore to bed beneath my pillow and flipping up the covers so it was made. Kind of.

As I opened my bedroom door, the scent of coffee hit me first, followed by something sweeter.

Was he... cooking?

Noises came from the kitchen and the bedroom door where Garrett slept in was opened, so I figured he was at least attempting the feat I'd rarely seen him do before. To my utter surprise, I found him in the kitchen, scrolling through the screen on his phone, standing in a mess that could only be described as the aftermath of a bomb exploding.

"Um. What the hell?" I asked before I could censor myself.

I wasn't a neat freak by any means, but this? There was what looked like pancake batter dripping off the counter's edge. The blender I only pulled out for the rare margarita had some sort of thick, yellow-ish substance in it. Banana peels were piled at the edge of the island. Egg shells were cracked and opened, pooling on my white marble countertops. The mere sight of everything threatened to have my morning sickness make a return appearance.

"Shit." Garrett dropped his phone to the counter. "I meant to have it cleaned before you woke up."

"What is all this?" I took a cautious step into my usually stark white and impersonal but large kitchen, careful to keep an eye on the flour on the floor and headed toward the coffee. Once I popped in a pod, I grabbed a mug from the stand next to it and settled everything, inhaling my favorite aroma as it brewed.

It had the added bonus of muting the other scents in the room that still made me feel a shade of green.

"Banana oat muffins and a banana smoothie." At my look, which had to be saying something close to *What the hell for?* he grinned sheepishly. "I read online it's good for morning sickness."

Oh. *Ohhhh.* My heart squeezed as he turned from me and picked up banana peels and eggshells and threw them in the trash.

"That was... that was really sweet of you. Thank you. How long have you been awake?"

It was barely seven. Garrett was an early riser, but for him to not only make all of this, plus go to the store to buy everything? What time had he woken up? It had to have been crazy early.

He cleared his throat and brought his coffee to his mouth. Over the rim, he said, "I didn't sleep well last night.

Guilt hit me like a swift kick to the ribs. "I'm sorry," I whispered. "For all of this."

"I know." He took a drink and set down his coffee and began cleaning the mess he'd left on the counter.

I didn't usually eat bananas and my morning breakfast had consisted of toast with the occasional swipe of peanut butter for protein, but the muffins didn't look too bad. I grabbed one and scooted around to the other side of the island. Peeling off a small chunk, I plopped it into my mouth, preparing myself for it to taste like cardboard or for the texture to ignite my gag reflex.

Fortunately—and surprisingly—it was pretty decent. I caught Garrett watching out of the corner of his eye.

"It's not bad," I said and tore off another chunk.

"Thanks for the compliment," he teased and rinsed out the dishcloth.

As he cleaned, I ate. It was with a stony silence and not the comfortable peace between us. I squirmed on my seat, not knowing how to begin what we needed to talk about.

He didn't seem to be in a rush, or maybe he was as lost as I was because he didn't say a thing to me while I ate.

Once I finished the muffin, and he was still cleaning, I asked, "Can I try the smoothie?"

"You sure?"

I shrugged one shoulder. "The muffin didn't kill me."

"Smartass." He turned and flipped the switch, refreshing the mixture that looked goopy and gloppy, but I could try this. If bananas helped and if I could swallow it, I'd try anything to have a settled stomach.

He slid it in front of me and I swiped a small area where it'd overflowed around the glass. I brought my finger to my mouth and licked it off, catching Garrett's gaze on me.

And that gaze?

It was *heated*. A warm sensation slid down my spine as I repeated the move. It was sweet, with a slight tang. The taste didn't matter. I could have been drinking poured cardboard for as much as I was paying attention to it.

I must have let out a sound because Garrett's gaze darted to me and then quickly away.

"How would you feel about getting out of here and going for a walk?"

"A walk?"

"Yeah." He glanced over his shoulder. "Do you feel well enough to do that?"

Better now than later when my human body would take the form of a sloth for the remainder of the afternoon.

"Sure."

6

GARRETT

I'd slept like crap all night, despite the bed being new and comfortable. With Lizzie down the hall from me and very vivid memories of what our last time together was like, able to relax that close to her and so far away at the same tie was near impossible. Add in it was the last time I'd had sex, and my rock-hard dick kept me awake as much as my frustration with the situation we were in.

I'd finally crawled out of bed around four-thirty, pulled up a twenty-four-hour gym where I could get a free weekend pass. I'd worked out, stopped at the grocery store, and been back at her place, showered and cooking breakfast, when she woke up.

Now, we were headed down Michigan Avenue, weaving our way around professionals in suits on their way to work and retail workers preparing to open the stores on the Magnificent Mile. The wind was brisk and chilly, not unusual due to the time of year, and I took a deep breath, inhaling the familiar scents of exhaust and water and dirt and excitement and anticipation.

Three months. It'd barely been three months since I was in Chicago, but damn, I missed this city.

Next to me, Lizzie was bundled in her winter coat with lightweight gloves on her hands and shoved into her pockets. She'd thrown on leggings and furry boots that almost came up to her knees. She was dressed more for February than mid-March, but that was normal. As much as she loved the city, she despised any weather below fifty degrees.

"Do you miss it?" she asked.

"I miss everything about the city." I was still hoping Vegas would eventually begin to feel like home, but I doubted I'd ever get used to living in the desert. My backyard didn't have grass, for crying out loud, but dirt and rock. My neighbors had mostly cemented their backyard and added a pool. The pool I'd consider, but a cement backyard? I was used to trees. City buildings and rooftop parks at the very least—not dust and scorpions.

She pushed her lips out, a move she made when she was thinking of something and debating how to say it.

I gave her a minute. Two. We crossed the street and headed toward Millennial Park, and she still hadn't said anything.

"I'm keeping it," she blurted quietly, stunning me so badly my knees locked and my boots froze to the slushy pavement.

"What?"

She rubbed her hands together and stared at her own boots before she slowly lifted her eyes to meet mine. "The baby. I'm keeping it. I just... I thought you should know that."

A rushing wind rolled through me, stunning me. "I hadn't considered you'd do anything different, Lizzie. Not with our baby."

"Okay. Good. I just... I didn't know... you... and Vegas... and..."

The apples of her cheeks, visible above her scarf, turned a pink that had nothing to do with the chilly weather.

"Lizzie." I sighed, my shoulders drooping. She was *such* a pain in my ass. All she had to do was talk to me. "There's nothing going on with me and Nadia. Stop skirting around what you want to say or ask and just ask me. *Talk* to me."

I wouldn't beg her for anything. Never again. But this was coming awfully close.

"There's not?" Her lips parted and she sucked her bottom one between her teeth. Her gaze flickered toward the lake, an inky black topped with dirty white caps at the top of the waves. "Oh. You looked really happy with her."

She shuffled on her feet and I frowned, trying to piece together what she was saying. Or implying. Because she said it past tense. Not now. Not like the picture we took last week before we headed out to Chicago hadn't just been days ago.

"What are you not telling me?"

"You have a ton of pictures with her."

Good freaking Christ. Was she seriously going to make me do this? Irritation bloomed and was quickly followed by anger.

She'd run from me. She'd avoided me. She hadn't called and she didn't tell me she was pregnant when she found out. No, instead, she orchestrated showing up at my hotel while I should have been focused on my team and my games. Lizzie had never been someone who played games, but suddenly I felt like I was the marble inside a pinball machine with no hope of escape.

"Why can't you just be honest with me for once?" I asked, practically spitting the words between gritted teeth.

"And as far as Nadia. I don't think I owe you any explanation outside of what I said already. If you can't trust that..."

"I do." She nodded, and fucking hell, I was sure those were tears making her eyes glisten. "I just... *shit*. I keep making everything worse."

"I don't know what you mean by that."

"When I found out. When I found out I was pregnant, I was online, making plans to come to Vegas to see you. To tell you, because I wanted to tell you face to face. And then I saw that first picture of you and Nadia, and you were smiling at her, looking so happy. I didn't know what to do, if you'd want anything... from me. It scared me that I'd lost you, and it was my fault, but I had this part of you and I didn't.... I didn't want to be that girl. The girl who shows up knocked up and begs you to take me back or anything, not if you were dating someone."

Take me back. Goddamn this woman. How could she not know I'd always want her? How could she think I'd go from loving her, telling her I wanted us to be together to moving on so quick? Irritation spiked, frustration with her and her doubt in me as it did the entire situation. "You are such a pain in my ass."

I growled the words as my hand cupped the back of her head. Before she could blink, I slammed my mouth to hers.

Immediately, sparks flew, the chemistry that always swirled around us sparked and sizzled in every molecule of my body. Lizzie tensed at my first contact. Her hands flew to my chest at my coat and it took only a minute before she melted against me and began to kiss me back.

At the first touch of her tongue against mine, a groan slipped from my mouth. She tasted like sweet air, fresh mint, and cool Chicago weather.

"I'm sorry," she murmured, whispering against my mouth. "I'm so sorry for everything."

"Come here." I wrapped my arms around her shoulders, hugging her tight to me. "We'll figure this out. But you have to know that if you're having my baby, I'm going to be involved. In everything, Lizzie. I want to be at appointments. I want to see our child grow both before it's here and after. You can't keep that from me."

"I wouldn't." She said it into my chest as I held her, practically squeezed the life out of her. I was so strung tight from the last twenty-four hours and I only had so much time before I had to get back.

But her admission? That she had no plans to keep this baby from me? It was all I needed to know.

The rest we could figure out with time.

"As much as I really like that kiss," she said, tipping her head back. "I kind of feel like I need to throw up. Can we head back?"

"Of course." I slung my arm over her shoulder. We hurried back to her condo where I learned she hadn't been joking.

"YOU OKAY?" I had a warm washcloth and a can of ginger ale on the coffee table in front of where Lizzie plopped down on the couch. From the sounds of it, the bananas I'd given her for breakfast were no longer working for her. I squatted down in front of the couch and wiped her forehead with the warm cloth, hoping it'd help.

"Good now. For a while at least. Thanks for the pop."

She was sick. I was helpless. I was a problem solver by

nature. Not being able to solve this for her rattled something loose inside my chest. "What do you need?"

"Crackers." She groaned and collapsed back onto the couch. "My mom's been buying saltine crackers for me in bulk. My pantry should be full of them."

"I'll go get you some."

I went to stand, but her hand covered my wrist. "Wait."

"What is it?" I tossed the cloth to the table.

"Just... can you just sit here with me? For a few minutes?"

I'd do anything for her, even as upset as I'd been, and as confused as I was, she was my friend. One of my best friends. I'd give her anything she ever needed without question.

"Yeah. Come here." She pushed up and I slid beneath her shoulders so her head rested on my lap. I grabbed a pillow, settled it beneath her cheek, and then leaned forward and picked up the ginger ale. Once I was settled, I slid my hands through her silky hair, brushing it with my fingers.

I was with Lizzie.

And she was having my baby.

What that meant for us specifically, I wasn't sure, even though I knew what I wanted. I wanted a family. And I wanted it with her. But that could come later. We had other decisions to make first.

"When you were going to come to Vegas..." I started, keeping my eyes on the blank television screen in front of us. I wasn't quite prepared to see the look in hers. "How long were you planning on staying?"

"I was thinking two weeks, originally. I have some time off, but some of that would have depended on how you reacted."

"You'd know I'd never be pissed about this, right? It's a hell of a damn shock, but I'm not mad."

"I was afraid you'd hate me. After North Carolina and then not calling you."

She sniffed and I settled my hand on her shoulder, cupping it with my palm and squeezing. "Never. I could never hate you. I was hurt, yeah, but hate? That could never be me and you."

"Thanks. I'm glad." She settled, curled her legs up so she was in a ball. Even as she spoke, her words slowed and slurred until she blew out a breath and fell asleep.

I grabbed the massive blanket draped over the back of her couch and covered her, careful not to jostle her as I slipped off the couch.

I picked up her copy of *What To Expect When You're Expecting*. It was the top book on a stack of paperbacks on her coffee table and while she napped, I read.

I was behind the ball and needed to catch up if I could figure out how to be the best help to Lizzie moving forward.

7

LIZZIE

I groaned, waking from sleep and stretching. Somehow, I was tangled in a thick gray blanket and a pillow from my bed was beneath my cheek. I sat up, wiping my face, and flinched when I saw Garrett.

He was here. It took me another second to swipe the grogginess from my brain. He was *here*. And I'd fallen asleep in his lap. At some point he'd moved, but I didn't wake with the couch pillow beneath my cheek like I'd fallen asleep with. At some point, he'd made the effort to go to my room and grab the one I always used. Plus my big blanket from the back of the couch.

He'd always been like this. Always knew exactly what I needed and then he didn't hesitate to make it happen. I was the idiot who didn't see it for far too long.

"Hey." My voice was still thick with sleep and my gaze dropped to where his brows were pinched, a book held in his hand with more draped over his lap.

The rest I'd left out were strewn about the coffee table in front of me. *Starting Your Own Business. Build Your Empire*

Your Way. Hell, he'd even opened my file folder and had spreadsheets laying out.

He waved the back in his hand in my direction. *Entrepreneurship 101.* "What's this?"

His tone was too tight to be happy or curious. The flat line of his lips a hint of his frustration.

My stomach rolled, and not because I hated that look on his face.

"Excuse me," I mumbled, and his quiet but fierce curse followed me as I hurried off the couch and into the bathroom. I made it to my knees in front of the toilet before the little bean inside of me woke up and gave me its standard hello. I'd rather think of someone trying to reassure me they were okay than moaning about being so damn sick.

Since I'd barely had anything in my stomach, it didn't last long. By the time I splashed water on my face and gave my teeth a quick brush, I felt a hundred times better.

I opened the door to the bathroom and found Garrett in the kitchen. He was plating up crackers, the kind I'd asked him to get me, and then declined, before I fell asleep. On it were chunks of cheese from my fridge and some peanut butter. I'd be amazed that he knew me so well except we'd had many arguments about whether peanut butter or cheese went better with crackers.

"No banana this time?" I teased and hid my smile as his shoulders fell.

He was so damn protective. And not only that, he had initiative. He didn't even ask if I needed anything, just got to work trying to figure out what might help. Maybe it was because he grew up without a father and was the man of the house well before he should have been, but this trait was, hands down, one of his sexiest.

"Will this work?" he asked, sliding the plate across from him at the island. "You'll have to tell me what you can eat."

"I can take care of myself, you know."

"Yeah, but now you don't have to, at least not all the time." At the reminder of the issues we still needed to figure out, his expression blanked. He turned to the fridge, grabbing a bottled water from it. "Do you need more pop?"

"Please. Actually, how long did I sleep?"

"Not long. An hour I guess."

"I'll get the one from the living room then." I went to slide off my stool but he stopped me, holding out his hand.

"I'll get it. You sit." He pointed a finger at my plated food. "Eat."

I was munching on the crackers when he returned, although munch was a stretch. Nibbling it in mouse-sized bites was closer to reality.

"I didn't mean to snoop," he started. "I saw the baby books on top and figured I'd get caught up with what you're reading and going through, but then I saw the business books."

"I'm not mad at you for being curious." I took a sip of my ginger ale and waited to make sure it'd stay down before taking a larger bite of the cracker. "I've been considering doing something different."

Vulnerability was never something I excelled at. Confidence? Sass? Charisma? All that I had in spades. I commanded boardrooms full of men and earned their respect in a way they didn't call me a *bitch* behind my back. I spoke in front of full auditoriums, filled with a corporation's employees while I explained changes to their retirement accounts, enrollment processes and based on their age and agendas, how they should be funding their plans. I could gain control of a party and crowd with the snap of my fingers and I could be the best smart aleck, but vulnerability? I preferred to hide that deep behind my intelligence and confidence, thank you very much.

Being this way with Garrett? It was a million times harder. Ridiculous since he was the only man I'd ever truly trusted outside my dad.

His fingers tapped impatiently on the countertop. Twisted veins popped from beneath his muscular arms and the backs of his hands as he held himself back from pushing me. He'd learned long ago I went at my own pace and that pace quickly alternated between a high-speed chase and a turtle crawl.

I took a bite of another cracker. Washed it down with ginger ale. Across from me, his irritation pulsed like a quickly growing storm. One of those that whipped down the street and wiped out summer humidity as quickly as it appeared.

I could do this. I *had* to do this. If anything, I owed him.

Blinking, I lifted my head, barely able to meet his dark expression. "I was thinking of starting my own company. Maybe moving to individual financial planning for a while, starting over." I chewed my bottom lip. Had it gotten hot in here? I grabbed the front of my shirt and shook it to cool me down. It was hard to tell with the way my body temperature could swing like a chimpanzee on a tree, back and forth from frigid to burning these days.

"Where?" he asked, and it came out on a rasp, so rough I barely heard him.

I shoved my tongue to my teeth, tried to settle the nerves prickling my skin and on a rushed exhale, answered, "Vegas."

His lids closed, his lashes fanned out in a way beauty

products couldn't replicate with the best of their efforts and his shoulders slumped.

"You were thinking of starting a business in Vegas?" He lifted his head torturously slow and all those emotions racketing my body, bouncing around and confusing my libido as well as my stability made my chest ache and my core pulse.

"I decided as soon as I found out I was pregnant. Yeah."

"You were moving there for me."

For us, but... "Yeah."

Something beautiful and heavy swirled between us, something so real, so tangible, if I'd lifted my hand it was entirely possible to *feel* the way he loved me even though he hadn't moved a single inch.

Garrett pushed off the counter and strolled to me with panther-like grace and stealth, but there was nothing peaceful or graceful in the hard etched lines digging into his features.

He reached me and I swiveled on my stool before he pressed a leg between my knees and stepped in between my spread legs. It was the only place we touched. His denim covered legs pressed to my inner thighs and still it felt like he was making love to me with his hands and his mouth and the rest of him.

"What stopped you?" His voice was full of grit and emotion, and I flinched.

"Nadia," I whispered. "That picture. You two looked happy, and I was worried you'd moved on and then I didn't know what to do."

His hands slid to the sides of my neck and his forehead dropped, so close the messy strands of his wild and untamed hair brushed against my flesh. The pads of his fingers burned a brand straight to my soul.

"Garrett."

"You didn't give me any warning."

I should have. I should have called before I planned on showing up so we could talk. Then I could have arrived on his doorstep with my bags and a clear conscience and hard conversations out of the way. "I thought you'd like the surprise."

His lips parted on a soft laugh and his eyes closed. He was killing me. Garrett was never great at hiding his emotions, not from me. We'd had *years* to memorize what our looks meant. This one was new. Deeper.

"I would have. I would have loved that surprise."

"I freaked and I'm sorry for making things harder."

"There's nothing going on with Nadia and me. She's a teammate's sister. She needed some help, I needed a plus one for some events. I swear to you, that's all it was."

Something flashed in his eyes but disappeared quickly, leaving me with nothing but the truth. I pushed away that hesitation I thought I'd seen. Maybe it was my imagination. Trying to find something wrong when everything right was standing in front of me, peering down at me like he couldn't decide whether he wanted to devour me or throttle me.

"So... what happens now?"

8

GARRETT

I t'd taken everything in me not to wake her up once I saw her business plans. The books. At first, tension and fear knotted itself deep in my chest as I started reading the baby books. I'd never known there was so much to know about pregnancy, about the changes women go through, what was going to happen. As soon as I saw a page that happened to mention the way organs were squeezed up into their ribs and then their backs, I'd needed a break.

How did women do this? Especially someone as thin as Lizzie. Where'd she *fit* everything? What if she was hurt? What if the worst happened and she lost the baby? Would the baby be healthy? How could I be the dad I wanted to be when we lived so far apart? How could I travel and leave my son or daughter at home? How could I *fly*?

And. Oh. Holy. Shit. I almost jumped off the couch and went in search for some Tums in a medicine cabinet. How in the *hell* did women go through all this? No wonder my mom looked so frazzled when we were little and Dad was deployed. If I was having these thoughts after five minutes, what in the hell would happen to me after *years* of worrying?

Shit.

I'd tossed the baby books down and scrubbed my hands over my face until the panic racing through me changed to memories from when I was ten, officers showing up at our house to tell us my dad had died in a training exercise. I was ten the day I became the oldest man in my house. All because of a flight gone wrong.

Somehow, I wasn't afraid of flying. My dad flew jets for the military. Anything could happen when he was in the air. That wasn't the same as flying commercial although I wasn't great with smaller, private planes. It was Lizzie who was terrified of flying. But how would all that fear manifest when I had to travel so much, be in the air so much, once I had someone carrying around half my heart and soul in their tiny body?

But this?

Vegas.

She'd been planning on moving there. Yeah, I was pissed she hadn't returned my calls or texts, that she'd left me in the dark. Pissed she'd been planning on a way to bridge that space between us while not bothering to pick up the phone.

The surprise would have been hella nice.

Much better than a damn phone call.

I brushed my thumbs over the column of her throat. She was so soft, so sweet even if she was paler than usual and had light purple half-moons beneath her eyes.

Her pulse spiked as I brushed my thumb over the sides of her throat, up the line of her jaw until my thumbs were at her chin, running along her bottom lip.

"There're a lot of things I want to do now," I admitted, my gaze staying on hers.

Her cheeks turned pink and the tip of her tongue slid across my thumbs.

One tiny touch from her and my body was hot and strung tight. I wanted it. *Her*. When it came to Lizzie, I was always willing to take what she'd give.

Perhaps that was what created this mess in the first place.

Clearing my throat to push down the quickly bubbling lust growing inside of me, steeling my spine and hardening my dick, I pressed my lips to her forehead and stepped back.

"I'm not sure which ones are the smart ones and I don't want to fuck this up again."

"I know," she rasped, that tongue swiping her lips again as I dropped my hands from her body, but damn it was difficult.

Every time I was around her I wanted her thrown against the wall, her legs spread, and me pounding deep inside of her until she clawed at my back and rattled the windows with her screams.

Fuck.

I swiped a hand across my mouth and stepped away, putting my back to her. Reaching down, I adjusted myself and bit back the groan caught in my throat. Carnal need, something stronger than plain old lust and desire, sizzled my blood.

Once I had myself under a decent amount of control where I wasn't at risk of doing all the things I'd just fantasized about, I blew out a breath. "Are you hungry? For more than that snack?" It was well after lunchtime, and we had twenty-four hours before I needed to be on a plane.

"Garrett."

"Yeah?" I faced her, dragging my gaze to meet hers despite the worry of what I'd see there.

Her expression slayed me. There was desire mixed with concern and no small amount of fear. "I can still come to Vegas with you."

I'd never have to miss a doctor appointment. I'd get to see our child grow inside her stomach and be there for her every step of the way. I'd get to be the man and father I'd dreamed of for so long.

But would I be able to do it with Lizzie? Us as partners? *Together* in the way I'd always wanted to be?

It'd kill me if we couldn't make it work, and I wasn't sure now was the right time to take the risk.

"Not forever," she quickly said, dashing all my hopes like a puck to the groin without proper gear on.

"What?"

"I just meant—maybe, maybe we can take our time with all this? But I can come back with you. I still have that time, and I could stay a few weeks, do some work, find a midwife or OB or something."

My head fell and I stared at the wood floor beneath my feet. For a moment, as brief as it was, she'd offered me everything. Yanked it back like a yo-yo. And I was so damn tired of being her toy.

"Lizzie—"

"Just to take our time. I *want* it, I do. But it's not like I can move in twenty-four hours."

She wasn't wrong. Somewhere along the way, possibly the first, or the second time she tore out my heart, I'd stopped fully trusting her.

She was taking that step, though. She was willing to consider doing this. For our baby. Maybe for us.

She loved this city more than she might possibly love herself. Offering to give all of it up for me, the comfort of her family and friends she'd had since kindergarten and her career she'd worked so hard for. Hell, even the view of her apartment was a thousand times better than anything I'd ever had and definitely better than my red dirt back yard.

Two days ago, I'd doubted I see her while I was in Chicago. Now so much had changed. There really was no sense in rushing it.

"I'd like that," I finally said. "I'd like for you to come back with me. And as for the rest, we'll take it a step at a time, okay?"

Surprise paled her face until she slumped back in the stool. *Fuck.* She wanted that. But we'd been here before. "Oh. Sure. I get it."

She slid off the stool, yawning behind her hand. "I'm not really hungry, but I should probably—probably go call my boss. You know, make sure she's still okay with everything…"

She rambled and seeing her so shaken killed me. I'd never once turned Lizzie down when she wanted or needed something for me.

"I don't want to screw anything up. Not now. Not when there's so much at stake."

"I know." She rolled her lips together. "I get it."

She spun on her heels, disappeared down the hall and once the door to her bedroom clicked close at the end of the hall, I stared at the vast, black lake in the distance.

I'd fucked that up somehow. She'd offered me everything, clear in her gaze, and for the first time in the years I'd known Lizzie, I'd said no.

She was vulnerable, honest, all the things I'd needed from her, but something was holding me back and I could only hope I could get her to see that for now, *tonight*, it was absolutely the right decision, despite her pain.

I turned, grabbed her snack plate and ginger ale, tossing the food left behind into the trash and cleaned up the kitchen. I was starving, so I pulled up UberEATS and ordered us food from a local Mexican restaurant. Lizzie might have said she wasn't hungry, but there was no way she'd ignore a bag of nacho chips or salsa and queso from her favorite place.

Hopefully, it was enough of an apology.

As suspected, Lizzie made an entrance in the kitchen an hour later. I was almost done eating the triple burrito meal with a side of two enchiladas I'd ordered myself but her chips and queso were toasty warm in the oven.

"That smells incredible," she said, glancing around as if she was waiting to see a Styrofoam container. At her disappointment, I grinned around the fork in my mouth.

"You said you weren't hungry and didn't want anything to eat."

"Right." She rubbed her lips together and turned to the fridge.

Did she really think I'd do that?

"Lizzie," I said, forcing down a laugh.

"Hmm?"

"Your food is in the oven. Dork."

She shot me a look, cautious at first that spread into a barely there smile with the corners of her lips kicked up. "Thanks. You're the best."

"I know."

I grinned again and shoveled in the last few bites of my enchilada. This we could do. We'd locked down flirting, friendly teasing, and playful banter to an art form years ago. It was all the other stuff, *feelings and shit*, that tangled everything up.

She was shaking her head, and a beautiful moan slipped from her lips as she popped off the queso top. Leaning forward, she had her hair in a fist at one shoulder and she breathed in the spicy cheese scent.

Gross.

Also, maybe getting tangled up wasn't such a bad idea. My dick certainly perked up at that moan.

She lifted her eyes and, for a moment, terror struck me. Had I said that out loud.

"I really appreciate this. And it's perfect. I can't eat much at a time but cheese seems to be something I can always eat."

I shoveled that into my memory bank for later when she was hangry. Feed her cheese. Done.

"It's not a problem. How you feeling?"

"Good." She grabbed a large bowl from next to her oven, bumped a button with her finger to turn off the warmer, and dumped the entire bag of chips into it.

There were lots of things Lizzie and I had in common. Loyalty. Similar senses of humor. Our love of traveling despite her hatred of flying.

And Mexican food.

She set the bowl on the table, grabbed the salsa and queso, and plopped down across from me. "Mmm. This even smells so good. Nothing smells good anymore, although that's getting better I guess, but I think I could drink this entire bowl of cheese."

She dipped a chip, took her first bite and as she did, another one of those delectable moans she made shot straight to my dick.

"Lizzie?"

She dipped another chip into the cheese, scooping it up

and covering the chip. But really, was there any other way to eat it?

"Yeah?"

"Stop making that damn sound and eat your food."

Her lips parted, jaw relaxed, and then she rubbed her lips together. A brightness hit her eyes and her shoulders shook with laughter even as her cheeks turned a deep red. "Right. Sorry."

Fuck me sideways.

How in the hell was I supposed to go slow with her?

9

LIZZIE

"I called my parents."

At that, all the teasing and I swore the *lust* in Garrett's expression fled. "How are they?"

"My mom was happy you were here. She's been telling me I need to tell you." I dipped another chip and nibbled on it, careful not to make the noises Garrett accused me of. Could he fault me? Hot and salty tortilla chips with queso from LaVallerta Mexican was orgasmic.

"How have they been? You know..." He flung his hand out and swirled it in the air in my direction. "With everything?"

My parents knew Garrett well. He'd eaten dinner with us, spent holidays at our house when he didn't have time in between games to get back to Seattle to be with his mom and sister. Hell, more than once, my parents had flown Rachel and Gabrielle in to see him on Christmas. They *loved* Garrett.

Were they pleased I was pregnant and not married and we weren't even together? Not exactly a conversation I wanted to have with my dad, even if I was twenty-eight years old.

"They were worried. Upset, but you know they love you. And my mom's been great. Bringing me food and everything, checking on me."

"Of course she would. Did you tell them about Vegas?"

"They're not so thrilled about that, sad mostly." I paused and dipped another chip. "They want to see us before you leave."

Garrett's back straightened and he pushed his cleaned off plates away from him. "Your dad is still a pacifist, right?"

I pointed the cheese covered chip in his direction and scowled. "He's not going to shoot you."

"We're leaving tomorrow."

"That's why I told them to come tonight."

His thick brows arched and the look he gave me made me squirm in my seat. Not like that was much different than how I usually reacted to *any* look he gave me, even if I was still hurt from what he'd said earlier. Stupid of me to expect he'd just say, "Hey, you're pregnant, haven't talked to me in three months, but yeah, let's just jump in to being how we were last time we saw each other." Hell, before then, we hadn't talked in a year. If I was being logical, I'd completely understand. Whenever Garrett and I acted on our emotions and feelings for each other, miscommunications turned into bombs.

I chalked it up to the fact we *felt* so much. We wanted so much. But we could never figure out how to make it happen.

"Tonight? Shit." He scrubbed his face and groaned. "I wasn't prepared to see your dad."

"He's not mad at you."

"You said that, but it's one thing for him to *say* it and then it's another for him to look the man who knocked up his daughter face-to-face and not feel the urge to punch him."

"Pacifist, remember?" I mumbled around another chip doused with cheese.

If we were somewhere else, if we were *anything*, I'd reach my hand across the table, grab his from his face and hold it, brush my thumb along his palm and inner wrist because I knew it would make him calm down.

But we weren't there. We weren't anything. He loved me, and I'd never had the guts to say it back to him. No wonder why he wanted to take this slow.

He didn't want me to run again or avoid the hard conversations I always had before.

He didn't trust me not to hurt him again, and I couldn't fault him for that. It would be me that would have to step up.

Later. I'd give him that later.

"When will they be here?"

I shrugged. "They said later. It's only what, four?" I glanced at the clock. "Probably not until seven."

"All right." He shoved away from the table and stood, gathering his emptied plates.

"Where are you going?"

"Store. If your dad is coming for dinner, I'm going to butter both him and your mom up with my lasagna."

This man. A soft laugh fell from me as I twisted, another soaking chip dipped in queso frozen halfway to my mouth. The cheese dripped to the palm of my hand beneath it. "You are such a dork."

He winked a wink that did funny things to my insides. "You love me."

I did. He was teasing. But I did.

He dumped the trash and slid his plates to the counter

and left the room, his keys jingling in his hands before I could tell him the truth.

Later.

Before we reached Las Vegas, there'd be no more miscommunications, no more hidden secrets between us. We'd step off the plane with a fresh, clean slate... and our baby growing inside me.

~

MY MOM'S hugs were epic. I swore she had to practice them by hugging a tackling dummy or something in secret.

She squeezed me tight as soon as they walked into my apartment and the familiar scent of her floral perfume wafted into the air.

"Hey Mom."

"How are you?" She pulled back and cupped my cheeks with her palms. "Things good?"

She said it quietly, but Garrett was close enough to hear, mostly because as soon as we got the call from security they were here, he'd settled a hand at my lower back and stayed close. Whether or not it was for me or for his own protection, I didn't know.

"We're good, Amy," he said and my mom's gaze narrowed on me, waiting for my nod before she let me go and gave Garrett the same bone-crushing hug. "Good to see you."

"Always great to see you, Garrett. I'm glad you're here." She grinned up at him. "Not so glad you're taking our girl away, but it's a good thing. For all of you."

As she said it, she glanced down at my stomach and back to Garrett, whose expression had softened. "I'll take care of her."

"I know you will. Now..." She stepped back and finally

dropped her purse on a sideboard table and clasped her hands together. "It smells incredible in here. What can I help with?"

Mom hurried off to the kitchen, where everything was done and ready to serve, which would leave her feeling helpless in about thirty seconds. Mom loved to be needed, to care for everyone around her.

"My turn," my dad said, and gave me the same warm and strong hug Mom had. "Good to see you, Lizzie. Thanks for having us tonight."

"Of course." I stepped back as he clasped Garrett's hand. "Garrett. Always good to see you, son."

My dad had called Garrett son since the first time they met. It was the kind of man he was, welcomed everyone he met into the family fold without hesitation.

"You too, sir," Garrett said, tripping over the sir.

I covered my mouth, choking down a laugh.

Sir hadn't been used by Garrett since that first meeting. That he used it now told me how nervous he was.

My dad laughed and clasped him on the shoulder. "No better man I'd want as a father to Lizzie's kids. You know that. None of the sir crap. We've been over this."

"Right. Dan." Garrett slid me a look that said he wasn't so certain. I, for one, was having too much fun trying not to laugh at his unease.

"Dad, Garrett's worried you're going to punch him."

Garrett's blue eyes narrowed. "This isn't funny."

"It's hilarious." I shoved past both of them. "I'm going to help my mom in the kitchen. Let you men sort yourselves out."

"Everything's done," Garrett called out to my back.

"I know."

I was pretty certain I heard him mumble something to

my dad that sounded an awful like *she's a pain in my ass* to which my dad returned *all the good ones are, son.*

As suspected, Mom looked lost as she stood at my kitchen island. The garlic bread was sliced and in a bowl, covered with a cloth napkin. The salad was prepared with a variety of salad dressings on the table. The lasagna was on the stove, cooling. Garrett had even set the table with placemats and picked up a couple bottles of red wine like we were preparing for a Thanksgiving meal instead of time with my family.

"He's nervous," I told my mom as an explanation.

"Looks like it," she muttered. Her hip bumped into mine and we both laughed.

Garrett didn't cook a lot, but there were a hand full of meals he did really well. Lasagna was one of them.

"Can I get you something to drink?" I asked, already reaching for one of the bottles of wine.

"That'd be great. Thanks, honey."

Garrett and Dad entered the kitchen, Garrett looking no less nervous, but resigned and my dad went immediately to the fridge where he grabbed a beer Garrett must have told him he bought.

Of course, Dad's favorite, too.

"Want a beer, son?" he asked, and Garrett's shoulders finally unclenched from being up to his ears. Dad was treating him like he always did. I figured eventually Garrett would relax. Apparently all it took was an offering of alcohol.

"Yeah, Dan. That'd be great. Thanks."

The men popped the tops on their bottles, I poured Mom a glass of wine, and filled a glass with water and lemon for myself. Once drinks were filled and settled at the table, we grabbed plates, filled our food, and it took absolutely no time at all for the friendly and familiar chatter to make things like they always were.

"You like the new team?" Dad asked once we were seated. "They look good."

Garrett's eyes widened and I swore a color brightened his cheeks. "You're watching?"

Dad was more of a football fan, but he watched the occasional game. What I didn't think Garrett ever knew is that Dad *always* watched him play.

I truly believed Garrett was the son my dad never had and always wanted.

"Of course I'm watching you. Wish you were still here, though, but it seems like a good fit. Guys good?"

"Yeah." Garrett cleared his throat and then swiped his mouth over his with a napkin. "Almost all of them are great. They treated me as one of their own as soon as I got there, which was good. Doesn't always work that way and with their goalie injured and them not going to their back-up permanently, that can be tricky. But so far, there's only been one or two guys I don't really like. Most of them have made me feel right at home."

"Happy you have that. Change can be hard." He tore off a chunk of his garlic bread and waved it back and forth between Garrett and me. "Speaking of, what's the plan for you two?"

"Dan—" Mom started.

"Simple question."

Ah. So the understanding Dad shtick was just that. A ruse to lure us into comfort. This was the protective dad Garrett had been so worried about. Probably why when I glanced at him, he was looking at me like he had a gun to his head, stunned into silence.

"I'll be there for two weeks." I took a sip of my water,

eyeing my mom's wineglass. If there was ever a time I could use a drink, this was it. "I want to get a feel for the area, call some obstetricians or midwives to see if I can get in for consults. Shawna's already said I can work remotely as often as I need. So..." I shrugged and flashed a nervous smile to Garrett. We hadn't actually *talked* about this part, but he'd definitely indicated he'd be okay with it. "After that, I figure I'll come back, pack, get this place ready to sell, and then... move."

"Move?" Garrett asked, and the one word sounded like it'd been dragged over gravel it was so rough.

"I mean, yeah." I shrugged, settled my hands in my lap and wiped them down my thighs. "I figured, well, that'd be best. For all of us."

Garrett speared me with a look that ignited my core. Told me all in a look exactly how much he'd show me he wanted that if we were more settled, if my parents weren't in the room.

Based on the look on my mom's face as she rolled her lips together and flashed me wide, amused eyes, she totally *read* exactly what Garrett wasn't saying.

"That's good," she said, and picked at her salad. "That's wonderful for you two. A baby should have both his parents nearby."

"Let us know what you need help with," Dad said, and took a bite of food.

That was it. Plans made. Parent approved.

And Garrett? He was still looking at me like there was no one else in the room—no, in the universe.

I WAS JOSTLED SOFTLY and opened my eyes.

"Hey," I whispered, blinking to clear away the haze of sleep.

Garrett was leaning over me, one arm beneath my shoulders, moving me to sitting. "It's late, and your parents are taking off."

"Oh." *Oh.* I must have passed out while the guys were watching TV. "I'm so sorry," I said, jumping off the couch. The quick move made the room spin and Garrett held me until I was steady.

"It's okay," my mom said in that soft, compassionate voice of hers and wrapped me in a hug. Softer this time. Tears sparked my eyes. Other than my few years in England, I'd never gone more than a week or two without seeing my parents.

"Call us when you're there. Let me know how things are going but most of all, take care of yourself and my grand-baby, okay?" She leaned back and pressed her hand to my cheek. "I love you, Lizzie-Lou. Be safe." She leaned in and squeezed me again, and whispered, "He loves you. You love him. Everything else will work itself out."

"Thanks."

My dad's goodbyes were similar, minus the tears in his eyes, and then his hand brushed against my stomach. I wasn't convinced I was showing, but my stomach bloated at night. Mostly I looked like I ate way too much LaVallerta. Which really, not a problem.

"Pictures. Keep us updated on everything, right?"

"I will." I nodded, and he went blurry through my tears.

Garrett stepped up beside me and shook his hand. Surprise widened his eyes as my dad took that handshake and yanked him forward into a man hug. "Take care of her."

"Always," he promised, his gaze sliding to me.

The seriousness in those dark brown eyes of his warmed me from the tips of my toes straight to my scalp.

He would.

Garrett would take care of me.

We walked my parents to the door, waited while they tugged on coats and slid into shoes and then there was another quick round of hugs, more tears, and a few exasperated looks from the men. Once they were gone, Garrett wrapped his arm around my shoulders and held me tight to him.

"You'll be good."

"I know."

"You're planning on moving to Vegas."

He said it like I hadn't already mentioned it. Like I hadn't already talked about my plans to start my own business out there, even before I knew about the baby.

Maybe hearing me say it to my parents made it more of a reality.

"Yeah. Of course that's what I wanted."

His head dipped and his lips pressed to my forehead as he wrapped me in a hug. It wasn't exactly the reaction I hoped for, or what his look said he wanted to do earlier. "I want that too. Always want you with me."

He let me go when I thought he'd push for more, turning out the lights as he guided us down the hall.

He stopped at his bedroom and opened his door. He wanted slow. I could give him that if he needed it, but he needed to know that wasn't what I needed.

I settled my hand on his chest. Now was the time. To tell him everything I thought, everything I *felt* and hadn't had the courage to say.

He *loved* me.

Because of that, I needed to swallow my own fear and be

honest with him. "That night... the last time we were together?"

His eyes closed and his head fell forward, pressing his forehead against mine. "You don't have to—"

I didn't need to. I wanted to tell him all the things I'd held back. There was no reason for any of it, not anymore.

"I should have said it back. I should have told you I loved you."

He blinked. "Lizzie—"

"You don't have to say anything. But I want you to know that. I get why you want to go slow and I get why you don't trust me, but I was willing to move to Vegas because I loved you and had made my choice, Garrett. There are no regrets here."

Before he opened his eyes, his hands were at my cheeks, thumbs skimming the apples of them.

My body burned with arousal at that first, seductive touch.

"I—"

"I don't need to hear anymore," he murmured, and then fused his mouth to mine.

10

GARRETT

This was not the slow I intended.

Slow didn't exist in the realm when I knew what she felt like, what she tasted like.

And hearing those words? How in the hell would I ever remove my mouth from hers when all I wanted to do was slip my tongue down the column of her throat, to her breasts, teasing her nipples with nips of my teeth and licks of my tongue, drawing a trail to her navel and beyond?

This was *Lizzie.*

My woman.

Mine.

She whimpered into my mouth, her hands at my hips. I'd almost gone absolutely insane when I saw her dad brush his hand at her stomach earlier. I hadn't even noticed, hadn't seen the slight swell of her lower stomach, but I saw it then.

Holding her with one hand, I did the same as her dad had done, dropped one of my hands and pushed it between us. Her stomach was small, but larger, too. It didn't take long to feel that gentle curve around the waistband of her sweats and as I did it, she huffed and pulled back, ending our kiss.

But hell.

Maybe before now, the fact we were having a baby had been some *out-there* idea. But she was changing. *Growing.* With our child and it was insanely hot as hell.

"Fuck," I whispered, as she covered my hand with mine.

"It's just bloating right now. Normal. It's not..."

"I don't care. You're carrying my baby." *And you love me.*

She blinked, looked up at me through her lashes and whispered, "Yeah. Crazy, right?"

It was, and at the same time, anything but. It was perfect.

"No. It's beautiful." I dropped my forehead to hers, and we stood like that in the hall, her fingers between the gaps in mine at her stomach and I let the peace of that moment wash over us. "You know how I feel about you."

"I know."

"I don't want us to mess it up again but going slow with you is a special kind of hell."

Her fingers between mine pressed in until she was holding my hand at her stomach. She turned her head, kissed the side of my throat. "We'll figure it out."

We would. We absolutely would. I wouldn't stop fighting for Lizzie. Ever.

"I should go to bed," she whispered, as if either of us talking any louder would interrupt this peace we'd found. "Early day tomorrow and lots to do."

"All right." I kissed her forehead, and slid my hand from hers, instantly losing the soft warmth of her. "Good night, Lizzie."

"Night, Garrett."

She stepped away first, yawning as she did and I waited in the hallway, hands curling into fists at my sides and locking my knees so I didn't dive after her, tear her off her feet and toss her to her bed and ravage her until we didn't get a single moment of sleep.

But back in my room? That was a whole different story.

My dick was hard, almost bursting through the zipper of my jeans. Usually, I'd fight this, but it'd been months since I held Lizzie in my arms and despite the fact I was a grown man with a decent sense of self-control, that all fled and turned me into an animal when I was covered with her scent, the taste of her lips, and the knowledge my DNA was growing inside her.

I tore off the button of my jeans and undid my zipper. I barely had my jeans and boxers to my knees before I stumbled to the bed and spit into my hand.

At the first swipe of my hand down my hard, pulsing length, I gritted my teeth so I didn't shout for her to get into the damn room and finish this.

At the second swipe, the pinch at my tip, I closed my eyes and pictured Lizzie. Her full breasts. Her hips. The berry scent of her lips and the way her eyes would gaze with lust as soon as I sunk inside her tight heat.

At the third pull, I shoved back into the bed, and then imagined her stomach swollen, her breasts even larger. I imagined what it'd feel like to see my child grow inside of her and how it'd change us and how we'd handle living together in Vegas. And fuck. It was a fantasy I'd had for *years* coming true in less than forty-eight hours.

The woman I loved more than life itself, more than hockey, was willing to move to be with me because she *loved* me.

"Fuck," I grunted. I tried to keep quiet, tried to not sound like a complete fucking pervert, but like always happened when Lizzie was nearby, all that shit went out the window.

Precum helped the ease of my hand, sliding down my

dick while I pictured Lizzie's dark pink lips wrapping around the tip and taking me deep, gagging, eyes watering, on her knees like she liked it so damn much.

My balls grew tight and I worked faster. The sounds she'd make. How wild would she get once she didn't feel like throwing up so much?

How I'd take care of her as much as I possibly could to make her know what she was doing was the best damn decision she'd ever make.

Yeah.

I'd give Lizzie everything. A home. Love. Safety and protection. And she? She'd give me the one thing I'd always wanted. A family.

I'd reassure her of all of it more than anything in the world.

I grunted, teeth gritted. It was a wonder I didn't crack a crown and then I came, groaning out her name beneath my breath so she didn't think I was being murdered by the sounds I was making.

My seed slid all over my hand and it took seconds, minutes, hell it could have been hours until I felt like I was steady enough to stand and clean myself up. Blood roared through my ears, and my limbs were loose.

If I'd had a game to play, I wouldn't be able to stand on my skates.

Once I was capable and had cleared all the visions of Lizzie out of my brain, I tore off my shirt and used it to clean myself off. With my jeans pulled up but still undone, I opened the door to use the bathroom in the hall.

"Hey, I was just thinking—" Lizzie stared and then froze.

Her gaze dropped to my chest, the shirt wrapped around my hands and my undone jeans in a split second, and her eyes went wide.

And kill me. Fucking kill me now. I wasn't sure of the expression on my face, but as Lizzie rolled her lips together, fought between laughing and screaming based on the way her shoulders shook and she covered her mouth, I figured it wasn't good.

"Did you just—"

No way in *hell* was I telling her anything. "Go to bed, Lizzie."

"In my guest room?"

"Fucking hell." My head fell to the wall, and I banged the back of my head against it. *Thump. Thump. Thump.* Could anything be more embarrassing? Emasculating?

And she was laughing at me?

I turned, tried to glare at her. "Cut me some slack here."

She chortled. Yes. A mixture of a cough and a choke echoed in the hall and she swirled her finger in a circle pointed in my direction. "That's your sex face. You did, didn't you. You just totally—"

Fuck this. I would not be ashamed that I just beat it like a fifteen-year-old after his first date and got caught. "I did. I just came all over my hand and stomach and I did it thinking of all the things I want *and* will do to you someday. Is that what you want to hear?"

As I spoke, her humor fled and her jaw dropped. *Jesus.* Was she surprised I'd think of her when I did that? Especially after that kiss?

Color turned her cheeks pink and I stepped forward. She could try to embarrass me, but I'd win this. I'd win every damn round. "Do you want me to tell you what I was thinking? The sounds you make and how they turn me on, the way I was thinking about dragging my tongue down every single inch of your body until you came so loud your neighbors called the cops. The fact that even though it's been months, I can still taste you on my tongue?"

She licked her lips. For a second, I thought she might say yes. That she didn't only want to *hear* it, but participate.

"I just wanted to know what time the flight left tomorrow so I know when I need to set my alarm."

Sure. Of course.

This woman. That's not what she wanted—sure, it might have been then, but it sure as hell wasn't now.

"We'll need to leave here by noon."

"Good."

"Yup."

Her eyes glittered. "Thanks."

"You're welcome." I stayed stoic. It drove her crazy. And as she struggled for words, I took that shirt I'd used to clean up and pretended to finish wiping myself off my hands.

Her chin fell, her gaze zeroed in on that move and she shuffled on her feet.

"Lizzie?"

"H-huh?"

"If you don't want me to turn those images I just branded into your brain into action in the next five seconds, I suggest you get to bed."

It was the only warning I'd give. I could do this with her all night. Fuck slow if she didn't need it.

Hell, I wasn't even certain I did anymore. There was no slow when it came to us. It was either all brakes or all gas.

I blinked, counted to one in my head. By two, her soft padded feet hurried away from me. By three, her door clicked shut.

Smart girl.

We'd have time anyway.

"You okay?"

"I'm good." I had my arm draped over Lizzie's shoulders. The flight had been smooth and easy, but without Lizzie able to take her motion sickness meds or have a drink or two, she'd clung to me like a starfish from the moment we got in line to board the plane.

The flight, for her, had been hell. Couple her fear of flying with her morning sickness and I now owed our travel coordinator, Gabe, a bottle of his favorite liquor since he'd been able to get us both first class seats. I'd given Lizzie the aisle seat, first row, and she'd spent more time puking in the bathroom than any woman her size could possibly be able to manage. She smelled like shit—not that I'd tell her—and her face held a green hue to it. No amount of crackers or ginger ale had helped.

"Let's sit." I ushered her to a chair in baggage claim and she dropped into it, pressing her arms to her knees, and held her face in her hands.

"I'm fine."

She was two seconds from puking again. I grabbed the ginger ale, a sleeve of crackers and pushed them into her lap. "Stay here with the carry-ons while I grab the rest of our bags."

She'd packed almost her entire closet and dresser and bathroom items. By the time she was done that morning rushing around, one suitcase alone for all of her business stuff and books, leaving behind a pile of boxed things she'd said her mom would send to her, it looked like she was getting ready to move permanently.

Four suitcases later, I returned to Lizzie, whose color

had returned to her cheeks and she'd emptied the ginger ale.

"This airport sucks," she stated, and glared at a row of slot machines like she wanted to tear them out with her hands. "It's bad when you have a headache, but all that noise is mind-boggling."

I didn't blame her for that. The constant dinging and ringing of the slot machines throughout the airport were abrasive at best.

"My area is nice and quiet," I assured her. "Come on. I've already contacted the valet and they're bringing up my Suburban now." I gave a quick glance to the massive pile of suitcases like we were a family of twelve headed back from a six-month European extravaganza trip. "I hope it all fits."

Her hand slapped my stomach, and I feigned a pained grunt.

"You're a jerk," she teased.

I grabbed her hand before she could yank it back and pulled her to her feet. "Yeah. Maybe. But I'm *your* jerk."

Her grin softened and those eyes of hers glazed over with that expression I loved so much. "Yeah," she whispered.

"How far do you live from the Strip?"

We were flying through the streets of Las Vegas, and in the distance, I could see a massive Ferris wheel I knew was right down there. But so far, Las Vegas didn't look anything like I'd expected it to. Not a fan of gambling or one hundred plus degree heat, it'd never been a city I'd wanted to visit. But now, I wanted to go down there, just to say I had. To see what the fuss was about.

"About thirty minutes west of it depending on traffic." He glanced over at me, his left arm holding the steering wheel at twelve o'clock, right elbow braced on the wide console between us. He looked relaxed, maybe slightly humored at my question, and one hundred percent sexy man. "I could have driven you through it if you wanted to see it. But traffic is a pain in the ass."

"It's okay. Maybe some other time."

His lips lifted into a slow, sexy grin. "Yeah. Some other time."

That damn gorgeous look. It made me think of crazy

things. Like how I'd busted him last night after beating off in my own home. I'd never been more thankful to leave my own home. I'd never be able to step foot into my guest bedroom and not imagine him and all his *glory* spread out on my bed, hips arching into his fist, eyes squeezed closed while he thought of me. Thought of us.

Some other time.

I was preparing to throw away everything I'd spent my life building for this man. A life with him. We had time for everything and anything we wanted.

"Yeah," I said, returning him that soft smile, letting him know what I was thinking with my eyes. Based on the way his narrowed and brightened, he understood.

He reached across the console and set his hand, palm up, wiggling his fingers—an open invitation.

I slid my hand into his and our fingers tangled together.

"You doing okay? Feeling okay?"

"Yeah." My hands squeezed his. "Never better, I think."

His grip on mine tightened, sending a flash of warmth straight up my arm to the organ behind my ribs.

He liked that.

Ten minutes later, we entered a gated neighborhood. He flashed his security card to the guard standing in a small security center, and the gates rose.

"Security neighborhood, huh?"

"Yeah. There are a couple guys on the team who recommended this area. It's safe and quiet, a lot of money back here, so no one really thinks twice about having an athlete living next door. Joey doesn't live too far away actually."

Like me, he'd lived in a high-rise apartment building, north of where I lived, but much fancier and more modern. Had to give it to Garrett, he had style, with both his clothing and his house.

I leaned forward, watched a tight row of one and two-story homes built from stucco with red, curved tiles for roofs. Typical, and what I'd think of when I thought of Las Vegas, but wow, they were really smashed close together.

"Do you ever feel like you're living in a sardine can out here?"

He chuckled. "Sometimes. Yards are the size of postage stamps. Some of them even have fake turf for yards. Or all bricks. Mine is a yard full of red dirt."

"Dirt?"

"Yup. I plan on putting in a pool. Hot tub. That kind of thing."

"Sounds good." And yet, he'd considered doing all this without me. Moving on. Starting a life here with new teammates and friends I hadn't yet met. A burst of nerves made my stomach flip. What would they think of me? The girl who got knocked up? *Shit.* What would bloggers and gossips say?

My hand went to my stomach to settle it, but nothing helped.

"Hang on tight," he said. "Few minutes and I'll get you out of this car."

It wasn't the car, or the motion, making me sick.

It was fear.

In Chicago, I'd known the team. Garrett and I had been so close, I'd hung out with them often. Yeah, we'd been teased about being friends or more or whatever else the guys said, but I'd *known* them.

"I'm not sick, I'm nervous," I admitted. "About the guys on your team. The people here."

"It'll be fine. I'll make sure of it and hell, you know Joey won't let anyone say shit about you."

Joey Taylor, the youngest of the Taylor brothers. One of

his older brothers, Jude, was married to my best friend, Katie.

"You're right. It'll be fine." I wasn't so sure. There was still Nadia, who he'd told me there wasn't anything going on, but her brother was on the team. What did he know? Or think? And outside the pictures of them, he hadn't said what had happened between them.

"You look like you're going to throw up."

"Yeah, well... that's my standard look these days."

He huffed, but there was no humor in this. Now that we were *here*, pulling through his neighborhood, the car slowed down and he was pulling into a driveway, three-car garage—two straight ahead, one to the left with a gated door between them—that ball of nerves in my stomach climbed to my throat.

He had to park the Suburban at an angle inside his garage in order to get it to fit and I climbed down, sliding my hands down my jeans and already hating my choice in clothing.

"It feels gorgeous." I lifted my hands in the air, soaked in the warm weather, the sun heating my skin instantly.

"Tell me about it. Hence the reason why I want the pool." He popped open the back of his SUV. "Which suitcases do you need immediately? Any of them? I'll come get the rest later once we get settled and I show you around."

"Oh, um..." I couldn't even remember what I'd packed or what I'd thrown where outside the suitcase containing my bathroom items and my carry-on. And crap. Had I really packed *everything* I owned. I looked up at Garrett, embarrassed and shocked. Welcome to my daily kind of crazy. "I have no idea where anything is."

He laughed, bent down, and brushed his lips over my

cheek. "I'm not surprised. Come on. I want you to see my place." He held out his hand and like magnets, mine found his. "I'm really happy you're here with me."

And just like that, the ball of nerves in my stomach popped like a balloon. Maybe all I needed was Garrett, smiling down at me with his slightly crooked smile, partly hidden by his beard. His wild, untamed curly hair was way too long but sexy as hell, and he looked down at me with that look in his eyes that proved his honesty.

"Me too."

His gaze darkened and heated before he let go and reached into the back. Yanking out three bags, he threw one strap over his shoulders and carried the others in. I followed him around the SUV, through the sparkling clean and sparse garage—nary a yard cleaning tool or speck of grass in sight—and into his house. He opened the door and those nerves took flight again, but this time, not out of fear. With excitement.

This was his *home*. A place where he would live for the hopefully, foreseeable future, and he'd not only invited me into it, he wanted me there. We hit a mudroom slash laundry room first. Piles of hockey gear were stacked in one corner, skates hung from hooks, and practice jerseys and athletic shorts were in piles. Other than that, it was large and spacious with cream tile everywhere leading into what looked like the kitchen just beyond.

"I'll leave this shit here and we can sort through everything in a while and after I bring in the rest of your stuff."

"I can help with that."

His gaze dipped to my stomach and then lifted, slowly. "No. You can't."

One of my hands flew to my hip. "I'm pregnant, not an

invalid or incapable. Women *have* been doing this since the beginning of time, you know."

"I do." He stalked toward me, closing the small space in two quick strides and moving so fast I was pinned to the wall behind us before he stopped. "But you're also pregnant with *my* baby. And you're you. So I'm not taking chances and you're just going to have to deal with the fact that while I know exactly who you are, and that you're capable of every damn thing you set your mind to, this..." His hand settled at my hip and slid to my stomach, creating a maelstrom of emotions flooding my body and sent prickles of lust down my spine. "This is something you don't have to do alone. I'm here to take care of you—both of you—so you're just going to have to deal and let me do my job. Got it?"

He was teasing. Those lips of his curled with humor, but his eyes told a different story. They were heated. They were *hot* with desire. And probably his need to protect me.

"I get it." I nodded and breathed out the words on a sigh that held not a small amount of lust right back. "I'll try to be more accommodating in the future."

He smirked at my sass and bent down, kissing my forehead. "See that you do."

I huffed and shoved him off me. This was where we excelled. Flirting and playfulness. It shouldn't have surprised me we'd be able to be *us* so quickly, with so much between us, but it shouldn't have shocked me either. We'd always been friends. It was the *more than* friends where we stumbled.

We'd figure it out though. With time. Possibly a communication coach on speed dial.

"Come on. I want you to see my house."

He gripped my hand and strolled us into the kitchen. It was large, impersonal, like he hadn't had time to decorate a thing, but his furniture from Chicago was all there. All modern and chrome and black leather looking completely out of place with the cream tile, light oak cabinets. and off-white walls.

But the space was gorgeous. A kitchen island with cream marble countertops, four barstools, opened straight out to the living area where a massive television screen was plastered onto the wall. The kitchen was enormous. Two double ovens, a six-burner stove top. The island even had one of those smaller, veggie washing sinks in addition to the large kitchen sink that overlooked the backyard.

"This is great," I said, trying to think of all the positives. In truth, the space was. The rest? It wasn't him. At all.

"It's shit, but it was the best thing I could find in the location I wanted. I want to have it redone, make it more me eventually. Was planning on doing it this off season."

That made more sense.

"I think it needs to be lightened. Match the furniture more."

"We'll figure it out." He said it without a second thought. That *we'd* figure it out. Not him. And that nervous excitement pulsing through me spread faster, hotter.

We might have still had things between us to overcome and we both knew it, but he had no doubt I'd be there to do so.

That... that made me want to drop to my knees, thank him with my mouth, right then and there. I cleared my throat so I didn't do something that stupid. *Slow,* he'd said he wanted.

I'd give him that—even if it meant I'd probably spend a lot of nights in his guest room pulling off what he'd done in mine.

We turned a corner where he took me down a large

hallway where there was an office, an actual library room with a vaulted ceiling and a ladder that took you to the highest shelves. They were mostly empty. Garrett wasn't a big reader. But there was a gorgeous, dark brown leather chair in one corner that looked brand new.

"This is... this is incredible." I spun in a slow circle, envisioned all the books I could fill those shelves with while looking out in the backyard that he hadn't been joking about. There was a six-foot privacy fence made of brick. What should have been the yard was all dirt and stone. Desert living. Palm trees and other scarce plants that probably thrived with no rain.

"I'm thinking this could be yours." He scrubbed the side of his jaw. "You know. Your office, if you want."

My vision blurred as I took him in, shuffling on his feet like he was as nervous as I was.

"I'd like that," I whispered, my throat thick. I couldn't hold back. He might want slow, but he had to know I was all in. I went to him and pressed my hands to his cheek. Pulling him down, I rolled to my toes and met him halfway. I kissed him, slowly slid my lips over his and kept it chaste, pouring my emotion into it at the same time. "Thank you. This is perfect."

"Good." His hand slid to my back and he held me against him until I settled back on my feet. "Then let's see the rest."

He showed me his workout room and we headed up the stairs where he quietly pointed out three more bedrooms. Not a lot of furniture in there, he said, but there were beds for his mom and sister. But not me. He didn't give me a chance to look in the rooms, or choose which one I'd be staying in, before he walked toward the end of the hallway to a door that was closed.

"This is my room," he whispered, for whatever reason, possibly he was trying to figure out sleeping arrangements like I was. He opened the door, stepped in, and then, to my utter shock, stopped so fast I ran into his back like it was a wall of steel as he bellowed out, "What the fuck are you doing here?"

12

GARRETT

Nadia.

She scrambled off the bed faster than I'd ever seen anyone move.

"What the hell are you doing here?" I barked out. Holy Mother of God. How had our wires gotten so damn crossed?

Two small hands pushed at my back and then to the door and Lizzie skated in next to me asking, "What is it—Oh..."

Oh was right. Her jaw dropped and as she came into view, Nadia shrieked, reached for something silky and scrambled off the bed faster than I'd ever seen anyone move.

"Oh I'm sorry. So sorry. I didn't... I didn't think anyone would be here."

She moved, throwing on that robe over something I assumed was supposed to be sexy lingerie, but I averted my eyes to above her face.

"Nadia—"

"Nadia?" Lizzie asked. Next to me, she froze, but I reached out and grabbed her hand, moving us both into the bedroom and out of the doorway.

"I'm sorry. So sorry. I just... I thought... I hoped..."

"You hoped *wrong.*"

This wasn't happening. André was going to have my ass if he knew this was happening. Hell, he was going to kick me straight to his mother country if he thought I'd screwed over his sister. The whole reason I'd agreed to the charade in the first place was because all three of us knew the score.

How in the hell did I just lose the game?

And this was happening *now*? When I told her about Lizzie? When I told her we weren't going to the next event?

Fuck me sideways.

"I'll just..." She was still grabbing shoes, a small bag she'd brought. Every time she grabbed something else, my eyes widened. What in the hell was she thinking? "I'll just... I'll get out of here."

She took off then, leaving both Lizzie and I alone in my room in the dust from her quick running.

Something banged into the wall, followed by her curse, and I was left gaping at my bed, the messed-up duvet with Lizzie still holding my hand in complete silence.

"I swear to you, on my life," I growled, shaken, pissed, and humiliated. "Nothing fucking happened between us. Nothing ever would."

"I believe you," she said and she squeezed my hand. "You've already said that, so I believe you. But she was really upset. You should... you should go talk to her. Calm her down before she gets behind the wheel."

Had she not just witnessed the same insanity I had? "You want me to do what?"

"Garrett.... that was intense. At least for her. She was in serious pain and I don't know if she hurt herself, but obviously she thought something... so go talk to her. Clear the air. And then later... maybe explain why she thought she could do that."

"Fuck." I scrubbed a hand down my face. She was right. Of course she was. Normally I wouldn't react that harshly—to any woman. But hell. That wasn't what I expected.

"Go." Lizzie shoved at me and got me moving. This was not the conversation I wanted to have, even if I'd shown up at home all alone.

I ran down the stairs right as the front door closed. The metal gated door slammed shut in the small outdoor patio area and I caught it and flung my way through it.

"Nadia!" I called out but she kept running, still barefoot. Her arms full of whatever she'd brought with her.

Shit. I hadn't even noticed her car at the curb I'd been so caught up with Lizzie and thinking of what she'd think of my place.

"I'm sorry. So sorry. Again. Crap. I am so embarrassed." She said it all in a rush as she reached her car. Everything in her hands fell to the street as she opened her purse.

I bent to help pick things up, and she slapped my hand away. "No. I have done enough trouble. Stop. You do not need to help with this."

"Nadia." I stood. Setting my hand on the car. "Stop. Calm down. Please."

She didn't. She dug through her purse until she locked on her keys and the doors unlocked.

"I need to go."

"You need to take a minute. Or five and take some deep breaths so you don't crash once you get behind the wheel."

She shook her head. She still hadn't looked at me. Nadia was gorgeous. Of course she was. She was still in school getting her master's in landscape architecture. She'd done it all with her brother's help. Their parents had both died years ago, right after André made the pros in the US. He brought his sister over, and he'd helped pay for her education ever since.

They were good people. Knowing I'd hurt her—however unintentionally—*killed*.

"Please. Look at me," I said, trying to soften my voice and kick the remaining rage out of it. Had Lizzie not been Lizzie—that entrance could have gone so vastly differently.

Her head lifted, tears stained her flushed cheeks. "I'm sorry. I know what we were. Or that we weren't anything. But you're so good and so nice. I started thinking... well, and then you said you couldn't go to the gala next week and I just... I hoped I could make something happen."

Shit. Shit!

"Nadia."

"No." She held up her hand. "I know. I understand. This was my fault. Very much so. Let me, please, just let me go now."

"Nadia." I felt absolutely nothing more than concern for a friend I'd hurt and the urgent need to go check on Lizzie. "You sure you're okay?"

"I will be. And please, tell her I'm sorry."

"I think she understood."

"Good. That is good." She squinted at the sunlight and pursed her lips together. "You are a good man. I'm sorry I did that to you. I will move on, but after—after Toby—it felt *good* to be treated well. It just... misfired inside my brain a little."

"You deserve the absolute best. I'm not that guy for you, but there is one out there. I promise."

"Thank you."

"Can I help you now?"

She looked down at her feet, giving an embarrassed laugh. "Sure, good guy. I will let you help."

I crouched down, a grin on my face. Nadia was a great woman. I meant everything I said. Had Lizzie never been on my brain, I still didn't think she would have been my type. Outside of this small fiasco, she was generally too serious for me. But she absolutely deserved a man who appreciated that in her.

I gathered up her things, ignoring the lacy items and bathroom items she'd packed as if she'd hoped to stay for a weekend and didn't act like I saw a thing when I tossed it all into her back seat. "Drive safe, Nadia."

She slid into the driver's seat, hands still trembling. "I will." She peeked up at me, sunglasses now slid over her eyes so I couldn't see her. "And... I am happy for you. I am."

"Thank you." I stepped around the car, back to the side-walk on my front lawn, and I waited until she got her car started.

Once she pulled out and down the street, I headed back inside, not surprised at all to find Lizzie in the kitchen, pretending that she hadn't been pacing or, most likely staring out the windows and watching.

"Is she okay?"

My heart grew three sizes. It stretched and grew and put pressure against my sternum so harsh I rubbed the area that felt the force of my love for this woman.

Had Lizzie not been as incredible as she was, this could have had a drastically different beginning to her welcome to Vegas. Instead, all she cared about was Nadia.

"She will be, and I'm really, really damn sorry this was how you met her because I swear, under a different set of circumstances, you two would be trouble together."

"So—"

I lifted my hand to stop her. "She has an ex-boyfriend. Toby or something or other I don't even remember but the guy was causing her problems, refusing to accept she'd broken up with him. André, her brother, asked me if I'd bring her as my date to a holiday fundraiser we had. Swear to God" —I placed my hand on my chest— "I told her straight up where I was, that I was happy to play the part if it got her ex to realize she was over him. I also told her most definitely that I was not at all in any position or place to want *any* kind of relationship right now. I'm new to the team, finding my footing and I want to come together with these guys, which isn't easy after being in Chicago for so long."

She came to me, that soft smile making me think of sex on lazy Sunday mornings where we moved slow and unhurried. "I think I understand."

"I don't know how she got a different idea, and I talked to her, since she called when we met that night. We had another thing to go to next week, and I figured that's why she was calling and when I got back to my room, after calming down, I called her back and told her exactly why I wouldn't be able to go to any more events with her. She sounded hurt, but I didn't think... I didn't think she really thought she had a chance. Or that she'd do this. I never even kissed her, Lizzie."

I played back through our interactions, running a hand through my hair and staring at the ceiling. Was there a time I'd flirted? Maybe, but it was harmless. Had I led her on? No. I'd told her how much I loved Lizzie, how much I wished things could have been different with us. The only time I'd ever touched her was to help her out of a car or usher her through a photo line or through a doorway.

"I can see why she'd be attracted to you."

She said it with that same lazy smile, but now humor sparkled in her grass green eyes.

"What?"

"Yeah." She shrugged and took another step toward me. Every move closer to me sent a spark of heat to my spine. "You're a good guy. You were probably a really good friend, made her laugh and forget her problems. Made her think something better was out there and when she thought she'd lost you, well, women who have had losers or jerks can see a good thing and will do anything to keep them. It's not your fault, though."

"So, what you're saying is, I'm better than her asshole cheating narcissistic ex so she might as well shoot her shot."

She laughed, threw her head back and her throat bobbed as she laughed her lyrical tune. "Yeah, I'm saying she found something *just* above the bottom of the barrel."

"Thank you," I breathed out. She really wasn't pissed and, better, she trusted me. Believed me. "For not freaking out about this and believing me." I whipped out my arm and grabbed her hand, yanking her to me until she slammed against my chest.

The urge to kiss her and take and devour and slake my desire deep inside hit me strong and fast, shooting straight to my dick and stealing my breath as I inhaled her sweet scent and felt the silky strands of her hair brush against my arms. I kissed her instead, pressed my lips to hers tenderly, fighting back the base urges fighting for dominance until her lips parted, and I slipped my tongue inside her mouth.

Kissing Lizzie was nirvana, a religious experience. She gave herself to it like she gave herself to everything she did —full of passion and with one hundred and ten percent. I could have kissed her forever, held her in my arms and stood in my kitchen until the world ended.

But I'd promised her slow, and as much as I loved her, I needed to be a man of word on that.

There was no way I was screwing us up by going back to our old ways.

I slowed the kiss, lingering at her lips as her hands fisted my shirt at the back and then rested my forehead to hers.

"What do you say we do dinner out somewhere and go have some fun on your first night in Vegas? Unless you're too tired?"

Her eyes glimmered with the diminishing haze of lust and excitement. "Can we go to the Strip?"

"We can do anything you want."

Always. Forever. As long as she did it with me at her side.

13

LIZZIE

I was still swaying on my feet, fingers pressed to my lips to seal in the taste of his kiss and feel of his mouth, not to mention the passion he poured forth into that kiss when Garrett stepped back and picked up his cell phone.

"I hate to do this, but I should call André. Make sure he knows about Nadia. At least so he can check in to make sure she's okay. They're really close."

Right. At least I pulled off the compassionate not-girl-friend baby-mama role. Inside, the mere mention of her name tightened a fist inside my chest. This woman wasn't just absolutely, breathtakingly gorgeous, something I could one hundred percent admit to, she'd been splayed out on Garrett's bed, in his *house*, like a sex goddess offering to heal all his wounds and take him to heaven with a crook of her fingers.

At least he'd been as shocked, and as fiercely angry at the sight of her as I was.

"Of course," I murmured and stepped away to give him

privacy. He didn't let me go far before he took my hand in his and squeezed.

He didn't let me go as he brought his phone to his ear. With his focus on me, I hid the jealousy and pain I'd actually experienced. He sent her home, and I believed what he said. The problem was I was going to have to see this girl again. Hell, she was the sister of a teammate. If I stayed here, I'd most likely see her frequently, and now I had to introduce myself to her at some point knowing her bra size as well as the fact she obviously made frequent trips to get waxed.

"Hey, it's Garrett," he said into the phone, his other hand firmly wrapped around mine. I didn't know if he wanted me close for him or for me, but I went to his side and rested against him. He dropped my hand and wrapped his arm around my back, settling it at my hip. "Listen. Yeah. I just got back a bit ago." Garrett's lips pressed to my temple and stayed there as he murmured. "It went well, man, Lizzie's actually here with me." He laughed and then, "Yeah. No shit. It's good, but that's not what I'm calling, it's about Nadia."

I closed my eyes, tried to find peace in the rumble of his voice and the beat of his pulse at my ear while he told André what happened—minus the details of the barely there lingerie. No brother needed to know that.

Who must have been pissed because through the phone I heard a muffled, "Oh fucking no. That is not good."

"Yeah, that's what I thought. But anyway, I talked to her, and she left in her car. Just wanted you to know so you can check on her if you want, make sure she got home safely or in case she ends up at your house."

More muffled, masculine, and accented words came through the phone I couldn't make out and Garrett chuckled. "It's all good. Lizzie knows what's going on, or that there isn't anything. It's good. Like I said, she was shaken up, so I thought you'd want to know." More pause, more murmured tones and then, "Yeah. I'll be at practice tomorrow. I'll talk to Lizzie, but we can probably make it. She loves Joey."

At the mention of Joey, my interest piqued. I twisted so I could see Garrett's expression. His full lips tipped into a smile. His fingers at my hip drew small circles. The man wasn't traditionally magazine model sexy but all his imperfections made him more attractive to me than a photoshopped man who probably tanned and got more Botox than my mom.

He ended the call and before he could say anything, I asked, "Joey?"

"Guess he's invited the team over for drinks tomorrow after practice. You in?"

"I'd love to see him." I hadn't seen him since North Carolina at Christmas and he was pretty wrecked then. He'd trusted me with information he hadn't told his family yet. "Has he said anything?"

"That he and Lenora got divorced without telling anyone, yeah. Did Katie tell you?"

"No. He did. Back at Jude's."

His eyes widened with surprise, and he swiped his hand through his hair. "No shit? Do you know why, because he's been pretty tight-lipped about the whole thing."

I didn't blame him one bit, but Joey's story was his to share.

"If he hasn't said anything, I'm not sure it's my place. Sorry." And I was, because Joey needed his friends. Mostly, he needed to get over Lenora. It'd give me a great amount of pleasure to be locked in a room with her for five minutes.

"He hasn't said shit. Totally tight-lipped about it."

"Then it's not my story to share."

"Of course not. I wouldn't ask that of you, but are you in? Want to see him?"

Joey? Absolutely. The rest of the team and their wives who might not take too kindly to the ex-friend who was knocked up invading? Not the most exciting thing I could imagine doing. Slightly more entertaining than shoving toothpicks beneath my fingernails on my list of painful experiences.

"I suppose the first time meeting your new teammates, it'd be more comfortable with Joey there."

"They'll like you. Hell, they barely know me and for the most part, they've treated me like they've known me as long as Joey."

Didn't surprise me. Garrett was a likable guy. Plus, as successful as he was, his ego was the size of a peanut. He didn't have a cocky, asshole bone in his body and I knew because I'd explored his plenty over the years. Still, I smiled. I was happy for him. Truly. Not all teams had great chemistry but he seemed to make the case his did. "That's good. I'm glad you have a good team here."

"Me too. Come on, if you're not tired or need a nap or anything, how about we go do some touristy bullshit and get some food in us."

"Sounds great. I just need a few minutes to get freshened up."

After being on the plane and puking and then the whirlwind that was Nadia, I needed a few minutes to settle myself.

I was really here. In Vegas. With Garrett. Pregnant with his baby.

We could go to anything. Explore Vegas. Take on the world—

As long as we were home by eight so I could pass out on the couch.

WE ATE dinner at Hexx Kitchen, one of the few menus we scanned before leaving where I thought I could find something that would sit well with me. As it was, Garrett ate a massive rib eye with a second order of seared scallops. It was the steak that had sounded good to me as well but by the time we arrived, my tiny bean decided a French dip, torn apart so I could eat the meat dipped in horseradish and au jus separately, with no bread, was the best thing since well, sliced bread. Two sides of asparagus, an extra order of macaroni and cheese. Between the two of us, we had so much food it'd make a table of four look like they over ordered.

I didn't know if it was the flight, the excitement or stress —either or, possibly both—of the last few days, but I didn't feel like I wanted to crawl into the nearest couch and sleep for eight months by the time we were done.

Instead, I was invigorated by the noises and sights, the Bellagio fountains that went off at their timed intervals through the palm trees across the street. Even the club soda with lime I chose over a simple pop tasted like liquid gold.

But mostly, it was the company. Across from me, Garrett told me all the stories he'd already compiled about his new team. Starting with André, the back-up goalie, he then skipped over Joey since I knew him. We talked about Dominick Masters, the team's first line defenseman who also had more goals than any defenseman in the league. The right and left wingers, Alix and Max. All were single, including Joey now, younger than both of us, and had no problems living the high life with VIP services at the nearby casinos' hotel bars complete with bottle service and all the tail they could chase. Garrett's description, not mine.

"So, Alix is the player? And the bad boy?" I leaned forward, my elbow on the table, and curled my hand into a fist. I popped my chin onto that fist and gave Garrett a salacious wink. "Girls like the bad boys, you know?"

Garrett stabbed his fork in my direction. "He's not a bad boy, but yes. Even if I'd die for him, I still wouldn't let my sister within five feet of that guy. If he comes tomorrow, your required minimum distance to maintain will be ten feet."

I threw my hand back and laughed, slapping my hand on the table. "You silly ogre. You can't tell me what to do."

He winged up his brows and glanced down at my stomach, hidden beneath the table but the heat in his eyes made it clear. "You're carrying half of me in you. I can so."

"Half of me." I chuckled and speared an asparagus with my fork. "You make it sound like I'm already the size of that Eiffel Tower behind me."

He chuckled and raised his hand. "The baby book I downloaded, specifically for dads, told me to *never* comment on your size so I'll claim the fifth on that one."

My mouth might as well have dropped to the table. Electricity jolted through my veins as I watched his smile spread. "You... you downloaded a baby book? About dads?"

And oh dear. Why did I suddenly feel like crying? He went blurry and I blinked, trying to clear my eyes but it was no use.

"Yeah." He cleared his throat. "Is that... is that making you cry?"

"Shut up." I flung the rest of my asparagus at him. He nabbed it out of the air like it was a puck heading straight at his face and tossed it into his mouth. "I cry all the time."

"You're a pretty crier. Beautiful all the time, but you cry pretty, too."

"God," I moaned and dropped my face into my hands. "You're going to make it worse."

His knee bumped into mine beneath the table and then one of his hands reached out, pulling down my fisted hand. "Hey. I'm in this. I'm all in. I want to know everything, be there for you, be there for *us* and the baby. Of course I want to understand what you're going through." He stopped, glanced toward the fountains again as they lit up and he cleared his throat. "I won't be able to be there. Not all the time. Not with travel and you know…" If I went back to Chicago after these next few weeks.

"Garrett—" I practically breathed his name but he continued before I could think of anything else to say. I couldn't, wouldn't, make promises I couldn't keep and luckily, he soldiered on with what was on his mind.

"Anyway, I want to be involved. Here for you. I can't do that if I don't know what's going on."

At the end of my first trimester, I was still trying to wrap my head around everything. It'd taken me three weeks before I started reading baby books, before the reality settled. Sure, I'd known enough to start taking prenatal vitamins, to call my OB-GYN's office and for the first time, schedule an appointment for something more than my annual exam. They'd handed me pamphlets. Done a vaginal ultrasound. Only then, once I heard the wild whoosh of a heartbeat that was most definitely not mine, had I finally broken down and ordered my baby and pregnancy books.

It'd taken Garrett days. Of course it had. Because that was the level-headed, excited, and involved kind of dad he would be.

"I want this." I squeezed his hand back and my second

hand dropped to my stomach. "I want this with you. All of it."

"Good."

We shoved away our plates and soon the server came with our check. Once Garrett signed it and slid in a tip I would have stabbed someone for in my high school years, we walked the Strip.

We wandered down to the gondola rides in front of the Venetian before turning around. On the way back, I convinced him to walk through Flamingo Hotel's casino even though neither of us wanted to gamble. We took pictures in front of the Eiffel Tower. Strolled through Caesar's Palace and then back toward the Bellagio. By the time we stopped at the fence, the sun was setting and I was thankful I'd grabbed a heavier cardigan. I wrapped it around my waist, tucking my arms in close as Garrett caged me in at his chest and curled his hands around the handrail. He brushed his chest to my back before settling his chin at my shoulder.

The scrape of his beard sent shivers down my arms but the heat of his body warmed me straight to my toes.

His lips brushed over my cheek, back to my ear, intensifying my reactions, and I loved every single moment. There was not another man alive who could ever make me feel like Garrett.

"I'm so damn glad you're here with me. No joke, Lizzie. I want this."

I uncurled my arms from my stomach and settled my hands over his on the railing. "I do too."

The fountains burst in front of us, water changing colors from the lights and the music played. People lined the railings, all of them mesmerized by the sights in front of us, but all I could think of was Garrett, and this chance I'd been given to make things right with us.

Please don't let me screw this up.

As the thought hit me, my backside pressed close to his vibrated. Once. Twice. Then again. "Is that your phone or are you happy to see me?"

His chuckle rumbled through his chest, against my back. "Group text from the guys on the team."

"Do you need to go check it?"

"No. There's nothing more important than what I'm doing now."

Holy swoon. Thank God I wasn't wearing a corset and was being held up against him or else I risked fainting straight into the fountains. Yeah, I really needed not to screw this up.

I let go of him, turned my back to the railing and pressed my hands to his cheeks. "Thanks for making this so easy."

His head bent and he brushed his lips over mine. "I love you. It's as simple as that."

"Right," I rasped, and slid my hands down his body, over the curve of his chest and wrapped my arms around him. I snuggled up close, turning so we could finish the show. As it came to a gentle close, dozens of tourists clapped and the chatter around us increased, Garrett held me to the side.

"Let's get out of here. I want to hit the store to make sure you have what you can eat and then I want to get home."

14

LIZZIE

Garrett stocked up on groceries like the world was ending. Our cart was overflowing to an insane degree and we had more bags in the back of his Suburban than a family of eight had to have for a two-week grocery trip. I couldn't stop teasing him for it. Every time I said something sounded good, he threw three in the cart. Add in the fact he had a week-long home stretch of games and he consumed more calories a day than an elephant, I was practically doubled over in laughter by the time we pulled into his garage.

He was still shaking his head at me like I was being ridiculous, probably because I was, and I was still laughing. I couldn't help myself from egging him on further.

"So. Is there anyone else who has a key to your place?"

His smile fell. "Are you fucking with me?"

"Too soon?"

"It will always be too soon for that joke, dumbass." He leaned across the console and kissed me. "Get out of my truck. Go inside. I'll get the groceries in."

"I can help."

"Yup. You're a capable, strong, independent woman. I know this. I also know when you're not laughing, you're yawning, so you're getting tired. So go inside, get into whatever clothes you'll wear when you fall asleep in twenty minutes or less, and relax. I'll get the food in."

I shot him with a playful glare, but opened my door. "You know. Sometimes it sucks how well you know me."

"You'll get used to it."

I stuck my tongue out at him. "For that, I'm even going to let you put all the food away, too. I should see you in, what? Three weeks?"

His chest shook and his rumbling laughter filled the garage. "Go inside, you fool."

Inside, my suitcases were still mostly left in the mudroom except for the one I'd taken to a room earlier to get refreshed. Luckily, that suitcase held the clothes I wore most these days, which included loose jogger sweats and oversized sweatshirts. In fact... oh, yeah, I knew exactly what I was going to throw on.

Garrett's Chicago College sweatshirt I stole from him within the first few weeks we started messing around. Now seven years old, the letters had faded. The wrists were so worn there were holes in them, perfect enough I could thread my thumbs through them.

It drove Garrett crazy every time he saw me in it. More than once, it'd ended with me thrown over his shoulder and tossed to the nearest piece of soft furniture. Sometimes, a hard surface did equally well.

I hurried up the stairs to the suitcase and dug through it. Whipping out the red sweatshirt with the faded gray lettering, I also pulled out my favorite pair of jogger sweats. Bought a size larger than I usually wore, they fit my bloated stomach perfectly at night.

Another yawn hit me as I stripped out of my jeans. I didn't need to wear maternity clothes yet, but I'd wrapped a hair tie around the button and through the hole like I'd learned on Pinterest since I couldn't close them the right way anymore. I caught my reflection in the mirror and turned, grimacing as I saw my boobs bursting out of my bra that was quickly undone and fell to the floor.

Wowzers. They were big. And so sore. All the time. One day I accidentally smacked one on a doorframe and fell to my knees, crying out in pain. If that hurt that bad, how in the hell was I going to manage childbirth.

I shook the thought away. I'd been trying not to read too far ahead to keep from panicking about the horrors headed my way. The last thing I needed was to start freaking out now.

I turned from the mirror, tugged on my sweats and threw on the sweatshirt, forgoing putting on a bralette I'd taken to wearing.

Screw bras for the next six months—maybe forever—who needed them anyway.

Dressed looking like I was a poor college student who'd gained the freshman fifteen, I grabbed a hair clip, twisted my hair, flipped it, and then settled the clip. Hair wisps at my temples and the base of my neck flew in every which way and hair sprung from the clip, making it look like I'd just shoved my fingers into an electric socket.

Perfect.

I snagged a bottled water I'd kept on the nightstand earlier to take it back to the kitchen and headed down the stairs.

When I reached the landing, I smothered another laugh.

Garrett's kitchen counters were full of grocery bags along with a large pile of them on the floor. I found him at the fridge, both doors open, hands braced around the French door handles, giving the fridge the most perplexed look.

I leaned my shoulder against the wall and took the time I had to study him. The curve of his backside in his jeans that clung to his ass and thighs. The stretch of his arms, muscles bulging. It was a little-known secret Garrett used to take figure skating and yoga, still did the yoga, to work on his flexibility as goalie. I was one of the few he allowed to tease him about it, but looking at him now, there was not a single inch of him I wanted to tease him about.

The man was perfection, even as he scratched his jaw and caught me standing there, my mouth watered at the sight of him.

"Don't say it," he said and glanced at the groceries with no home and from what it looked like, no home to go to, before he brought his eyes back to me and they dropped. Beneath his jaw, his irritated tic appeared. "That's my sweatshirt."

I shrugged. "It's my favorite."

"Yeah, I remember how much I liked it half a decade ago, too." His gaze stayed at my chest, but there was no doubt he wasn't seeing the faded lettering, but the memory of what was beneath.

I stood, arched my back and ignored the fact without a bra my breasts, even with their sudden new growth, were well hidden beneath the oversized sweatshirt.

"What's going on with the groceries? Do we need to take half the supply to a food shelter?"

"Just about." His mouth cracked into a smile. "I already ordered a deep freezer online for the frozen stuff."

"You did what?"

He shut the fridge doors and came toward me, hand

snaking out and grabbing a fistful of thick material at my stomach. "Should be here tomorrow. We'll make the rest work tonight."

I grew up with money. I'd never hidden that. Granted, Garrett's contracts would have put him well above even my own parents' pay grades, but to buy a deep freezer because he overbought groceries *once*? Talk about excessive.

"That's ridiculous. How about next time you go to the store, like in six months, you just don't stock up for Armageddon?"

"I won't make any promises." He brushed his lips over mine. "We should get this stuff put away, but I have a question for you first. And you can say no…"

"What is it?"

"Can I—" His fist loosened on my top and then settled at my hip, drifting up and down in what didn't feel like a calm gesture. He was tense. "Can I touch your stomach?"

That was what had him nervous? "You've seen every inch of my body. Hell, there's probably parts of me you know more than me." The best parts, if I was being honest.

Maybe it wasn't the time to tease him about it because he blinked slowly and exhaled. "I know… but this… this is different."

"Hey." I took his hand in mine and with my other, I lifted the sweatshirt to just below my breasts. He was right. This was different, a different flavor of vulnerability, and I was never good with that. This was… my body changing. Even so soon. And what would he think when I was stretched out like an inflatable pool toy?

I must have looked as uncertain as him as I settled his hand on my stomach and then slid both of ours beneath the waistband of my sweats. "I don't have to."

"You're right. This is strange."

"It's your stomach, and your same soft skin but it's so much more too."

Tears burned my eyes as his lids closed and the tenseness in his body melted. That was... possibly the sweetest thing he'd ever said to me. Better than all the dirty talk.

He opened his eyes, and the shimmer in them stole my breath and blurred my vision further. Was he... *crying?*

"Garrett," I breathed out. He was. And the floor beneath my feet shuddered from the weight of his expression. His happiness.

"We're having a baby," he muttered, almost as if he was just finally realizing it.

"Yeah." I laughed, and my hand on his squeezed. "I already said that."

"I just... it keeps coming in small hits and waves but this... you're changing and I hope you know I mean that in the most amazing way possible."

"Get ready. Soon I'll look like I swallowed a Mini-Cooper car."

"And you'll still be the most beautiful woman I've ever seen."

How in the hell had I been so stupid to take this long to reach out to him?

The tears slid from his eyes like he willed them to and he stepped back, shuddering on an inhale and swiping his hands through his hair. He turned back to the mess all over the counter and dropped his hands to his sides.

"Fuck. What the fuck was I thinking?"

I laughed and shoved my shoulder into his. "Want some help?"

～

"LIZZIE. WAKE UP." Garrett's deep voice rumbled in my ear and I slowly opened my eyes. The first thing I saw was him hovering over me and to the right was the television.

"Did I fall asleep?"

The last thing I remembered was resting on the couch while he flipped through a variety of streaming apps while we argued over what to watch. I wanted a comedy, something light-hearted. Garrett wanted something that would blow vehicles or buildings or people sky-high. When it came to what we watched, unless it was hockey, we rarely agreed.

"Did I fall asleep because it was taking you too long to make a decision?" I asked, voice groggy from sleep.

"Sure. We can go with that." He settled his hand at my back and brought me to sitting, sliding my feet to the floor. "It's late. I didn't want you to spend the night out here."

"Thanks." He guided me to my feet and then settled a hand at my back as we headed toward his stairs.

"Do you need some water?"

"Oh. Please."

I went to turn, but he stopped me. "Head on up. I'll go get it."

"Thanks." Between sleep, the day, and all the activity, my ankles might as well have had ten-pound weights strapped to them. Moving was difficult, slow, and I took each step like I was at the peak of Mount Everest. I was barely to the top of the stairs when Garrett's quick steps vibrated on the stairs and he reached me.

"You're so tired you're almost falling over the railing."

"I know. But I'm told it gets better. Couple of weeks and I should have more energy."

"Good. That's good."

We pulled to a stop outside the bedroom. The bed

looked inviting, but I couldn't bring myself to tear away from Garrett's gentle touch at my back.

"I should let you get your sleep," he said, clearing his throat.

Hmm. If I wasn't mistaken, he was having the same thought I was.

"Good night." I peered up at him, hoping to see the look in his eyes that said he didn't want this. That he wanted me to come with him. I craved that familiar and memorable look of heated desire that could turn me wet in a nanosecond. Instead, all I saw was conflict.

I hated it. I'd caused it. He might have been happy I was here, excited about the baby. But *us?* That would take more time.

I'd give it to him after I'd so royally screwed up.

He opened his mouth, but before I could hear apologies or excuses, all of which were valid, but would still send my emotions into overdrive, I rolled to my toes and kissed him.

"I get it, and it's okay," I whispered. "Sleep well."

A rumble built in his chest, similar to a growl. I stepped away before he could do anything he wasn't ready for. I'd hurt him. I'd own that. But I couldn't see him looking so conflicted and feel the guilt of that. We had enough to figure out without weighing me down more.

I closed the door behind me, rested against it and as a yawn shook my body, I pushed off the door then headed toward the bathroom. There, I washed my face, cleaned up, did all my nightly duties with eyes half opened and a sluggishness weighing me down and slowing my movements.

I needed this second trimester and the "energy burst" I'd heard of to happen and happen soon.

I expected, once I finally fell into bed, to not remember falling asleep again.

Instead, wearing only an oversized T-shirt and my long hair braided to keep it tangle-free, I tossed and turned. I got out of bed and flicked on the ceiling fan. Back to bed and kicked off covers. Threw them back over me.

It wasn't the heat or exhaustion making sleep difficult.

It was Garrett. The sound of the shower running. The creaks of floors and quiet thumps of doors closing.

It was being so close to him, three nights in a row and not being able to fall asleep curled in his large and hot frame. Feel the gentle brush of his arm hair on my body as he held me.

It was all it took. Memories of us together scrolled through my mind until I was so restless, the only one way I'd sleep was to take care of the need heating my body, making me wet.

Knowing him, he was resting, one arm bent behind him on a pile of pillows while he watched whatever game was on, hockey or not, or SportsCenter. His chest, with the perfect amount of hair across his pecs and down the delineation between his abs would be bare, the covers draped at his waist.

My sex throbbed at the thought, and I closed my eyes, pictured him there, remote in his hand or resting on his stomach. Maybe playing with his phone. Responding to his team's group text and one side of his lips curled into a smile.

And I could have been there with him, had I not screwed us up.

I shoved down the irritation, the arousal building between my thighs. Three months without sex wasn't anything I wasn't used to, but suddenly my body felt like it'd been years.

But for now, I could think of him—and take care of myself.

I slid my hand down my belly, to the apex of my thighs where my clit was already swollen and I was already drenched. Biting down on my lip to keep a groan muffled, I slid two fingers through my center, gathering moisture before I pressed them in circles around my clit, hips arching into my timid, but familiar movement. Eyes closed, I pictured Garrett. The weight of him on me, how full I felt when he was inside of me. Two fingers pressed inside me, then three. It didn't matter what I did to myself, there was no substitution for Garrett's thick and long dick inside of me. A groan of frustration fell from me as I sought what he gave me so well, and I went back to rubbing my clit, the easiest way to take care of myself but even then I imagined Garrett's mouth, his tongue, and the way he bit and sucked and flicked and played my body like his own personal orchestra.

He was gifted at *everything*, at least when it came to knowing how to play with my body.

I couldn't hold it back. My fingers moved in rapid pace, with my other hand, I pinched and pulled on my nipple, squeezed my breast, tugged it until there was the slight sting of pain like when Garrett would bite them and everything culminated. My spine went white hot, my thighs trembled and right as my orgasm hit, I lost the hold on my bottom lip and a small cry of pleasure burst from me as I came, thinking of Garrett... which he could do for me so I wouldn't only be half-satisfied.

My heart racing, I slowly came down and froze as a creak of wood floor whispered through the door.

Another creak.

Oh shit.

There was a quiet thump on the wall outside my room and then footsteps.

My breath stalled as I waited, my fingers still rubbing my sex.

Would he come in? Walk away?

More footsteps faded and I finally exhaled.

Oh dear God. He'd *heard* me. He had to have.

Mortification settled before a vision of him last night, bare-chested, with his T-shirt wrapped around his hands as he cleaned off his own aftermath. Served him right, I figured. Now we were even.

I grabbed my phone and sent him a text, telling him exactly that.

His reply was almost immediate. **Wasn't nearly as funny to me as it was to you last night.**

I could apologize, but I wasn't sorry. I could say it wouldn't happen again, but I wasn't a liar.

Me: Next time I'll be quieter.

Garrett: Next time, I'll be in the room with you and it won't be your fingers getting you off.

Oh....

I couldn't wipe the smile off my face before exhaustion took me and I fell asleep.

But my dreams that night? Divine.

15

GARRETT

Killing me. She was killing me and it'd been less than twenty-four hours since we got off the plane. Lizzie in my kitchen, face slightly green, sipping her one cup of coffee with her hair pulled back, a beautiful mess with her sleepy eyes sliding to me as I entered was a thing of absolute beauty.

Also, pure fucking torture after what I heard her doing last night. Ironically, doing it while I was on my way to convince her to come to my room despite not wanting to move too fast. But that's what we did, we jumped into the fire and then were burned by the flames.

I'd paused to turn around, head back to my room to go *slow*—a torture in itself—when I'd recognized that gasp, that mewl she made whenever I was deep inside her and she couldn't hide.

She might have caught me in the aftermath of getting off, but hearing it?

Slamming my head into the wall couldn't have been more painful.

It was nearly as bad as seeing that sweatshirt of mine she

swiped back in college. The way it hung on her frame, hid every one of her curves. It didn't matter. I'd long since seared the image of her body in my memory. But it did something to me to see her wearing her clothes, like she'd declared herself mine.

After a restless night of sleep, leaving me tired for my practice I had to get going to, the last thing I needed was to walk into the kitchen and have Lizzie sitting at a barstool, nibbling on crackers like a rabbit, and sipping coffee like she belonged in it. She blushed as soon as she saw me and turned her focus to her phone.

"Morning," I muttered, my voice gruff from sleep and irritation. "Sleep well?"

"Like a baby," she said, grinning while still blushing.

So we were going to skip right over the fact we'd both been caught pleasuring ourselves in the last twenty-four hours. Cool.

I went to the freezer, grabbed a bag of cut up frozen fruits and veggies I used in my morning smoothies and carried it to the blender. As I mixed everything and the whir of the blender permeated the air, Lizzie dumped her plate in the dishwasher and then turned, resting against the counter.

"You have practice today?"

I cut off the blender and grabbed a large cup from the cupboard. "Yeah. All day. Film and workouts and practice."

Shit. I hadn't even considered. For the next two weeks, I had no idea what she'd do during the day. I picked up my key ring and began twisting off one of my keys. It was to my Range Rover I had in Chicago when I signed my first contract. "I have my Rover in the one-car garage, if you need to go anywhere. Will you... be okay while I'm gone?"

She rolled her eyes and palmed the key. "I'll be fine. I'll get some work done and might make some calls to obstetricians and midwives. See if I can get in for some consults while I'm here."

I was halfway through a drink of my smoothie and started choking on it when I heard the midwife. "You're going to call doctors?"

She'd already mentioned moving here, taking the time to do this. It shouldn't have hit me so hard.

Perhaps there was still a large part of me assuming she'd take off. "Lizzie…" I could barely speak. My throat closed up. I didn't want to jump the gun on this, but this was something I had to know.

Lizzie looked at me wide-eyed. Maybe like I'd gone a bit crazy. And she was absolutely nonchalant as she said, "Yeah. When I move, it'll help to have that settled already."

"When?" She said when. Not if. "You just said *when*." It came out on a breath. My knees were shaking. We'd talked. We'd talked a lot. Back in Chicago, she'd said she was considering it, but this *sounded definite.*

She gave me a rapid-fire blink, still looking at me like I was crazed. "I thought I guess you knew that. I mean, I even mentioned it at dinner with my parents."

"I just." Shit, she was really doing this. What in the hell was my hold up with her? Why couldn't I trust she truly meant all of this? "You'd do that. You'd give up everything in Chicago. For me."

Goddamn it. I was not going to cry before practice, and hell, I had to get going so I didn't even have the time to break down, but shit. Last December, she'd said we'd figure it out and then essentially ghosted me. I'd truly doubted this would happen.

"Garrett. I love you. And we're having a child. Starting a family. I already told you I want this with you." Her head tilted to the side, adorable little confusion twisted her lips as she asked, "Where else would I be?"

Nowhere. That was where, because she belonged here. "Goddamn, I love you."

I pulled her to me and slammed my mouth to hers before she could—or couldn't say it back. She hadn't yet. Not really.

Before I lost complete control, I set her back down, slowed the kiss and made sure we were both steady on our feet before I slid my hand down the side of her face, cupping her cheek. "If you couldn't figure it out, that makes me really damn happy." She laughed, but I had to get this back on track. I needed to get to practice and now I had to get rid of my erection along with the swelling in my chest. "So... midwives? Like a home birth or something?"

"No." She shook her head. "Some do that, but I'd already looked in to some out here. They deliver in birthing centers, connected to hospitals but the moms are allowed a bit more freedom to move around."

"Are you thinking a natural birth?" I had enough teammates to have heard a dozen horror stories of giving birth. How terrifying it could be. Emergency deliveries or surgeries. Women strapped with crap around their stomachs and unable to get out of bed.

"I don't know." She fidgeted with the key in her hand. "I guess I just want options. Hell, I might just decide to schedule a C-section and be done with it. I've had some friends do that, and with your schedule... maybe that'd be easier."

"You're due right around when pre-season begins." Damn. That meant I'd have a newborn. Hell, maybe on the road when she went into labor. Maybe she had a point.

"We have time to make those decisions," she said, cocking her head. "Don't you need to get going?"

Yeah, but my heart rate was spiking, the back of my neck was sweaty and I was pretty sure if I tried to take a step, my knees would buckle. I gripped the counter and choked down the rest of my smoothie. "I think the reality of this is just starting to hit me and I might be having a panic attack," I admitted.

Lizzie laughed, a throaty chuckle and shook her head like I was adorable. I was anything but. I wasn't kidding about the panic attack, but the last time I had one was in my very first pro game I started as goalie. Pretty sure I swallowed more puke during that game and drank more water from my Gatorade bottle I kept on top of the net than was humanly healthy.

She came to me and ran her hands down my arms, up again, trying to soothe me, but one simple touch from Lizzie had the opposite effect on me. This time was different, even as her eyes glimmered with amusement as she laughed at me.

"This isn't funny."

"It's not," she agreed. "And it is. This is pretty much the massive roller coaster I've been on for weeks. Welcome to the club."

"Oh fuck... it's starting... what's that called? Sympathy pains?"

"You're fine." She was still laughing at me, head tilted back and she was losing the green hue to her skin. "I think you're doing great."

Her hands rubbed my arms and all panic melted. This was normal, right? To be so damn excited? So damn scared out of your freaking brain? And holy crap. This was just the pregnancy part, the part I had very little involvement in.

What was I going to be like when there was a helpless little baby in my arms? Or a sassy little toddler? A son who treated girls like dawgs? Or, hell, heaven forbid, a daughter who dated assholes... and I wouldn't even *be here* for those dates to threaten to murder little punks who showed up on a motorcycle to take my little girl out.

"I am so fucked," I moaned and dropped my forehead to Lizzie's. "I think I need to quit. Maybe I can coach. Go back to school and become an accountant. No way in hell our daughter is getting on the back of a bike."

"What?" Lizzie's garbled laugh made me groan. "What are you talking about?"

"I just saw my future flash in front of my eyes and it was fucking terrifying."

She was still laughing as her hands slid behind my back. On instinct, I did the same to her, forced her to cling to me like we were double-sided tape.

"We've got this," she said, but her chest was still rumbling with laughter, breasts pressing against my chest every time she chuckled. "I swear it. You're going to be a great dad."

"Goddamn you," I muttered, but I didn't mean it, and the way she squeezed me back told me she knew exactly what that meant to me.

Fucking *everything*.

"Speaking of," I whispered. "Wait until we have to call my mom and Gabby and let them know."

She stepped back, eyes wide with terror. "They're not pacifists like my parents."

"Nope." I kissed the top of her head and stepped back. "Have a good day, honey!"

"You know I'm going to spend the rest of the day freaking out about what your mom's going to say, right?"

My mom would lose her ever-loving mind. And then scream so loud we could hear her all the way in Las Vegas, over eleven hundred miles away.

Her hand came swinging out, but I jumped, avoided her playful slap and was in the mudroom grabbing my gear as she screamed out, "I hate you!"

I opened the door to the garage, grinning like a maniac, all fears gone. For now. "Liar. You love me."

She huffed. I'd won that round.

But I had no doubt Lizzie would get me back and it'd be equally painful.

JOEY SAUNTERED into the team's locker room while I was tying up my goalie pants, the rest of my massive amount of gear in a pile in front of me. As the goalie, I not only had the most gear and the largest locker, I created the largest mess, so I was at the end of the row. Across from me, Joey tossed his bag into his own locker before sitting down and smirking at me.

"So I hear Lizzie is back with you."

Back with me. I wished. I hoped so.

"We worked some things out while I stayed in Chicago, yeah. But she's only here for a couple of weeks."

He nodded, his black hair like all the Taylors flopping while he did it. Joey was the perfect mix of Jason and Jude. Jude's face shape, Jason's hair. He was faster than either of them but had the same wit. Their same loyalty. He clasped his hands together, elbows on his knees. "She tell you?" he asked, voice lowering while he glanced around the room.

No one was paying attention to us, they were all dragging their own gear on and giving each other shit.

"She told me you told her about your divorce back in December but that was it. Said the rest is your story."

"Yeah." He huffed and rubbed the back of his neck. "Not quite ready to talk about all that."

"I'm not prying, Joey. And even if she *had* told me everything you told her, you gotta know me well enough by now to know I wouldn't say shit, wouldn't judge it."

"Right. Yeah. I got that."

"Good. Then are you going to let me get outta here and warmed up or are we going to break out into a heart-to-heart."

He laughed, shook off whatever laying of sludge was covering him and stood. "You guys coming tonight?"

I grabbed my knee pads and started yanking them on. "She's excited to see you again, so yeah. We're coming."

"I'm happy for you. You know that, right? I hope it works out this time."

All the nerves, and all the excitement and everything I'd been facing for the last few days surfaced. I'd already screwed up a game. I couldn't afford to screw up more because my head was messed up. I could trust Joey. Hell, I didn't even know if Katie or Jude knew anything. My gut said no. Lizzie wouldn't have put our friends in that position.

I abandoned my knee pad, halfway pulled up and headed over to him. Joey's brow furrowed as I bent my head so only he could hear me. "She's pregnant."

His eyes widened. "No shit? Is it—"

"Mine. Yeah. Back in December. But I'm just now finding out, so yeah, she's here. She's talking about staying, but I know her. She could shove her head in the sand and take off and it's fucking with me. So, go easy on her."

His jaw jutted out like I'd pissed him off but that wasn't my intention.

"Don't be a dick. I'm just saying don't give her a hard time. Don't tell her..."

That'd I spent all of New Year's drunk off my ass and miserable. Or that while I might have played well when she wasn't talking to me because I used that fury to fuel my fire for the game, afterward I was a massive wreck. Not the greatest first impression I gave my new team even if Joey knew why.

"We still have stuff to work through. Us, mostly, and I just... I don't want her feeling that guilt. Staying for that reason."

He blew out a breath and nodded, anger softening and turned to something else. "I wouldn't do that to you. I want you two together. You need my help. You've got it, you know that. I've known you too long."

I clasped his shoulder and gave him a quick shake. "You Taylors are the best men I've ever met. Hope you know that offer goes right back to you. You ever need to talk..."

"You're there. I know."

But it wouldn't be now. His gaze ping-ponged to the guys in the locker room growing rowdier as they grabbed their gear and helmets and most started to head out to the ice. Damn. I always like to be the first one out there. Have a few seconds, if not minutes, to center myself, my thoughts, and stretch.

"I mean it, J. Always."

"Right." His jaw hardened again, ending the conversation with a tight-lipped look and one tinged with embarrassment.

It left me more curious, but whatever. I had enough problems not to take on more unless he brought them to me.

I turned back to my area, plopped my ass down and got

dressed. Knee pads, skates, full leg pads. Arm pads and blockers, chest pads. By the time I was done I was about fifty pounds heavier and waddling my ass out to the rink.

The ice was my home, and it didn't matter if I was on a frozen pond or an arena filled with thousands. My dad taught me to skate when I was three, something he'd done his entire life. It was in between his earliest deployments and after that first taste of being on the ice, skating in between legs before he let me go only to fall flat on my ass, I was hooked. Two more days of us at the rink and I was skating in circles, talking to it like it'd been set in my DNA before I came into the world.

There was no place that existed in the world where I was more comfortable, more confident, and more at home.

Unless I was with Lizzie.

I tapped my stick on the ice before starting my warm-ups.

Christ, I hoped like hell she stayed.

16

LIZZIE

For the first time in what felt like years, it was three o'clock in the afternoon and I didn't feel the desperate need to curl up into a ball and sleep until September. I hadn't even felt that nauseous when I woke up but had eaten crackers just in case. Perhaps things were getting better. I wasn't going to look the gift horse in the mouth. I was just going to be thankful I didn't spend the morning repeatedly brushing my teeth after throwing up.

I'd even managed to call a few obstetricians and midwives and some of them were able to fit me in for consult appointments before I left next week. I'd checked Garrett's calendar, and if he wanted, he could come with me to a couple of them but after this week, he was back on the road and only at home a night or two over a ten-day period. It wasn't necessary he came with me, simply because they weren't real prenatal appointments, but were more to help me find someone I'd want delivering our baby. Still, he'd want to be involved.

After, and since I wasn't in *will pass out at any moment even if I'm standing up* mode, I decided to finally be an adult.

I'd already shared all my secrets with Garrett. My parents knew everything. It was time to unload everything else on the only other person I'd lied to and kept things from. Katie had sent me numerous texts over the last few days asking if I saw Garrett, all of which I ignored. What could I tell her that night I left the hotel and he'd stalked off? What could I tell her the next day when he showed up and demanded to stay? What could I tell her the next day when I was packing bags to come with him to Vegas?

Now it was time for me to suck it up before she sent the SWAT team to my condo in Chicago and then alerted the FBI I'd been kidnapped.

With my laptop on my lap, I pulled up the FaceTime app to call her.

Her voice came through the computer before her grainy face materialized clearly. "It's about freaking time, girl. I was about ready to call the cops on you!"

Yeah. I knew her well.

"Sorry," I said, and immediately grinned at her face on the screen. But it wasn't my best friend that captured my attention, it was the tuft of dark hair at her chest, mostly hidden beneath a blanket. Marissa's tiny little hand rested on Katie's chest and from the lack of bra strap or anything on her shoulder, I figured Marissa was eating. "Did I interrupt lunchtime?"

She rolled her eyes in the loving way moms did and grinned down at her baby. My uterus squeezed.

In six months, that was going to be *me*. Having another human connected to me. The screen blurred before I could blink back the emotion.

"So, I take it the meeting didn't go well?" Katie asked.

"No." I shook my head, sniffed, and finally pulled my gaze off Marissa. There was no way to filter out all the things

I wanted to say so in a rush, it all fell out in a breath. "I'm pregnant and I told him and now I'm in Vegas with him."

"I'm sorry... what?" she choked, eyes widening, jaw falling and then her eyes went *huge*, shimmered with tears and her smile grew so big I could see all her teeth. "Are you serious?"

She shrieked and Marissa popped off, scrunching up her face. "Oh shit. Hold on a sec." She jumped, giving me a full flash of one of her boobs, moved out of screen and when she returned, Marissa had a pacifier in her mouth and Katie was covered up. "What in the hell? How did this *happen?!*"

I was too worked up to tease her. My typical sarcasm along the lines of well, Katie, when a boy and a girl have *sex...*

Instead, more tears fell. I'd held this in for so long, and now... now I could finally tell her everything. "In December, that weekend... and then I got sick, and freaked, and he'd told me he was coming to Las Vegas but that he loved me. Then I found out I was pregnant, and I was going to come here to tell him, but I saw him with that Nadia girl and I just... I didn't know what to do."

"Oh honey." Her blue eyes were as wet as mine and we laughed stupidly, swiping at our cheeks. "You could have told me. You didn't have to hold this in."

"I know, but I didn't want you to have to keep it from Jude, and then it took a while for it to be real, but my parents got so mad at me for not telling him right away."

"Holy crap! I'm like bursting with excitement and pissed I can't hug you. I mean.. you're pregnant, Lizzie. Our babies are going to be like, what *a year* apart? And you're in Vegas, so I'm guessing Garrett wasn't pissed."

I flinched as I recalled how angry he'd been that night I told him. When he sat in the booth and swore, told me he needed time. Demanded I give it to him. He'd left and I hadn't known if I'd see him again, or if I'd be here. Crazy that was only days ago.

"He was. Huge. At first. The night I went to the hotel he stormed out and I was so damn terrified, but then he showed up the next night..."

I told her everything. She listened and we cried and I stupidly even told her about Nadia being here when we arrived. And poor Katie. She was more pissed she couldn't have been here to hug me through all of this and had so many questions. How I was feeling... when I was due... what Garrett and I were doing.

"And now tonight, Joey's having guys over I guess so Garrett wants me to come." I chewed my bottom lip. "What if his team hates me?"

"Please." She snorted. "There isn't a single man you've ever met you couldn't charm. You'll be fine. And Garrett and Joey wouldn't let anything happen to you. What's really freaking you out?"

She knew me like the back of her hand. "I'm terrified to give up everything I've worked for up until now. To move here, start all over..."

"Yeah. I know what's that like."

How stupid of me. Of course she did. When Jude hobbled back into Katie's life after having ACL surgery, she'd been his physical therapist. Months later, she was quitting her job, moving to North Carolina, all for a second chance at the guy she'd always loved.

"It all worked out for me," she said, smoothing her hand across the back of Marissa's head and she did it so softly, I doubted she realized she was even doing it.

"It's terrifying," I admitted. "All of it. At least you and Jude were together and Garrett... I don't think he trusts me anymore, but I'm having his baby. *We're* having a child. And we're not even dating."

"Please." She rolled her eyes playfully. "I give that about another forty-eight hours. It's always been you for him and him for you. Stop *fighting* it, and now you don't have to. Some advice?"

"Always." She was the most levelheaded person I knew. Always had been. I'd take anything she said more seriously than the Bible.

"Enjoy every damn minute of this adventure. The two of you. The pregnancy. It's a wild ride, and I know it won't always be easy, but you two keep finding your way back to each other. Don't fight it. Don't run... unless you're running to Garrett. He's always been there for you."

Smart was my best friend.

"Thanks." I swiped new tears from my cheeks and nodded to Marissa. "How's the girl?"

We talked for what felt like forever and when it was finally after four and I figured Garrett would be home soon, we signed off with her final warning.

Pointing her finger at me and glaring, Katie said, "Keep another secret from me and you're not my BFF anymore. Got it?"

Her threats were as useless as mine and we both knew it. "Got it Katy-bug."

"Love you."

The screen barely had time to turn black before Garrett's garage door started opening. I shoved off the couch, determined to do what Katie suggested.

She was right.

We'd known each other for seven years. I'd loved him at least half of those. I was going to move here. We were going to have a child... and the rest?

The rest would work out exactly the way it was supposed to.

He stepped through the door from the mudroom and I launched myself into his arms.

"Oomph," he muttered, but that was all he got out before my mouth was on his and I was declaring, "I love you so damn much Garrett Dubiak, and I really, really don't like this idea of going slow."

He didn't say a word. Not my Garrett. His hands on my ass gripped me tighter and he slanted his head, sealed our lips together and at the first touch of his lips, every part of my body became his.

Who was I kidding? Every part of me already belonged to him.

He carried me, kissing, me moaning into his mouth with the ferocity of the weight of everything I'd realized, finally admitted to him, while he carried me into the kitchen, and the cool marble of his countertop seeped through my joggers. Then his hands were at my hips, at my sides, shoving up my shirt and tearing it off my body.

I hadn't bothered throwing on a bra, and as soon as my top was removed, the chilly air slid across my skin, making me shiver even while I was boiling with need.

"I have no idea what happened while I was gone," he panted, the dark amber of his eyes burning with a fire I'd never seen, "but if you're done with slow, then so am I. Lie back, honey."

With pleasure. I was so turned on, so primed from a kiss and his presence, I was already lifting my hips, pushing down my sweats, bare beneath and exposing myself to him on his kitchen counter while his hands languidly ran down my thighs, pulling off my clothes. He paused only to rip off his own shirt, his hair curly, bounced around his ears, the frame of his face and then he planted his palms next to my hips and stepped in between my legs.

Staring down at me, I'd never felt so exposed—so protected. The dichotomy only Garrett could provide warmed me from the tips of my toes and sent a pulse of heady desire straight to where I was opened for him.

"Garrett," I breathed as he bent over me. His cock, hard beneath his athletic pants, pressed against me in that exact spot.

One of his hands pressed to my sternum and slid to my breast. His gaze never left mine, stuck on me like I was on him, and then he licked his lips and my core spasmed. "I've been so hard for you since last Thursday I don't know where to start. Or how gentle I need to be." As he said it, his hand drifted low to the area of my stomach that was no longer concaved or flat but had a slight roundness to it. "I don't want to hurt you."

"It's fine. It's totally safe. And bonus…" I winked, wrapping my hand around his wrist and then splaying my fingers between his at my stomach. "We no longer have to worry about not having condoms nearby."

His head fell and he barked out a laugh which meant as he kissed me again, he was still smiling, still laughing. "Let me take care of you, and then later, after Joey's thing, we can come back here and play together. That work for you?"

I wanted to feel his hard, thick length inside of me more than I could remember wanting anything more in the world but before I could argue or tell him how much, his fingers, experienced and confident and sure because he knew me so well, were sliding through my folds, dipping into my dripping wet sex and moving with a slow, maddening pace he knew drove me out of this world.

I mewled into his mouth, grasping for any leverage I

could find, my feet on the counter's edge, my hand around his wrist as he worked me just so perfectly before he yanked off me, trailed his mouth down the column of my throat, my collarbone, to one of my nipples where he sucked as he played my clit and it took seconds, an embarrassingly short amount of time before I was coming, arching off the counter, pressing into him and clawing at his hair.

I cried out his name as my orgasm crashed into me, rolled through like a tidal wave and pulled me out to sea and back.

"Shit," I gasped, pressing my back to the counter, releasing my hold on his hair. When I could breathe again, I grinned up at him. "We're definitely doing that again later too."

He guided me back to sitting, sliding a hand beneath my shoulders to support me. "It'd be my pleasure. Whenever you want. Whenever you ask."

How in the hell did I get so lucky?

And why did I fight it for so long?

17

GARRETT

There'd never been a moment since I'd known Lizzie I wasn't honored to have her on my arm. Whether we were friends, or in one of our friends with benefits moments, walking into any room or club with Lizzie holding my bicep made me feel like I'd fought the hardest game of my life and came out the champion.

Tonight was no different.

In fact, it was more.

She loved me. She was here with me, preparing to get to know my new teammates and she was already in the process of figuring out how to start a life with me.

Plus, she was carrying my baby. I wasn't exactly sure when I thought that would stop being the sexiest thing I'd ever think in the world, but there was something about knowing she had a part of *me* in her, at all times, that simply made her *mine*, in every single way that mattered.

So yeah, I was feeling pretty damn good, Lizzie next to me, sipping on a bottled water, wearing a pair of jeans she'd cursed to hell and back while she tried to button them but still looked sexy as hell in them.

We were in Joey's kitchen, half the guys hanging in the living room, bottles of beer, glasses of Scotch, and bottled waters covering every flat surface. In the kitchen, Lizzie and I were hanging with Joey, André, and Kane, our team's powerful starting center. Most of the guys had come alone, but there were a couple of wives, one of whom was Sophie. She was married to our left winger Braxton, high school sweethearts since they were fifteen and at twenty-five, have now been married for three years. Some thought he was crazy for getting married so young, before he ever signed his first NHL contract. Personally, I admired them. Married three years, the travel and stressors of spending so much time apart and they still acted like they were on their first date. Those two knew what they had from the moment they found it, young as they were, and locked it down.

"You should come with me," Sophie was saying to Lizzie. "I can get an extra seat and then you won't have to sit alone."

Lizzie glanced at me and nodded. "I would like that. Thanks."

"No problem. Games are always better when you're not totally surrounded by strangers who couldn't make it to the junior league but still think they can play better than your man."

They were discussing our game in two nights. I hadn't even thought yet to get Lizzie tickets but Sophie was right. Lizzie would hate sitting in the stands alone and since she didn't know anyone, my second complimentary ticket I got for all home games would be empty.

"Where are your seats?" I asked Sophie. I was able to get pretty damn good seats for when my mom and sister came.

Also, a part of me, I think had always hoped Lizzie would see me play and I knew exactly where she loved to sit.

"Section Nineteen. I like to be able to see you all when you're on the bench. About halfway up."

"I got two behind my goal." I winked at Lizzie. "Ten rows up."

Her cheeks pinked and her hand that was still entwined in mine gripped harder. "Are you serious?"

"Even when I was pissed, I must have wanted you here."

"Awww." Sophie's hand went to her heart. "That's so sweet, and awesome." She focused on Lizzie and held up her glass of wine. "My seats Tuesday, your seats Thursday?"

Lizzie clinked the wineglass with her water bottle. "Deal. And thank you."

And just like that, within fifteen minutes of meeting someone, Lizzie had found a friend. Not that I was surprised. Everyone was drawn to her.

"Come on." Sophie linked her arm through Lizzie's. "Let me introduce you to the other wives and girlfriends." She glanced at me. "You don't mind if I steal her do you?"

"As long as you return her."

Lizzie chuckled and swatted her hand at my chest. "Where else would I ever go?"

Nowhere. You're stuck with me. I couldn't bring myself to say it, but based on the softening of her eyes, the gentle tilt at the corners of her lips, she knew exactly what I was thinking.

"Be back soon," she whispered, and kissed the hinge of my jaw.

I was two seconds from saying *fu ck this*, throwing her over my shoulder and back to my place. This afternoon's earlier taste of her left me craving more. *Everything.*

"Where you looking?" The question came from Joey and I refocused from watching Sophie lead Lizzie away back to the conversation at hand.

Arlo, recently called up from our AHL league team, was looking for a place to live. He was on the standard twenty-eight-day *prove yourself* contract and staying in a hotel by the stadium. We all knew he'd make the cut though. He was playing great, already had three goals in his first five games. I wouldn't be surprised if Coach told him after this home stretch to go find a place.

"Townhome, probably. Maybe rent a place, but I'm used to living off what I was making. I plan to save the rest." He shrugged and took a gulp of his water. "The only thing I'm worried about now is not fucking this up."

"We've all been there." Joey slapped him on the back, giving him a shake. "But so far, I think you've more than earned your place."

"Thanks, man."

"What's up with you and the sexy blonde?" Kane asked me, sipping his drink. His eyes had more than once dropped to Lizzie's ass through the night. As a teammate, he was a great leader. I didn't know him well off the ice but the way he kept checking out Lizzie's ass didn't make him an early favorite. "Known her long?"

"Seven years. Since college."

His gaze slid in the direction Lizzie had left. "Long time. No ring."

My jaw clenched. At six-four, I had some height on him. Some width too. I could take him. Although punching out a new teammate might not be my best choice.

"Yet," I all but growled.

"Hey man." He laughed, threw up his hands. "You haven't said a word about having a woman. How was I supposed to know?"

He wasn't. "It's complicated," I said, trying to tamp down my anger by chugging my water. Kane Andrews was a decent guy, and a player. Couldn't fault him for wanting her. He wasn't the first teammate I had that had the same questions. "You're also too damn young for her and she likes her man to know what he's doing in bed."

"Oh fuck off." He laughed and threw a chip at me. "Girls in my bed never complain."

"Bet that's why you don't have any repeats though," Joey razzed him.

"You assholes. That's by choice—*mine*," he said before we could give him hell for it. "You all suck."

"No no." I shook my head. "I'm pretty sure I heard that redhead at the bar a couple weeks ago say it was *you* who sucked."

The guys laughed, jumping on giving Kane crap, but he could take it. It was all in good nature anyway. He tipped his beer in my direction, grinning from cheek to cheek. "Remind me never to check out a girl you like. You play dirty."

There wouldn't be another woman in my life, ever. "Just keep your eyes off her ass and we'll be good."

"That you cannot blame me for. It's a damn fine ass."

Joey's shoulders shook with laughter. "You can't be pissed at him for that. It's true."

All the men craned their necks, checked out Lizzie's backside in her tight pair of jeans and shrugged and agreed.

I threw a handful of chips at all of them. "Traitors. You're all traitors. Eyes up, assholes."

"As MUCH FUN as I had with my team and seeing them all fall in love with you, I need you." My mouth fused with hers before she could argue. Not that I considered she would. We left Joey's after only a couple hours, once Lizzie started yawning and her laughs were softer.

She was getting tired, but if she was up for it, I'd already mapped all the ways I wanted to finish what we started earlier.

She responded to my kiss, dropping her purse to the floor and kicking off her shoes as she grabbed at my shirt.

"I've been thinking of this all night, for months, if I'm being honest."

Her words were a warm caress to my chest, sending heat to my limbs. My erection, already growing, punched at my zipper. For so long, Lizzie held her affection for me behind a wall.

Now that she dropped it, I just had to keep her from rebuilding the bricks. Replacing the mortar.

"Always. Always be honest." My hands went to her ass and I lifted, unsurprised when she linked her ankles behind my back, dug her hands into my shoulders and burrowed her face in my neck all while grinding her center against my hardening erection.

"Goddamn," I groaned, and hurried as fast as I could up the stairs.

I needed a bed. *My* bed. Immediately. One she'd hopefully never leave again.

I reached the room, flipping on the light switch and kicking off my shoes as I stumbled with Lizzie in my arms. Her soft laughter vibrated against my neck, sending shocks of desire through me, making me tighten my grip on her until I was on my knees on the bed, walking up and laying her down on my pillows. My bed was unmade from this morning, a feat I rarely managed to accomplish when I was in town, so I tugged the covers further down, resettled the pillows and finally, *finally*, pulled back.

Lizzie on my bed with her curled hair wild, her makeup a bit disheveled and her clothes askew was the most erotic sight. One I'd remember forever.

"Let's get these damn jeans off you," I said, leaning back and going straight for the zipper.

"Get scissors," she rasped, wiggling and lifting her hips. "I think they're fused to my hips and ass now."

She wasn't wrong. They were practically glued to her hips but as we wiggled and tugged, she breathed a sigh of relief, her hand fell to her lower stomach as I pulled them the rest of the way off.

"Oh thank goodness. I can breathe again. I might have to go buy new clothes soon." Her smile was crooked, a little nervous. If she, for one second, thought I gave a shit about any of that, she was wrong. Crawling back up the bed, I slid my hand over hers, fingers dipping beneath the waistband of her simple, white thong, and pressed my lips to her swollen area.

"Take my credit card. Go buy anything you need. Buy everything you don't need, I don't give a fuck, but don't ever look nervous with me about how your body looks." I peered up at her, her full breasts heaving beneath her shirt and her lips parted.

We'd known each other too damn long to be embarrassed about anything. Sure, I knew women thought shit about their bodies that men didn't give one single fuck about. Stretch marks, extra weight. It was all bullshit. There would never be a day that went by, regardless of changes she was going to go through, where Lizzie Winston wouldn't be my ideal woman.

"Garrett," she whispered, sliding her hand into my hair and giving a gentle tug. "I'm sorry. For last year. December. Waiting so long."

"Fuck." I closed my eyes, kissed her stomach and grabbed her hand, pulling her to sitting. I arranged us so she was straddling my lap and pulled her to me. Cupping her cheeks, I tilted her chin up so she was forced to meet the seriousness of my gaze. "We've both waited a long time for this."

I brushed hair behind her ear but didn't take my eyes off her for a second. She had to *hear* this. Move past it. "I ain't mad, Lizzie. I don't care how we ended up right where we are, I'm just damn glad we're here. K? Get all that shit outta your head."

"We could have had more time."

What was done was done. Yeah, the night we spent together over a year ago, where I'd laid my heart out and she hadn't done the same had hurt. Neither of us talking after, me waiting for her when I knew that wasn't her thing, her expecting me to always act like I had, and then December when she asked for time and took too damn long—that hurt.

"Honey..." I waited until she opened her eyes. "We have the rest of our lives. That's all that matters."

Her lips parted, giving me the perfect opening. I slid my lips against hers and dipped my tongue inside. I kissed away her worries and her doubts.

She was here. She might have to leave, but she'd be back. That much I knew.

Lizzie and I were meant to be together forever and I'd ensure nothing, absolutely nothing stopped us again.

18

LIZZIE

Sophie Lawson was a certifiable nut. While I'd always had to drag friends to Garrett's games in Chicago, or an occasional date which now made me feel like a pile of turd nuggets, Sophie *lived* for hockey. Shouldn't have surprised me since she'd told me she and Braxton started dating when they were teenagers and everyone in the small Wisconsin town where they were raised skated all winter or played hockey.

But this girl didn't just *love* the game. She was a maniac.

"Sit down," I grunted through a smile, tugging on her green and gold Vipers jersey with Braxton's name and number twenty-four on the back. "Before you get us kicked out."

The beautiful and sweet, almost innocent, looking brunette smirked at me. "Wouldn't be the first time."

Oh shit. I didn't think she was kidding. Unfortunately, the two drunken a-holes behind us weren't just drunk and rowdy, they were fans of St. Louis, probably in town to party it up before their team's game and hadn't stopped drinking since they arrived on the Strip.

They'd also made it clear they not only hated Lawson as a player, but *chicks who thought hockey was only about hard sticks*... their words.

So maybe it'd be worth getting kicked out for.

"Sit your ass down," one of the rumpled, drunk, and unshowered and unshaved men grumbled. "Your ass might be fine and tiny, but it's in my way."

"She'd look better without that jersey on, too," the other guy grumbled.

"Excuse me?" I whipped my head around. They were definitely worth getting kicked out for.

My hand was still tugging on Sophie's jersey, but instead of sitting, she grabbed my wrist and yanked me to my feet. So I was pregnant. So I was totally sober and completely over the reek of their beer breath in a way I could puke at their feet... they'd deserve that one.

"It's all right," she whispered. "Brax and I have a sign."

She winked, turned back around and thank God her husband was on the bench. He'd found her attention several times when his line wasn't on the ice, and as she patted her head, ran her hand over her chest three times, he was suddenly on his feet, whispering harshly to Coach and the security guard outside the home team's bench. The security guard glanced our way and then grabbed something clipped to his belt.

I glanced at her, her smug expression with her hands on her hips, ignoring the jeers coming from behind us.

"You're at risk of getting kicked out so often that you and Braxton have a *sign* for this?"

"Yep." And as she said it, behind me and toward the stairs, three security guards rushed down. She grinned at me. "I love hockey."

"Excuse me," one of the guards said to the men behind

us when Sophie pointed at the two of them. "We're going to need you to come with us. Harassing Mrs. Lawson isn't allowed in our arena."

As the men stuttered, jaw dropping as they realized exactly who they'd been jerks to, Sophie gave them a little wave of her fingers and a jaunty wink. "Enjoy your time in Vegas, boys."

"You fucking bitch!" one shouted. He lunged at her, but for her part, Sophie stood still, all five-foot-four of her. The guard stopped him, grabbed his arms, and I gaped at the men, the security team, *and* Sophie, while the crowd around us cheered on the removal of the other team's fans.

Once they were gone, Sophie grabbed my hand and plopped us back into our seats.

"I might have to change my mind about Friday's game," I said to her.

"Nonsense. This doesn't happen *every* game. Friday should be fine."

Yeah, but I'd be in a location where she couldn't easily get Braxton's attention if it wasn't. "You know I'm pregnant, right?"

She laughed, reached for a cup of soda and bumped her shoulder into me. For a tiny thing, she was damn strong. Probably all that hockey playing she did growing up. "You're hilarious."

I wasn't joking. She kind of terrified me.

In the end, the game went on without further need for security assistance, the Vipers won, Garrett didn't let a single puck through the net and afterward, I allowed Sophie to escort me down to the player entrance area beneath the stadium.

As soon as Garrett walked out, he found me, came straight to me and dropped his bag to hug me. "You're my good luck charm. That's the best game I've played since I've been here."

His hair was still wet from his shower and I ran my fingers along the back of his neck. "You were wonderful, and the entire team is incredible, but Sophie scares the batshit hell out of me."

He threw back his head and laughed, and I got so lost in the column of his corded muscled throat and his laughter bouncing off the cement halls, I almost missed when his shining eyes came back to mine. "It took me two weeks until I learned they had an actual sign for when she's about to get in some serious trouble."

"You knew?" I gasped and slapped him on his chest. "And didn't tell me?"

"Of course." He grabbed my hand, then his bag and we started walking down the hall with other players where *good game nice save* and all manners of congratulations were repeated by his teammates. "But I figured out of anyone, you'd love it. Did she let you watch at all?"

"Yeah." I squeezed his arm as we started walking. "I missed seeing you play. Tonight was incredible."

He playfully bumped his hip into me and then draped his arm over my shoulder. "And it's not even close to being over."

A delightful shiver tripped and traipsed its way straight to my happy place and gave a little dance of excitement.

Awareness slowly pulled me from sleep and I stretched, warm and rested, and as my feet moved, they brushed against something warm. Something hard.

What the? I rolled to my side, only to see Garrett, on his back, sleeping peacefully next to me. Blinking away the remains of sleep, I scanned his face, the peacefulness of his features, that square jaw, the bump in his nose he'd gotten from a fight in the junior leagues when he was a teenager. His lashes were thick, the same dark color as his hair but weren't long. Last night hadn't exactly ended up the way I'd hoped once we left the stadium.

At some point, on the quick drive home, I'd fallen asleep in the car. The game must have worn me out, and I'd barely been conscious when Garrett pulled into his garage, waking me to help me up to bed.

I'd been so out of it I hadn't even realized he'd brought me to his room.

His bed.

And yep. A quick check showed I was in one of his shirts.

I stretched again, feeling that pulse in my core as I took in Garrett's body. The warmth of him that seeped through the space between us and I rolled to my side, seeking out my saltines.

The nightstand was empty and I groaned, collapsing back into the bed, but...

Did I need them? I laid still, my eyes closed for several minutes to see if that all too familiar roll and dip of my stomach showed but when it didn't, there was still something remaining.

That pulse. Building to a low throb.

Oh *yeah*. This was familiar. There were lots of mornings I used to wake up and before ever rolling out bed, took the time to take care of that sensation. But it'd been so long, I'd almost forgotten what it felt like to wake up feeling like myself and not like I was on flu recovery.

But today... today I didn't have to rely on self-satisfaction.

I rolled over again, careful of my movements and after the shift still didn't unsettle my stomach, I was in the all-clear.

Reaching out, I brushed my hand over Garrett's stomach, the strength beneath the thickness there and as my fingers touched him, I slid upward toward the curve of his chest.

Scooting close, I waited a minute to see if I'd woken him up and when he didn't stir, I moved my hand down south, to the thick trail of hair below his stomach, over to a hip.

His eyelids fluttered, and a low groan left his slightly parted lips through his full, tan lips and I took that as my cue. He might not have been awake, but beneath my hand, his body stirred. He grew hard beneath my palm as I brushed my hand gently down his length.

"Fuck," he groaned and turned his face toward me. Garrett's eyes slowly opened and I was blessed with the rich blue in his eyes as he blinked before his lips kicked up at the corners. "You going to finish what you started or do you need food first?"

I choked down a laugh. Only Garrett would think of me first while my hand was wrapping around his hardening dick, stroking him.

"I love you," I said. Not a response, but a response all the same. "And I don't feel so sick right now."

"Good." He rolled toward me, his hand reaching out to cup the back of my neck and then his mouth was at my jaw, my throat. That throb so deep inside of me grew exponentially with every brush of his lips against my skin until he rolled me to my back and slid on top of me.

My hand worked him slowly, teased him and he continued to kiss me everywhere but my mouth because he knew how much I hated morning breath. Shifting to take care of my nipples instead, he was on them, grunting as I found that spot on his dick he liked so much and bucked into my hand.

"Oh goodness," I gasped, as he lightly bit one, tugged it playfully. A shiver racked my body, slid down my spine and coiled tight lower in my stomach. "I think my boobs are more sensitive."

Garrett rolled his lip over one, eyes meeting mine. "Yeah? Let's see just how sensitive they are then."

He tugged on one, pinched. Playing with my other with his mouth, he gave both equal treatment until he was bucking into my fist and I was arching, rolling, soaking wet and swollen and so ready to explode. He hadn't even touched me where I needed him most. I felt empty but full.

Hot. So damn hot.

"Garrett," I choked, digging my fingers into his hair. "I might come." And how in the hell was that possible. From my nipples alone?

"I might have just found my favorite thing about pregnancy." He grinned up at me. "Let's see if we can make that happen then."

He shifted, so he was directly on top of me and every time he pushed into my fist, my hips rolled. The tip of his dick brushed against my clit. I felt the wetness there, and he continued kissing. Teasing. Pulling. Grabbing my breasts and swirling his tongue around my hardened buds until it hit.

"Oh shit." I was orgasming from attention purely to my breasts and as it hit me, my hips went wild seeking to be filled, Garrett dropped his hand between us, pressed two fingers inside of me and found that place deep like he'd memorized my body. My orgasm rolled and rolled and took me under, sent me flying and I dug teeth into my mouth so I didn't wake the neighborhood.

"Holy shit."

"Lizzie..." Garrett groaned, and it was a warning, one I couldn't miss before he followed me, fucking my fist, losing control until he buried his face between my breasts and the heat of his release covered my hand and stomach.

Wow.

Once I could finally catch my breath, I tugged him up to me. Met his gaze. "Pregnancy sex is going to be awesome."

His eyes lit with amusement. I was awarded with a full, bright smile. "Everything about you is awesome. Let me get you cleaned up."

He gave me a quick kiss, pushed off and I kept my gaze on him, those thick thighs, his incredible ass as he disappeared into his bedroom.

"Do you have practice today?" I munched on a cracker and sipped my coffee while Garrett fried up his own full breakfast of eggs and bacon and toast along with one of his disgusting green smoothies. After we'd cleaned up and I'd pulled on some sweatpants and brushed my teeth, that familiar flipping of my stomach hit me.

Fortunately, I'd gotten crackers in my stomach in time, and now I was anxiously awaiting to steal a piece of bacon off his plate before he could get to it.

"Film this afternoon and workouts, after, but I won't be gone longer than a few hours. Why?" He glanced at me over his shoulder, giving me a view of his full back, trim hips as he moved comfortably around his space.

I had yet to find, all the years I'd known him, something Garrett didn't excel at. I figured some of that came from losing his dad so young. He'd *had* to learn so he could help out his mom.

He pointed his spatula at me. "Lizzie? Get distracted?"

"Yeah." I twirled my finger in the air at him. "You're just so... you."

I wasn't ashamed about it either.

"I'm so... *me?*" His grin appeared, along with a rare shot of a dimple on his right cheek.

I nodded. "Yeah. Awesome at everything. Skilled. Sexy. You know... you."

I sipped my coffee, enjoying the slight shake of his head, the curls that flipped over his ears and at the base of his neck. "Goofy. Back to my question."

"Oh. I have an appointment scheduled for today. It's just a consult, to see if I like them, but I was wondering if you wanted to come with me?"

His spatula froze in his hold and his face paled. "An OB appointment?"

"Yeah. I was able to get a hold of a couple on Monday." I tossed the rest of the cracker into my mouth.

"Yeah. I'd like that. A lot."

"Good." The bacon popped, regaining his attention, but that was okay.

I got to stare at his body some more while he finished cooking, and everything about Garrett was just as delicious as whatever breakfast he'd make.

19

GARRETT

This entire appointment was a mindfuck. As soon as we arrived, my palms started getting sweaty. All around me were women, all shapes and sizes and colors, and all of them looked as though they'd swallowed a watermelon or basketball. And this was going to be Lizzie. I kept glancing at her stomach, still mostly flat, slightly rounded at night, and tried to imagine how in the hell she was going to manage to grow like these other women. Yeah, she'd still be beautiful.

But would she be *hurt?*

In the pregnancy book for dads I'd downloaded, I hadn't had much time to read, but I kept imagining her hip bones stretching out. A living, breathing human shoved up beneath her ribs. How in the hell did babies come out of women like that, and how did they survive it? And hell... some didn't, right? I mean, it had to happen. Rare, sure because of modern medicine but Lizzie and I were just now finally figuring everything out. We were together, in all the ways I'd wanted to be for so damn long and what if the worst happened?

"Oh shit," I whispered, shoved my palms down my denim-covered thighs. Lizzie's hands settled on one of mine and curled around mine.

And just like that, her touch, calm and cool, gripping me because she could most likely read my mind, settled some of that.

We'd figure it out.

Her head fell to my shoulder and she squeezed my hands, whispering, "More sympathy pains?"

I chuckled and turned, kissed her temple. "More like terror. I'm imagining you and all the worst possible cases and it's fucking with me." I could tell her anything. She'd been my friend, held my hand through being drafted, possible trades early on in my career, tough losses, wins... everything. I had no reason to hide anything from this woman.

"I'll be just fine, honey."

"You'll be hurt."

She snickered. "Yeah because, assuming everything goes well, I'll be shoving something the size of a watermelon out the size of an orange, so..."

My brows arched. "That's the *good* picture?" Horror. Oh my God. And what would it do to that *part* of her I liked so much.

She shrugged and patted my hand. "Better than being sliced opened, I guess. At least in my opinion."

"This just keeps getting better." I rubbed my forehead. Sweat clung to my hairline and I wiped my clammy palms on my jeans again.

Her shoulders shook with quiet laughter and she grabbed my hand again. "Stop worrying. Everything will be fine."

When I managed to take a deep breath, I looked at her,

eyes shining, amusement making her eyes glimmer, biting her lip to keep her laughter in, I had a feeling she was right. Somehow. Someway.

Everything was going to be fine. "I don't want to see you in pain, not even for a second or for a good reason. And especially not in any way because of me."

"I know. That's why I love you so much."

I brushed my lips over hers right as her name was called.

Standing, it took a second for my legs to work right. More than the nerves, there was still the overwhelming, undeniable urge I had to drop to my knees and propose right there. In an obstetrician's waiting room, basketball-belly-carrying strangers the only ones in our midst.

"Wʜᴀᴛ'ᴅ ʏᴏᴜ ᴛʜɪɴᴋ ᴏꜰ ʜɪᴍ?"

Lizzie tucked hair behind her ear and shrugged. "He was okay. Good. I like the idea of those hot tubs, being able to soak. I hear that's nice for some women. I don't know how I like the idea of so many doctors in the practice, though. My midwives in Chicago only have three of them, so I feel like I'd get to know them. Trust them. But twelve? I mean, I only have like fifteen more appointments or something. I could end up with strangers delivering my baby. But the facility was nice."

She was rambling again.

Nervous.

Probably scared.

It was the last thing I wanted for her. So I said the last thing I wanted to, but for her, we'd make it work. "If you want, once off-season hits we can go back to Chicago."

The words stuck in my throat like I'd swallowed a puck. I

could figure it out. I'd still have to travel. Miss some time with her, but then she'd have her parents at least. Maybe that'd be better.

"What? No." Lizzie grabbed my hand from the steering wheel and clasped it in hers on the console. "No, Garrett. I don't want that."

"Are you sure?" I glanced at her quick.

"Of course. There are dozens of offices. I have time. It might be fine, it's just, I liked the small office I had, but that doesn't mean I can't find it here. But no, your life is here. Our life is going to start here. I don't need to go back to Chicago just to have to move everything with a newborn later while you're starting the season. I want to be here. Settled."

She was adamant. She stunned me. This woman. The reasons why I loved her grew every day.

I nodded. "Okay. Then we'll keep looking."

"I have another appointment set up for later this week, anyway. It's all women, which, no offense to men... I just think I might be more comfortable with a woman when the time comes."

I could see that. If I had an issue with my dick or my balls, I wanted a doc who had the same parts. Not that women couldn't be or weren't excellent doctors. But there were certain areas I'd rather have a man be there for. "Then we'll find you what you need."

"I don't doubt it." As she spoke, her other hand rested on her stomach. She'd complained about clothes. Needing more things. I imagined in a few weeks, at least a couple months, she would most definitely be needing maternity clothes or whatever they were called.

I could give her that.

A surprise, for when she was stuck here alone next week while I was on the road. A shopping spree. On me.

"When do you have to get to practice?" she asked, and I shoved the surprise I wanted to give her down. "Soon. I have just enough time to drop you off and change."

"Anything you'd like for dinner?"

"I can pick something up." I glanced at her as I pulled into my—our—neighborhood. "You don't have to cook."

"I want to. Besides, we've barely made a dent in the apocalypse stock up run."

Brat. She was never going to stop giving me shit for it, but she wasn't wrong. I had no idea what I was thinking the day we went to the store just that I wanted to make sure she had everything she needed or wanted.

"Then I'll eat whatever you cook for me." Although that was a dangerous promise.

Lizzie had been known to burn water boiling for box macaroni and cheese as easily as she could whip up coq au vin or rack of lamb... both meals I'd had from her before that were to die for.

But she didn't need to go all out.

On the other hand, how had we gotten so domestic? Talking baby doctors and dinners like we'd lived together for years.

At least for this, I wasn't scared at all.

FILMS WERE A BREEZE. Even with my not-so-great performance back in Chicago, we had no problems taking care of St. Louis and like I told Lizzie last night, I'd had the best game of my time with Vegas so far. Still, even with how well the team was working together, Coach Vik had honest, but harsh critiques for the forwards. The defense, getting them to work better at keeping the puck away from me for starts, but I wasn't worried. Alix and Dominick were two of the best in the league. Especially Dominick. He was our bruiser. The guy not afraid to throw down on behalf of whoever needs it. He was so damn good at it, I was pretty damn sure he played hockey solely for the pleasure of ripping off his gloves and pounding his fists into an opponent.

Coach Vik didn't take the same encouraging attitude mine in Chicago did, though. He wasn't quick at all to slap a shoulder with a *good game* or *nice play*. Always, out of his mouth, was ways to improve. Get better. Be faster. Be more alert. Not that I minded. I could rise to any occasion, but there were times I figured he was overly harsh with some of the new players, especially now, while he was barking at Arlo, whose expression was dropping by the second. I bumped into one of the defensemen, Max Mikolajczyk. "Coach always this rough with the new guys?"

As a veteran player and goalie, I was an island. I carried the weight of a win or a loss like no one else because while they all worked together, I worked alone. Sure, I took my licks, got screamed at, but it wasn't anything compared to this.

And Arlo was already nervous about his play, being sent back to the AHL.

"Vik's a dick. Hell of a coach, but if his players expect hearts and flowers, they won't last. Arlo's going to need to toughen up. Not let it affect his play."

He had his arms crossed over his chest and shrugged, leaning back in his chair. "We'll take the guy out. Get his mind off it and out of the hotel where he'll go back and pace. You want to come?"

I liked Max. As the captain, he watched all his players like they were a herd of puppies, so I wasn't the least bit surprised he already had a plan for Arlo.

"Can't. I only got so much time with Lizzie here."

"That the girl you brought to Joey's?"

"Yeah."

"You two together?"

"That's a complicated and long story with a lot of yesses and no's thrown at it, but now, yeah. She's it for me."

"Dubiak!" I whipped my head in the direction of Coach calling my name.

"Yes, Coach?"

"Go work on more stretches. You were looking too tight last night. I need you loose and limber for tomorrow."

"I bet that woman of yours would like that, too," Max muttered, punching me in the bicep.

"Nah." I grabbed my keys and phone off the table and pushed to my feet. "She likes it hard and long."

He spun his hat around backward and smirked. "Then what the hell is she doing with you?"

I could take the razzing. Had no problems with it, and I knew, even if Lizzie were here, she'd have an even better comeback for the playful joking. "Making all my dreams come true, man."

I fist bumped him, laughed as his jaw dropped and as I was walking away, he called out, "You shitting me? Good luck to you then, man!"

I lifted my hand in the air and got to work. Coach wanted us perfect and I wanted the Cup in my hands. I'd stretch all damn day and night if he asked in order to get what we both wanted.

∾

Mom: **Call me when you get a chance**

    Mom: **Hope your practice was nice.**

    Gabby: **We need to TALK**

    Gabby: **WTF**

    Mom: **Hope all is well**

    Mom: **Good luck tomorrow. Love you**

    What in the hell was going on?

    If I wasn't five minutes from home, I'd pull the car over.

    My phone, connected to the Bluetooth in my truck was losing its mind.

    Text after text popped up on my dashboard's screen.

    Gabby: **Are you ignoring me? Call your sister.**

    Gabby: **You got some explainin' to do.**

    Gabby: **Dude. For real?**

IT WAS Gabby's texts that almost had me yanking to the side and grabbing my phone, but I was in the neighborhood. Mom's texts weren't all that unusual except on the heels of Gabby's, suspicious.

    What in the hell was Gabby so worked up about? We texted. We talked. I called her when I could and she texted me after almost every game. My mom and sister were proud of me. I knew that. I was proud of them. Happy my mom picked herself up after Dad's death and worked her ass off to give us a good, happy home. She dated occasionally, but her job with the police department made it difficult. Seemed men, especially in Seattle's hippie-dippier area, were intimidated by a woman who could not only shoot a gun better than them but owned several for her own protection.

    And Gabby—she was a kick ass hair stylist. She'd done events for a few movies that were filmed in the area and she'd recently started talking about opening her own salon.

I'd talked to both of them last week. Sent Gabby a *thanks* text after she told me good game last night.

So what in the hell were they freaking out about?

I pulled the SUV into my garage, slammed the door and didn't bother grabbing my bag from the back. I wanted to say hello to Lizzie, see how she was feeling, and then I'd deal with the shitstorm still lighting up my screen.

"Hello?" I asked, and then was immediately hit by the perfect blend of garlic, peppers, onions... I knew that smell.

"Lizzie?" I asked, walking around the corner to the kitchen.

"Hey!" She grinned at me while she was slicing up garlic bread, a salad in a large wooden bowl Mom had bought for me for just that purpose. Wood tongs were shoved inside and on the stove was the black ceramic stock pot.

Mississippi Roast?

Mom found the recipe back when I was in high school, always wanting to try new foods or new spices on them when she got tired of cooking the same old boring thing for us all the time.

I hadn't had this in years. I'd even asked Mom to make it when they were here for Christmas but we'd run out of time.

"I love this meal," I said. Lizzie knew that, too.

She set down the knife and grinned. "I called your mom."

Oh. Now all those texts made sense. My phone vibrated in my hand and I looked down to see another text.

Gabby: CALL ME

"I hope that was okay?" Lizzie asked, nibbling on her bottom lip. "Because I'm sorry if..."

"No. No. It's great." I showed her my screen, scrolled down through all the texts I hadn't opened yet. "It just explains why my phone's been blowing up with texts from Mom and Gabby on my way home. I was starting to get worried."

Her brows puckered as she read the texts. "Gabby sounds pissed."

There was really no way of sugarcoating this. She knew Gabby, knew how protective she was of me. And Gabby had seen me days after Lizzie snuck out on me and had already ignored dozens of calls and texts. Now I knew at least then, she'd been sick, but Gabby could hold a grudge lasting a century. Or she could get over it with a snap of her fingers. Her texts told me she hadn't quite gotten to the finger snapping part.

"She wasn't all that happy with you. They were, upset, when I told them about the last time we saw each other."

Lizzie's brows jumped up to her forehead. "You told them?"

Internally, I cringed. Shit. But there'd been no way to hide how bothered I'd been.

"They helped me move in. Came in for the holidays and spent the week with me, so yeah, I couldn't hide that. Not from my mom."

"Rachel is a damn good detective." She worried her bottom lip and I went to her, slipping my hand to her lower back.

"Yeah. They love you, though, you know that. I'm sure your call just took them by surprise, is all. What if we Face-Time them after dinner? Can we tell them about the baby?"

"I'd love it if they knew. If they won't threaten to come down here and kill me for dragging you through the wringer."

I typed out a text. Told my sister to chill. Then opened up our family chat and typed out **FaceTime in one hour.**

Let me eat this dinner and then Lizzie and I will call. Now leave me alone. Everything is good. Retract the claws, Gabby.

I added a few emojis to take the sting out of that, knowing it'd piss Gabby off.

"No killing guaranteed. But I will warn you that Gabby was a bit more than upset."

"Right. I'll have to make that up to her." Lizzie's head tilted to the side and she tapped her chin with her pink painted fingernail. "Do you think an annual pass to the Château Ste. Michelle winery will help?"

I nipped at her finger and kissed her cheek. "It might smooth something over, yeah. But also, let her plan the baby shower?"

Gabby lived for that shit. After their initial anger or need to be protective of me, she'd come around. Mom always loved Lizzie anyway. Besides, we were together now. Something Mom had wanted for me for years. And I wouldn't even get started on how often she'd hinted about having grandbabies. Hell, I wouldn't be surprised if we told Mom what was going on and she showed up tomorrow with diapers and baby outfits.

"Oh shit." A laugh bubbled deep in her chest until her body shook with it and she placed a hand to my chest, grinning up at me. "We'll have a baby shower."

"You will." I stepped back, snagged a crouton from the salad, and popped it into my mouth. "I want no part of that. But when we register, I get to carry the gun."

20

LIZZIE

Gabrielle Dubiak was a force of nature. All silky black hair down to her waist, full lips, and almond-shaped eyes. This woman was a knock-out. She had all of her mom's features, making the Dubiak women some of the most beautiful women I'd ever met in my life. Coupled with Gabby's larger-than-life personality, not only had she and I become fast friends the first time we met, but I'd missed her a lot over the last year when things with Garrett and I were so messy. Her mom called her the wild child, aimless and prone to making decisions without measuring the risk. It was true, to an extent. When Gabby was twenty-one, her college boyfriend broke up with her and she ended up calling me the next day from a beach in Florida. She'd apparently decided to get out of town, drove to the airport, got a flight on the first one out and ended up in Miami. So sure, there was truth to what Rachel said about Gabby, but not fully.

Gabby lived for adventure and excitement. She didn't want to be stuck in one place forever. I couldn't fault her for that even if it differed from how I'd always pictured my life.

So did I expect her to be upset? Sure. She lived bouncing from whatever emotion she felt in the moment.

Upset was putting it mildly as soon as Garrett fired up his laptop, both of us sitting on the couch pressed together and the call connected.

What I hadn't expected was for her eyes to narrow as soon as the images cleared and for her to practically sneer when she saw Garrett's hand tangled with mine on his thigh.

"Garrett," she said, "hi."

Ignoring me completely, her mom on the split screen sighed her daughter's name and smiled at the both of us. "How was dinner?" she asked.

"Dinner?" Gabby asked. She spun her finger in a circle. "How about we start with what in the hell is going on between you two."

"Easy, Gabs," Garrett said, his voice barely over a growl. "We have things to say, and you love Lizzie, so I'm going to need you to take a step back or we're talking to Mom only."

She huffed, crossed her arms, and flopped back in the chair. For the first time since knowing Gabby, fear trickled down my spine. She was always protective of her big brother, but this was extreme, even for her.

And we were friends. Yeah, I'd hurt him. We'd hurt each other, but Garrett and I were moving past that.

"Gabby." I leaned forward and waited until she slid that glare of hers off her brother and to me. "I love him. All my heart, babe, I swear it. We're good."

As soon as the words were out of my mouth, Garrett leaned closer, kissed my temple. His lips were pressed into a smile I registered on the screen but what surprised me most was the glare sliding from Gabby's face and morphing into one of surprise.

"You *love* him."

"I do." I chuckled.

"Not as a friend."

"As a friend and more," I promised.

"Oh!" His mom clapped her hands together and smiled over her fingertips. "Isn't this wonderful? I always hoped you two would end up together. And if you're in Vegas, then that means..."

I glanced at Garrett, rose my brows. In for a penny, in for a pound was what my dad always said, but I'd leave it to him to spill the news. Gabby had barely stopped looking like she could reach the screen and throttle my skinny little neck.

"You want me to tell them?" he murmured.

"Tell me what?" Gabby demanded. "Someone better start."

His sister. She was a riot.

I turned back to the screen, saw apprehension on his mom's face, irritation and impatience on Gabby's.

"Tell them," I said to Garrett. "Before Gabby's face explodes."

She stuck her tongue out at me, barely managed to suck it back in so she didn't bite on it as Garrett said, "Lizzie's moving in with me."

"What?!" his mom shouted.

"Oh my God that's so amazing!" Gabby echoed from her apartment on the other side of town as her mom. As loud as it was, I imagined Rachel could hear her just fine. "For real?"

"For *realsies,*" I stressed.

Garrett chuckled and as both of them gave us their congratulations, Garrett lifted our hands, kissed the back of mine. Tears were making his mom and sister blurry and I sucked them back.

"One more thing," Garrett said, and waited until they quieted down. "We have something else to say."

"You're getting married," Gabby blurted.

"No," Garrett clipped.

She jumped on her chair. "You already *are?!*"

"What?" his mom gasped.

"We're not married," Garrett scolded Gabby and I didn't miss the pout his mom gave. "At least..." He turned to me and winked. "Not yet."

My chest tightened. Did he... Oh dear... he did. Of course he did.

It took me a moment to register that look in his eyes when he swung it back to his family's way and stated, "It's better. Lizzie's pregnant. We're having a baby."

Silence hit the screen. So silent, Garrett glanced at me. I gave him wide eyes. Maybe the microphone or speakers broke.

And then...

"Holy freak hot shit! I'm going to be an aunt!"

"Oh dear... this is... this is just... a surprise," his mom said, stuttering over her words, but her eyes were growing wet like mine and her smile was soft and loving as always. "You two... you're going to have a baby?"

"We are," I said. "I'm about thirteen weeks right now. Baby will be here in September."

"This is awesome! Where's the wine? Where's the champagne?" Gabby fled out of the camera's view but in the background, I could hear her flipping open cupboards and slamming them shut.

I didn't take my eyes off his mom. She'd always been so good to me. She knew how badly Garrett wanted kids of his own.

"I'm going to be a grandma," she whispered, chin wobbling. "Do your parents know, sweetheart?"

I squeezed Garrett's hand like my life was on the line. She looked so *happy*. "They do. They're happy. Now. Took a hot minute."

"Well, I bet I might have to call you two tomorrow to make sure this isn't a dream. But wow... a grandma. You're going to be a dad," she said to Garrett and those tears of hers slid down her cheeks. "You'll be a great one. I just know it."

"I'm back!" Gabby shouted, flying through the air and landing in her chair. Amazingly enough, she didn't spill a drop of wine from her glass.

"You hooker," I pouted. "Drinking in front of me when I can't."

"Don't worry. I'll drink for you for the next few months."

I had no doubt she would.

Next to me, Garrett snorted, kissed the top of my head. "We're really happy, Mom."

"Good. That's good and I am just... well, I am so thrilled for you. For being together. This is a surprise, for certain, but I always knew you'd find your way to each other and this. Well, it's everything. A baby," she sighed, and her eyes grew wetter. "What a sweet little blessing."

"Blessing my ass," Gabby said. "Think about how huge your tits are going to get!"

GARRETT LEANED FORWARD and closed the laptop and I fell into his shoulder as he draped his arm over me. "See? I told you they wouldn't stay mad."

We talked to both Gabby and Rachel for an hour. Tears

were shared. Gabby drank a half bottle of wine, and I swear she did it to rub it in my face. I wasn't even a big drinker. But there was something about knowing I couldn't have something that desperately made me willing to tackle her to the ground for a sip.

"I thought your sister was going to murder me at first," I mumbled into his chest.

Garrett adjusted us so, kept moving until we were on the couch, both of us pressed together chest to chest and he grabbed the remote from the arm of the couch and turned on the television.

"Only because she wants us both happy. She got over it quick."

"Yeah, by talking about my tits."

He laughed against the top of my head. "How big do you think we're talking here?"

I slapped his bicep. "Shut up."

"Come here and relax with me. I have another early day tomorrow with a morning skate before the game tomorrow night. Anything else happen today around here besides that incredible dinner you made for me?"

"Not really. I have another consult appointment on Friday with a smaller practice and I did some work. Went to the store for the peppers since that was the only thing you didn't buy in the entire store when we were there the other day."

"Brat," he replied playfully.

"You love me." I smirked at him and rolled over so my back was to his chest. His hand fell, slipped down to my stomach and his fingers splayed out on my small, swollen area.

"Yeah. And I love this little nugget too already."

My heart squeezed and a lump jumped into my throat. I'd always known Garrett was an awesome man.

But how was it possible he kept getting awesomer?

He turned on the television, found a basketball game when he couldn't find a hockey game, and like every other night where I ended up on the couch in a horizontal position, I closed my eyes and fell asleep before the first commercial break.

THIS. This was what I was looking for.

Across a small sitting area, coffee table in between us, Garrett and I were on one loveseat and two midwives, Serenity and Chelle, were on the other. Chelle was a surprise, but she popped into my appointment after she said her prenatal mama had to reschedule. As soon as I heard these two midwives call their patients moms or mamas, I was already sold. They were personal and calm with sweet senses of humors and they'd both answered all of my questions and some of Garrett's with blunt but kind honesty.

Ten minutes from the hospital, they went through the statistics of how many they'd had to transfer when it looked like their deliveries wouldn't be as simple as hoped for. No patient had been in a life-threatening scenario and they attributed that to the fact that they cared about their mamas and wouldn't risk their safety or baby's safety for their egos.

I'd originally wanted midwives who delivered in a hospital, looking to mesh the two experiences seamlessly, but already I wanted to beg them to take me on as a patient.

"I'd love a tour," I said.

"That'd be good. Thanks." Garrett took my hand and pulled me to my feet. "You like them," he said when the two midwives discussed which rooms were available. They had a mom currently in early labor in one room and two more in the waiting area that was more comforting than my parents' living room.

"I do. What do you think?"

"I think your comfort is more important than mine when it comes to what you'll have to be doing. The hospital being ten minutes away concerns me, but if you trust them." He shrugged. "I can do some research into this whole thing to settle my own nerves."

My hand pressed to his cheek. "Every single day you get more incredible."

"I just want what's best for you and our baby, that's it."

Yeah, but many men didn't. More, I'd heard from a number of coworkers and friends whose husbands weren't as checked in as this man in front of me.

"Okay, are you two ready?" Serenity asked. She stepped toward the doorway leading us down the hall to the prenatal rooms. The delivery rooms were what I most wanted to see. If they held the same homey, Zen vibe as the rest of that I'd seen so far, I'd drop to my knees and beg them to sign me that day.

"We are. Yes."

We followed her past the prenatal exam rooms and she said she'd show me them last. They had an ultrasound tech on staff, so they did a quick peek into that room. Admittedly, it looked as medicinal and cold as any other place I'd imagine, but Serenity assured me the other rooms were more like home. I suppose you didn't spend much time getting ultrasounds done so I didn't worry much about it but as she opened a door to a labor and delivery room, my jaw almost hit the wood floor.

Yes. Wood. Gleaming. Sparkling clean and the delivery

bed wasn't a twin hospital bed but what looked like a queen bed, complete with a headboard and soft bedding on top. In the corner was an enormous soaker tub that could easily fit Garrett and I if we'd wanted a romantic interlude in one, hell it was bigger than any tub I'd ever seen. Pillows were stacked next to it, along with towels rolled on a shelf. Everything appeared more like a luxury spa or hotel than where a baby would be born.

"Wow," I breathed, spinning in a slow circle. "You said a homey feel, but I didn't expect..."

It was decorated better than my own home, for crying out loud.

"We want our mamas to feel comfortable. We find labor progresses more naturally, more smoothly, when moms can be as at peace as possible, so we try to initiate that for them. The bed can be raised for delivery, much like what you'd find in a hospital. The bathroom has a step-in shower. Some women like the pressure of the water spray on their lower backs during contractions. We also do have the ability, along with an anesthesiologist on call from the hospital who is capable of doing epidurals and other medicinal pain management like we've discussed and if it's requested. In short, our job is to ensure you have a peaceful, healthy, and safe experience while welcoming your little baby into the world. We do whatever it takes to give that to you."

I was sold. Absolutely sold. Garrett's hand at my lower back spread a warm heat through my sweater to my flesh and spread outward, straight to my stomach. I swore, every time someone said the word baby, everything became more real for me. But this? I could imagine myself in here, plenty of space to pace. Maybe sitting on an exercise ball they could bring in for me. The fact I'd receive all the monitoring and opportunities but not be stuck in a sterile hospital made me want to squeal with joy.

"We'll have to talk about this," I said, not willing or wanting to jump too quickly into this. Yeah, Garrett said it was my choice, but if he had concerns, I still wanted to hear him out and that wouldn't happen here.

"I totally understand." Serenity, slightly graying brunette hair pulled into a low bun at the base of her neck, checked her watch and then smiled. "I still have about fifteen minutes before my next appointment. This went quicker than I anticipated. Since I have the time, would you like an exam while you're here? I won't worry about insurance today, but it'd give me an idea as well on how you're doing, and if you'll be low risk for us to accept you if you decide to allow us to help you."

"Um."

"Yes," Garrett said before I could. "If that's okay with Lizzie. I'd like that."

Of course he would. Because he hadn't been to any yet.

"Wonderful. Come this way and we'll get you situated."

We followed her to an exam room, where truly the only difference was the bed was a twin and not a queen, and the room was one third the size. She handed me what felt like a silk gown and not scratchy cotton. "These snap in the front, unlike a hospital gown. They tie below your hips. Mamas are welcome to bring their own clothes for labor but if they choose not to, this is what we offer. We also use this for exams when we need to do internal checks. For today, if you'd like, we'll try to see if we can hear your little one's heartbeat."

"That'd be amazing," I said, before I could stop myself. I'd heard it once, my eight-week exam with a vaginal ultrasound but I was far enough along now that I might not need it that way.

"Wonderful. I'll let you get settled and be back in a minute or two."

The door closed behind her and Garrett, for maybe the first time ever, looked uncertain.

"What?" I asked, already stripping out of my jogger sweats.

"Um. Do you... would you be more comfortable if I left? While you changed?"

"What?" I barked out a laugh and then as a dark hue slid onto his cheeks, felt horrible for laughing at him. "You've seen me naked at least a dozen times since I've been in Las Vegas alone."

"I know." He scratched the back of his neck, did that manly, lift the hat and swipe through the hair and replace thing. "But this is a doctor's appointment. Different."

"I think it's okay." I tried for a straight face, failed, and continued stripping out of my clothes.

He cleared his throat, muttered something that sounded like his usual, *"You're a pain in my ass,"* but it was low and I couldn't be sure.

He'd given me his back, so I quickly settled on the bed, draped the silk cloth over my lap. There wasn't a need to remove my top, so I reached out and poked him in the back of his thigh with my toes. "You can turn around now. I'm not naked."

Before he could, a light knock rapped on the door and creaked open. "Everything okay?"

"We're good." I grinned at Serenity and wiggled my fingers at Garrett. "Come up here and hold my hand."

As Serenity got settled, we talked about my last period, and how far along I was. I told her again, even though we'd already spoken about my current doctor, what they recommended, the prenatal vitamins I was taking. She went over the fact I was beginning the second trimester, what to expect in the upcoming weeks. How often my appointments would be. It was all stuff I knew from reading and other appointments, but the more I heard it, the more settled I became, and the more I trusted her.

Then came the moment where she smiled at Garrett and more to him than me, asked, "Would you like to hear your baby's heartbeat?"

"Yeah." He cleared his throat, squeezed my hand until I had to wiggle fingers to get him to loosen his grip. "I'd like that."

"Good." She squeezed cold jelly on my stomach, warning me first and then I laid back. As soon as her handheld Doppler landed on my stomach, nerves hit. What if we didn't hear it? What if something was wrong?

Serenity's brows pulled together as she wiggled it and all that remained was a static sound and those questions grew louder.

Until.

Whoosh whoosh whoosh whoosh.

"There it is." She smiled up at me. "The little one was hiding from me."

"Is that...?" Garrett choked over his words and they were all he managed to squeak out before he glanced at my stomach, and then gaped at me, mouth open, awe shining in his eyes.

"It's the baby's heartbeat. Strong and steady. A hundred fifty beats per minute, which is very healthy," Serenity confirmed.

The sound made me cry the first time I heard it and scared me equally. Not Garrett. Of course not him. Instead, his spine straightened and his shoulders pulled back, jaw hardening as the reality settled over him. The weight of how things were changing.

Like he was a soldier, given a mission. Protect at all costs and he was preparing for the battle.

I *loved* this man.

21

LIZZIE

"Come here." I barely managed to drag Garrett into the kitchen before my need became combustible.

How I'd managed to restrain myself after watching his reaction in the midwife's office, not jumping him right there and doing the deed on the exam table took herculean feats I didn't know I possessed.

How I managed not to convince him to climb into the back of his SUV before we pulled out of the parking lot was an even greater impressive act of self-control on my part.

But now we were home, my body primed, my heart squeezing so painfully in my chest because it beat so powerfully for him.

Garrett was mine. He was *ours.* And there was nothing. Nothing or no one who could change that for me.

I kicked off shoes, walking backward, tripping over my shoe as I fisted his shirt. Garrett came with me, a look on his face halfway between amusement at my bossiness and a filthy look that said he was planning something I would enjoy immensely.

"Lizzie." He shook his head, pressing his hands to my hips before I hit the counter and I was plopped on it, his legs widening mine until we were pressed together right where I was desperate for him. "I feel like we've been here before."

One of his hands trailed up my side, brushed over the side of my breast so softly I could have imagined the whole thing and then slipped his hand to the back of my head, tangling my hair in his fingers and making a fist.

With a gentle tug, sparks ignited along my skin as he tilted my head back and pressed his mouth to mine.

I gasped into his mouth. "The question though, is now that we're here again, what's going to happen this time?"

His mouth moved to my jaw, back to my ear and in a gravelly voice that sent those sparks to a raging storm, he whispered, "I'm not doing a damn thing with you and my baby on this cold, hard counter."

"Wha—"

Before I could ask what he meant, I shrieked, found myself in his arms like I was a bride and he was carrying me upstairs.

"You're crazy." I laughed, wrapping my arm around him and tucking in my feet so I didn't bang them on the stairs.

"Only for you and this baby we're having."

I tugged on the back of his neck, brought his mouth down to mine and kissed him. We kissed while he walked down the hall, to his room, and I tensed, expecting him to toss me on the bed and ravage me but instead, he sat at the edge of the bed, shifting me in his hold so I was straddling him.

"You can still be rough with me, you know. I'm not porcelain."

Sex between Garrett and I had always been combustible.

As much as I loved this sweet side, I didn't need soft and sweet and to be pampered.

"That's good because I wasn't planning on being gentle." He tore off my shirt and unclasped my bra and then his mouth dipped to my breasts, instantly taking one in his mouth. He bit it. That slight sting of pain I loved so much sent a shock of fire to my core. I rolled against him, his hard erection between us, brushing against my center.

Holy crap. The way he worked me so quickly was mind-boggling. I clung to the back of his neck, rocking against him as he bent his head, teasing and playing with my nipples.

"I need you," I gasped, writhing against him. "All of you. Inside of me."

He kissed me again, palmed the back of my head and tangled his fingers in my hair, pulling back. The slight sting radiated arousal through my body and I gaped at him, body on fire, my sex pulsing with need.

"Please."

"Oh. I like hearing you beg." He stood up, taking me with him and set me on my feet. "I might have to do that more often."

He would, too, but I'd beg for him every day if I could.

Once I was steady on my feet, Garrett fell to his knees, his hands at my waist, he tugged down my leggings. I stepped out of them, bracing my hand at his shoulder for balance, both of us laughing as they stuck to my ankles and he cursed.

And then all laughter stopped. Garrett grabbed my ass and yanked me to him, my crotch right at his face and then he *devoured* me. Legs spread and shaking, all I could do was hold on, throw my head back and moan through the intense pleasure his mouth on me created. Havoc racked my body as he used his fingers, licked his tongue around my clit and then dipped his tongue inside of me, using his fingers to replace his tongue. My hips bucked against him, rolled to create that perfect friction and right as I thought my knees were going to give out, he stood.

"I was so close," I gasped, gawking at him.

He winked. The devil. "I know."

His shirt was torn off him. His jeans dropped followed by boxers and then he climbed on the bed and laid down. "Now get your ass up here and sit on my face."

A rush of arousal dripped to my thighs at his command.

"You're a freak," I said, climbing over him and getting settled.

His hands clamped onto my hips and yanked me down. "You love it."

I loved him. Everything about him, but especially this. I clung to his headboard as he brought me right back to the precipice and in seconds, he threw me over. I bucked against him, cried out his name and white-knuckled his headboard while my orgasm crashed into me, pulled me out to sea and back again before Garrett's adjusting us both, lining me up above him and slammed me down onto his thick length.

"Oh God," I groaned and my head fell forward, hand to his chest. He was so big, so thick, it took a minute before I could breathe again and then I leaned down and kissed him. "I love you. So much."

"I know." He smirked, hair a mess, beard wet from me. "Now ride me and show me how much."

～

THE SUN WAS BARELY UP the next morning while I was sitting cross-legged in the middle of the bed. Garrett was throwing his toiletries and clothes into his bag.

Already dressed in a suit for the airplane, my fingers itched to grab his tie and yank him to me. We got out of bed last night long enough for him to feed me, went back, and then we spent the rest of the afternoon and night tangled up in each other. My thighs were sore. Other parts of me tender, but I'd woken up again without the need to hurl or the desperate need for crackers.

If he wasn't leaving for a full week, returning next Friday, it'd be the perfect day.

Once he returned, we'd have thirty-six hours together before I was set to fly back to Chicago. Which meant this week, I had a lot of decisions to make and I wasn't relishing the idea of having to make them with him flying up and down the West Coast for games.

Garrett zipped up his bag, tossed it to the side and then planted his hands next to my hips, towering over me. His hair was still wet from his shower, strands falling down over his ears and flipping out. He'd never looked sexier. "You'll be okay? Now I feel like an ass for having you here and leaving you alone."

I set my hand on that tie, a deep navy, and pretended I didn't want to tear him out of the suit and have my wicked way with him or that I wasn't going to miss him. This was part of the gig, right? Constantly saying goodbye and safe travels?

"I'm fine. Maybe I'll get into some trouble while you're gone."

He chuckled and leaned in closer. "Yeah? Close all the bars down, partying it up?"

He was teasing. I wasn't. Not entirely.

I shrugged. "No, I plan on calling some pool companies for backyard landscaping quotes." Yesterday, while we were naked, we'd caught sight of the backyard through the windows and he'd given me his whole spiel of what he wanted to do. A raised hot tub with a waterfall into the pool. The sides of the pool landscaped with boulders and large stones to make it feel like something rustic or mountainous. Anything to hide the cement walls fencing in his home that felt like you were imprisoned when you looked outside.

He scowled down at me, scrunching up his nose. I leaned in and kissed it. "Don't even think of doing that without me."

One or two wouldn't hurt. At least a starting point. "Okay."

"Promise me."

I kissed him and grinned. "I promise not to make life-changing decisions without your presence."

His eyes narrowed. "That's not what I said."

"Close enough."

Summer would be here soon. I'd be as large as the back-yard. And it'd be hot. *Sweltering.* I'd pay for the pool myself if I had to.

"Relax, Garrett." I laughed and gave him a shove off me. "I wouldn't do that without you." Not entirely. What harm could a few quotes do? They'd take days or weeks to get back the sketched designs, right? "I'll work. Find my way around town. Find a library. Boring stuff but I'll be okay here."

"If you need anything, call Sophie."

"She's already invited me to get together for dinner and to watch the game with some of the other wives and girl-friends."

Last night's game had been much more chill than the

previous. Maybe it was the seats and because we were surrounded by Viper fans, but security hadn't been called once and Sophie only screamed at the refs a handful of times. We'd laughed, she'd filled me in on what the guys were like, knowing them longer than Garrett, the ins and outs of Dominick, the defenseman who had the team title Bad Boy. I hadn't met him at Joey's. When I asked Sophie said it was because he *never* hung around the team. Ever.

He didn't, however, have any problems landing on the cover of gossip columns and being seen partying it up and down the Strip.

Sophie was fun. Easy to talk to. Easier to laugh with. I learned the other night that she was a private school teacher and rarely missed a home game.

"Good. I'm glad." His head fell again along with his shoulders. "I still hate leaving you."

I didn't think his nerves were altogether about the baby. The last time we'd been separated, I hadn't exactly been great with communication.

A ping of guilt pinched my chest. He might have said we were moving past everything, but did he trust me fully? I'd earn it.

I understood. So much of our issues had come from my hesitancy... for years, if I was being honest. But I was all in on this one. With him.

"Call me as often as you need," I said, showing him I understood. We could do this. We could make it work and if he needed to get a hold of me eighteen times a day to learn I'd always be there for him from here on out, I had no problems with it.

"Yeah. I love you. You know that, right?" His voice did that low dip with a slow drawl thing that made my core tingle. Damn him. We didn't even have time for him to fix that for me.

"Of course I do." I all but shoved him off of me. "And I love you. Now get going or you'll be late. I'll be fine, I promise."

"All right all right." He snagged me by the back of my neck and pulled me to him, tugging me to my knees on the bed. "But I need my good luck kiss."

He slammed his mouth to mine, kissed me until I was breathless and long after he finally dragged himself out the door, the taste of him still remained.

22

LIZZIE

I followed the GPS through the streets of Vegas, avoiding the Strip like Sophie had suggested and pulled up to a security gate. After giving my name to the guard, I kept following the map on Garrett's Range Rover's screen, a car I could most definitely get used to driving even though I hated driving in general, and a few minutes later, pulled up to a gorgeous white painted house with black windows and black roof. So unlike most of the rest of the homes I'd seen in Vegas, Sophie and Braxton Lawson's house looked like it could have been plucked out of a *Country Living* Magazine spread and plopped straight into the heat of the desert.

It was gorgeous, with a three-car garage to the right, space between that and the house where the driveway to what looked like a carriage house beyond. The driveway was curved, landscaping done so perfectly with a variety of bushes, flowering plants. and cacti they had to pay someone a fortune to maintain it all.

It was shocking, given how modest Sophie seemed. I'd anticipated a house more similar to Garrett's or even Jude and Katie's, but this home was more mansion-like and for the first time in a long time, my stomach flipped with nerves.

Fortunately, it had nothing to do with the baby bean inside me. After Garrett left earlier, I managed to drag myself out of bed, make myself my own banana smoothie, something I'd taken to liking after the first one he attempted in my own apartment, and managed a thirty-minute walk outside before needing to get to work. With the time difference, I was technically late, but Rachel didn't mind so I put in a few hours of work, did research on starting my own business in Las Vegas, and after lunch and a quick nap, called it a day so I could rest up before a late night.

Now, that lingering exhaustion was starting to kick in, but I hoped since Sophie said she'd invited other wives and girlfriends over to have a girls' night while we watched the men play, that the company would wake me up long enough to make it through their game.

In my purse, my phone vibrated as I climbed out of the car and I grabbed it immediately. Garrett had already called to tell me he'd gotten to Anaheim safely. He asked me what I was doing after their morning skate practice and I'd sent him three good luck memes sure to make him laugh before his game.

Checking the phone, I figured it'd be him, but instead it was Katie and I smiled as I read her text.

You call me to tell me you're pregnant and in Vegas and then I hear nothing? Brat. Call me!

I'm walking into a teammate's wife's house to watch the game. Call you tomorrow!

Before I reached the door, my phone vibrated again.

A shocked emoji and then, **New friends already?! Soon you'll forget all about me.** Followed by a crying emoji.

Because I was the brat she accused me of, I replied, my thumbs flying. **Little people. Always worried about being forgotten.**

Her reply was an F followed by symbols and then a B followed by more symbols.

Katie never liked being reminded she was always close to being one of the shortest people in a room at any given moment. Served her right.

You started it, I typed back and rang the doorbell.

A ghostly, mourning tone echoed through the house, giving off a spooky vibe. It was immediately replaced with Sophie's large smile and body decked out in Vipers gear as she flung open the door and shouted, "You're here! Yay! Now the party can really start!"

I'd been so nervous pulling up to her driveway, the fact there'd been other cars there hadn't clued me in on the fact I was late.

"Am I the last one here?"

Great. Way to be late and make an awesome first impression.

"No way." She tugged me in, yanking on my arm like we'd known each other as long as Katie and not a few days and slammed the door behind me. "You're totally fine. Everyone's in the kitchen though and since you and Paige are both knocked up, I even made some mock sangria for you to have if you want some."

Mock sangria? "Isn't that... juice?"

Sophie laughed and kept tugging me along like it was the funniest thing she'd ever heard. But seriously. Sangria without alcohol? What else would it be?

"Yes, you cow. It's juice, but fancy juice, so enjoy if you want."

"Ah. Fancy juice. That makes all the difference."

"I knew I was going to like you." Sophie smiled, dragged me through her ornate entryway with a massive staircase delineating it. The kind you'd see in old-school movies where the women wore dresses to keep them five feet from other people.

Glamorous and gorgeous and yet it was richly decorated with neutral tones, lots of greenery. The living room she guided me through was at least two stories high with a catwalk from one end of the house to the other and even though it was enormous, it was comfortable.

"All right, ladies," she called out as soon as we entered the kitchen. "This is Lizzie." She swung out an arm in a dramatic gesture, much like I was learning she did everything else. "Lizzie. This is everyone you haven't met yet. Paige, the other knocked up chick ruining all our fun. She's married to Seth McCabe and they're so adorable together they make us all want to puke." A pretty little blonde tipped her glass in my direction and winked. "That's Maisy, Willow..." Two brunettes wearing Vipers jerseys with different numbers on them lifted glasses of wine in my direction. "And that's Nadia. André's sister."

My hand squeezed Sophie's involuntarily as I took in the blonde. More beautiful than I remembered from her Instagram photos, three times as covered as I saw her the other day.

She looked as shocked as I was. Sophie, clueless to the tension mounting, more embarrassment than anything on my part, and based on the blush on her cheeks, Nadia's too, continued. "Nadia isn't a girlfriend, but she's living here. Her ex is a douche-canoe we all want to throw into the Grand Canyon if we ever had the opportunity."

"Hello," she quietly said, and sipped a bottled water, almost seeming to hide her face behind it.

It was her nerves that settled mine. It was obvious she was embarrassed, but whether that was because of her behavior or because she didn't get the shot she wanted kept me from being overly friendly. "Nadia."

No one else seemed to know we'd met before, a fact I was grateful for. If she was friends with these women, she hadn't spilled her plan—or the failure of it—to them.

But really... I needed a drink. "So... you said something about a mocktail?" I asked.

"It's delicious," Paige called out from her side of the island that was large enough to fit a row of eight barstools and grabbed a glass. "I'm on my third, which means I'm going to be up all night peeing like a racehorse, but it's really good."

"Ah. The things I have to look forward to."

Her stomach was already proudly declaring she was much further along than me, something she didn't bother hiding behind an oversized jersey. Her shirt was skintight, curving over her chest and full belly, stretching out the Vipers logo, a viper snake wrapped around a V.

It gave the illusion of a misshapen head, but she worked it. "How far along are you?"

Her hand stalled on the upper cover of her abdomen. "Thirty weeks. Only ten more to go but I swear, right now I wish it was two."

"You look great." I didn't blame her. I couldn't imagine being comfortable once I grew to her size.

"Thanks. I feel great too, most days. And you? You're still early on, right?'

"Thirteen weeks," I said, and glanced around. None of these women would know Garrett that well, or our history. Admitting I showed up on his doorstep pregnant after one night when we weren't in a relationship wasn't the best first impression.

She popped a chunk of cheese into her mouth while I took a sip of my sangria. "You two weren't dating, right?"

Paige sounded more curious than judgmental, but I felt the eyes of every woman in the kitchen on me. On instinct, like I needed to protect my unborn child, my hands went to my stomach. Hell, I'd see these women all the time. "Garrett and I are—were," I corrected because things seemed so simple recently, "complicated, I guess. But we've been great friends for years. Since college, actually."

"But you weren't dating?" one of the brunettes asked, Maisy or Willow. I couldn't remember. "Because I thought he and Nadia—"

"No," Nadia said, "Garrett and I were friends. We just..." she sighed, and the awkward levels in the room notched to uncomfortable levels. "He was helping me get Toby off my back. That is all." She smiled at me, hesitant, but no less beautiful than she seemed to look at any other time. "He is a good man. I am happy for you both. Truly. And the baby is wonderful news."

"Thanks, Nadia." A chunk of cotton stuck in my throat. Her sincerity was apparent, along with her sadness and for that, I felt for her.

I knew exactly how it was to lose a guy like Garrett because I'd lost him and gained him multiple times over the years.

"But you're together now?" the other brunette asked. "That's awesome."

"We are. I have to head back to Chicago next week but the plan, I think right now is to get my home ready to sell and then come back."

"That'll be wonderful for you and the baby," Paige

replied. "And if you need any help, pointers or have questions or need help finding a doctor or anything, let me know. Us mamas have to stick together."

"Thanks." I fought my chin wobble, tears and emotions threatening to erupt. "I will. Although I had a consult with a few places this week."

"Oh? Where?"

"A midwife Serenity—"

"Oh my goodness! That's where I'm delivering. Aren't they amazing?"

She clapped her hands and yanked me into a hug so surprising she almost jerked me off my feet. Goodness. "I thought so."

"You'll love them. Seriously. They've helped me with so much stress and everything. I couldn't have stayed so calm all the time through this without them."

"You've been *calm*?" someone asked and Paige glared at her.

"Yes Maisy. Calm. Well..." She shrugged and chugged her sangria like it had half a bottle of alcohol in it. "As calm as I can get anyway."

So the one who asked about Nadia was Maisy. She smirked at Paige, narrowed her eyes as her gaze danced over me, and then gave a fake smile to Sophie. "So, how about we go watch that game."

Everyone ushered out, but it was Paige who touched my hand as I went to grab a plate of cheese and crackers. "Don't mind Maisy. She's been dating Max, one of our defensemen for like six months and she thinks she's hot shit because he's the captain. None of us can stand her but we can't hang out and not invite her because then we seem like bitches. Can't have that when her social media following is six figures."

I smothered a laugh and rolled my lips together. "Thanks."

"No worries. Joey was so excited when he heard Garrett was being traded here he couldn't stop talking about how great he was. He mentioned you, too, seeing you at Christmas when he was with his family. You're good people, I can feel it, but that doesn't mean all the girls are, even if we try to like them."

She had no clue how much I needed this. Friends. People who understood I wasn't a gold digger or anything.

"Thanks Paige. I appreciate the help. Truly."

"Sophie and I are happy to help. Frankly, we're pretty kick ass, at least when I'm not carrying around an extra thirty pounds."

That I could understand. I was a lot more fun thirteen weeks ago myself.

We set down the snacks we'd brought from the kitchen on a massive, fabric covered ottoman and snuggled into a sectional couch that could fit twelve of us comfortably.

Soon, we were laughing at Sophie screaming at the television, laughing over everyone's stories of ridiculous things that have happened to them since dating a pro athlete, and by the time I got home, and crawled into bed I'd felt like I was beginning to have a new home.

Friends.

A growing family.

Why in the world would I ever want to leave?

23

GARRETT

"**D**amn. You deserve a drink after that last save." Alix Halvrick, one of our left wingers, slid a beer in front of me, and settled his elbow on the bar.

We were at the hotel bar after the game in Anaheim. We had another game there tomorrow before we hopped on a plane to fly up to San Jose to continue our West Coast series. Tonight's game was tough, but we won three-to-one and the save Alix mentioned almost made me pull a groin muscle I stretched so far to grab it.

Being a yoga master with all that flexibility was one of the things that made me such a good goalie.

"Thanks." I grabbed the drink and checked my phone. I'd already gotten a few texts from Lizzie, and I knew she was back at my place, in bed.

She was probably sleeping, but I couldn't stop thinking about her, knowing she was in *my* bed, sleeping because she was exhausted from carrying *my* baby. Sure, sure. Ours. Whatever.

It was still mine. Being on the road and leaving someone

I loved behind was a whole new dynamic I hadn't been prepared for.

"So, you think tomorrow will be as easy?"

I snorted into my beer. "No games are easy."

"Maybe not for your Chicago team, but we kick ass here in Vegas."

Alix had been in the league for three years, and he wasn't wrong. Vegas did kick ass. But being cocky never helped anyone. "With an ego like yours, it's a wonder you can fit through a doorway."

He shrugged. "Ain't ego if it's true. I'm the best."

"The hell you are," Joey said, coming up to him and shoving him away, laughing. "You've yet to beat me one on one."

Alix's blond hair shook as he laughed back, scratching his short beard. "Well, I'm better at soccer."

The guys tended to kick around a soccer ball for pregame warm-ups. It loosened us up, was something stupid and fun, and Alix was right on that account. He dribbled a soccer ball better than any of the other players. His solo record currently sat at forty-five.

"Too bad you can't shoot a puck like you can dribble a ball," I cut in, tipping my beer in his direction. "It's all right, little Halvrick. A little more practice and you'll be a big boy soon."

"Oh fuck off. I'm big in all the places that matter." He stuck out his tongue and glanced down at his junk.

"Don't care about your dick," I teased back. "But I wonder if there's anyone on the team you could beat in that contest one on one, either."

"Oh!" Joey called out, covering his mouth with his fist. "Shots fired."

"You're all idiots. Grow up." Max strolled up to my other

side, stern look on his face. At thirty, he was one of the older guys on the team. Still single, divorced actually, but in a relationship with some chick none of the guys could stand.

"We *do* grow." Alix smirked, full of mirth. "That's how it gets so *big*."

Max rolled his eyes and ordered another vodka tonic before standing from the bar. "Don't get too drunk tonight. I don't want to have to carry your hungover asses on the ice tomorrow."

"Okay Daddy. We'll behave, we promise." Joey and Alix said it at the same and I dropped my head, chuckling and trying to hide it. Being on a hockey team was a never-ending game of giving each other shit and not taking it personally. Fortunately, Max, as serious as he always was, took the ribbing good naturally and smacked Joey on the back of the head as he walked away.

"Don't be stupid," he called out, taking his drink to the elevator. He'd probably be upstairs, reading and passed out in thirty minutes. Typically, that was me, after a game. I only enjoyed a drink or two before needing the night to rest up for the next game. Tonight was no different. I would have headed up if Alix hadn't bought me a drink. But I was still getting used to my new team, so bowing out early wasn't the way to get in their good graces.

As it was, I was content sitting at the bar, hanging with men who came up to me, since they had to get up here anyway for more drinks.

Alix and Joey took off while I checked my phone like a psycho one more time.

Damn. Get a girl in my house. Get a baby in her belly and I turned into a neurotic loner.

A flash of long blonde hair appeared in my peripheral

and I turned, giving the woman a cursory glance before dipping my head back to my phone.

"Would you like another?"

I glanced up at the question, only to find the woman pointing to my drink. "I'm good. Thanks."

"You played really well tonight. I'm a huge fan of yours."

Ah. This could go one of two ways. She was actually a fan of hockey, or she was a fan of bedding hockey players. The first I was more than willing to be polite to. The second I started running from years ago. Now that I had Lizzie, I wasn't interested in either except the basic politeness required.

"Thanks. It was a good game. You're not an Anaheim fan?"

"I was at the game," she said, and pushed her breasts forward, straightening her back. "But I went to college in Illinois. Hard not to fall in love with the Storm when you're a student there. A guy I dated once got me hooked on hockey, and you, well, you're a great goalie."

Sounded about right. I was awesome. "Thanks."

If she was offended I wasn't giving her more than that, she didn't show it. Instead, she tucked a chunk of hair behind her ear, drifting her hand down the side of her neck as she dropped it back to the bar. "So, if you'd like that drink, we could take them up to my room."

Right. Called that one. "No thanks. I'm taken."

"Lucky girl." She shrugged. "No harm then, Garrett."

It never became less strange when strangers you didn't know knew you by name. Hell, she probably knew my height, my weight, and if she really was a fan, she could probably recall a goal I let slip through to lose the game for Chicago over the years. I had a few really shitty games in my long career.

And that was my cue to leave. As I turned to slide off the stool, Dominick Masters, top defenseman and all-around secluded asshole settled his forearms on the bar, giving the woman to my left a look up and down, stalling on breasts I'd just had none too covertly pressed in my direction.

"Have a good night," I said to the woman because if she was a fan, I didn't want to be a jerk. As I walked by Dominick, he grabbed my bicep and leaned in.

"That pretty little thing you had at the game the other night got you that wrapped up that quickly?"

Not only did Dominick not know a single thing about me, but he also hadn't made a single damn effort to *try* to get to know anything about me. For all he knew, Lizzie and I had been together for years. Whatever.

I had other names I could call him that rhymed with the end of his name. This was one guy I was glad I could sit in the goalie box and watch from a distance. The man was as cocky and arrogant as they came. Every team had one. Dominick Masters was ours.

"She's having my baby and I've loved her for years, so yeah."

At that, his brows jumped, and helmet me go.

"No shit? Didn't think you had a woman."

"And that's the problem when you're on a team but act like you're an island. You don't know shit about anyone."

By the time I was done, he was scowling at me, gripping his drink more tightly and finally let go of my arm.

"Yeah, I guess that's what you'd think of me."

He turned back to the bar, grinned at the woman who'd tried hitting on me, and that was most definitely my cue.

If he wanted her, he could have her, but I wasn't going to give a second thought to his cryptic statement.

I was exhausted, wanted to get up early to call Lizzie

before I had to meet with the goaltending coach for warm-ups and stretches.

"HEY. YOU'RE AWAKE."

Lizzie's sunny smile cleared on the screen of my phone.

Her blonde hair a mess on her head, wearing my sweat-shirt, a pair of sweats. Both would be so large they'd hide all of her glorious curves. She was already awake, in the kitchen, even though I'd hoped I caught her still in bed, preferably naked.

My dick definitely liked the idea and I groaned, running my hand over my stomach as she grinned at me through the screen call.

"What are you doing?" She leaned forward, elbow on the kitchen counter, and propped her chin into the palm of her hand.

"I *was* calling to see how last night went and how you're doing. Now, I'm thinking about what I'd do to you if I was there."

"Oh yeah?" She cleared her throat and her beautiful blush crept up her neck. "Like what?"

My hand settled at the waistband of my boxers. I had to be ready for the bus in an hour, but at least I'd gotten my own room this time. No worries about André getting a show.

"For starters," I drawled out, waited for her cheeks to have the blush settle at the apple of her cheekbones, and I grinned. "I'd steal back that sweatshirt of mine you're wearing."

Smiling, she shook her head. "No you wouldn't."

"I wouldn't?"

"No. Because you like stripping me out of it too much to not give it back to me."

She had a point. More, I liked seeing what was beneath that sweatshirt that was so damn faded it had to be one of her favorites. And hell if I didn't love that. That all through the years since college, she'd frequently covered herself in me.

I also wanted all of that right now. Her naked, running her hands down her body even if I couldn't be there, be the one touching her. Hell, a little morning orgasm could be just what I needed before I needed to get to Coach Campbell for stretching and an early warm-up.

It'd definitely leave me starting my day off relaxed.

"You're right," I said, tilting my chin up where I was propped on the pillows against my headboard. "But since I can't be there. How about you do it for me?"

She snickered and then her aqua eyes narrowed. "Are you seriously wanting phone sex with me right now?"

If she wasn't up for it, I'd back down in an instant but I knew Lizzie. Her middle name should have been Adventure instead of Louise, after her maternal grandmother.

I dragged my hand off my stomach and pushed it behind my head, letting her see my naked biceps I knew she loved. "There's probably one thing we should get clear, right off the bat."

"You mean the stick?" She snorted.

I rolled my eyes. Stick. Bat. Whatever. "Stick with me, yeah?"

"Sure." She giggled and popped a cracker into her mouth, wiggling her fingers toward her for me to continue. At the sight of the cracker, I paused my train of thought.

"How are you feeling?"

"Good. Cracker is to make sure I don't puke, but I woke

up feeling okay again. But that's not what we're getting straight, is it?"

As she asked, she started moving. My kitchen spun in the background and then the living room. Hell yeah, she was headed for the stairs.

"Right." I cleared my throat. "We need to get one thing straight. If we're together, and I'm thinking about you, I'm going to want to have sex with you. If we're on the phone and I see you, I'm going to want to have sex with you. If we're in the same room or building and I see you, I'm going to want to have sex with you. And all the other times when we're not together, I can pretty much guarantee, I'm spending most of that time thinking about how much I want to have sex with you."

"Well," she said, chuckling. "That's a lot of sex."

"I'm a guy in my late twenties with a *lot* of testosterone to expel, so yeah, that all right?"

She spun around. My bed was behind her to the right and then the phone shook. When she pulled back, she had both hands free. From the view, she'd set the phone on my dresser.

"Depends," she murmured, and then her arms crossed in front of her. Lifted, and with a quick whip, my sweatshirt was in her hand, her hair was flying, and my gaze zoomed in on her tits. Fuller than they used to be. A tiny thickening to her midsection. She was *changing*. And it seemed to be by the day. Definitely more at night.

At the sight of her, I readjusted and shoved my boxers down to my hips, freeing my erection. I palmed it immediately, cupped my balls and let loose a low growl of need.

"Grab your phone and get on the bed," I told her. "Lose the pants on the way."

"Bossy, bossy."

She hadn't seen bossy, not yet, but she liked it when I was in charge. Fortunately for me, when it came to Lizzie and her sass and her independence, she *liked* it when I told her what to do.

"Now, remember what you were doing that first night in my house when I heard you?"

She grinned at me and nodded. "Of course."

"Good. I want you to do that for me again. Show me what I missed out on."

She didn't waste a second. One hand cupped her breast while the other slid down her stomach, straight to her shaved pussy. She had the phone set perfectly, so I could see everything and I shoved back from the desk where I had my phone so she could see how hard she made me.

She whimpered as she played with herself, eyes glossy when she took in the sight of me and moaned. "It shouldn't be this normal to be so wet already. It's unbelievable how much you turn me on."

Her fingers glistened, shined on her pale pink painted fingertips as she dipped them inside and then rolled them around her clit.

I pumped my dick faster, reduced to grunts as I encouraged her, told her what to do. Add a finger. Pinch her nipple. "If I was there, I'd play with your tits until you came again. It was so damn hot."

"Your dick is hot," she fired back, but her voice was breathy and shaky, losing the fire intended. "I want to see you come. Want to swallow it down and feel you in the back of my throat."

She was going to kill me. I'd be late for the bus and the team would show up, finding me dead unconscious with my dick out and my pants at my ankles.

Who gave a shit. Precum pebbled at the tip of my dick

and I used it for moisture, fucking my fist like she was doing to herself with her own fingers.

"Shit Lizzie. You're so hot. I'm going to come."

"I want to see."

"You first."

Because even if we were apart, she came first. Always. In bed and out of it.

I staved off my climax, waiting until her back bowed off the bed and her thighs trembled. She cried out my name as if I was in the room with her, tunneling deep inside of her and it was all I needed.

I snapped. My orgasm hit, and I came into my fist, grunting and clenching my jaw to stay as quiet as possible. Damn hotels and teammates surrounding me.

"I miss you already," I said, and reached for the box of tissues. I cleaned up while she threw on that damn sweatshirt and then a phone call came through.

"What the hell?"

It was my neighborhood security guard.

"What is it?"

Lizzie was sitting on the bed, cross-legged, hair a mess and cheeks flushed from her orgasm but her eyes were narrowed, worried.

"Hold on. I need to take this call. My security guard at the gate is calling."

"What's that mean?"

"That I have a visitor. I'll give him your number to call when I talk to him, in case you have people over. Hold on a sec."

"Hello?"

"Hello Mr. Dubiak, a Miss Gabrielle Dubiak is here to see you?"

Oh shit. No way. She would have had to hop on a flight

at the butt crack of dawn to be in Vegas by now. My psychotic sister. Good luck, Lizzie. "Send her in. Thanks Joe, and while I have you on the phone, can you add Lizzie Winston to my call list for visitors? She's staying with me for a while."

"Sure thing, sir."

I gave him her number, said goodbye, and was laughing when I clicked back over.

"Lizzie?"

"Yeah, is everything okay?"

"For me, because I'm an hour plane ride away, for you, maybe not. Gabby's here."

"Oh crap on a cracker."

I laughed as her face paled and her jaw dropped.

Gabby might have been pissed initially, but she'd gotten over it. At least I hoped.

I scanned my wrist that was bare of a watch. "And oh, look at the time. I gotta get to practice. Love you!"

"You suck," she shrieked.

"You love me anyway."

"Yeah. Be safe today and good luck. If Gabby doesn't strangle me, we'll be cheering for you."

That's what I liked to hear.

"Love you, Garrett."

"You too, honey."

24

LIZZIE

G abrielle Dubiak wasn't just younger than her brother. At twenty-three, she had a protective streak larger than any human I'd ever met. I figured it was because they'd grown up depending on each other so much. She was only five when her dad died, so she grew up with Garrett being her go-to for everything man-related or necessary.

So even though she'd cooled it when we FaceTimed the other day and eventually was happy for us, I expected her to storm into Garrett's house, force me to promise never to hurt her brother again or she'd take my knees out with a baseball bat or something.

What I didn't expect was for her eyes to be puffy and swollen, in desperate need of Visine, and for her to drop her bags in the entry area and yawn into her hand.

"I'm exhausted and starving. Do you have any food or should I order something?"

She barely acknowledged me and I frowned, chasing after.

"Hey Gabby," I said, while she dug in the fridge. "Is... is everything okay?"

"Yeah, but that flight was killer and I'm wiped. Starving too. How are you feeling?"

Um. This was how this conversation was going to go?

Not at all what I anticipated. More like the Spanish Inquisition.

I rested against the wall, shoulder to it, ankles crossed, and waited until she was done rummaging through Garrett's refrigerator only to grab out a tub of Greek yogurt and grab a spoon from the island. "So, you're knocked up and playing house, huh? How's that going?"

Her tone was too blasé to trick me into thinking she didn't care. But worry made my brows tighten as I took in the paleness of her face, the purple rings beneath her eyes.

I ignored her question again and went to the other side of the island. As she sucked down the yogurt, I chewed the inside of my cheek. Gabrielle could be tricky, but we'd always been friends. Or at least I thought we had.

"What's going on?" I asked. She might have been protective but I highly doubted she flew all the way here just to eat her brother's food.

"Crappy week. Shitty month. A year full of regret." She shrugged like it meant nothing, but there was pain in her voice that made my gut squeeze.

"Gabby—"

"Don't." She pointed her spoon at me and then tossed it into the sink. The metal clinked against the ceramic sink, jarring my ears.

I didn't back down but kept my gaze on her as she tossed away her yogurt and went to the coffeepot.

"Fine," she huffed, glaring at me over her shoulder. "The

short version is that Kurt and I broke up. He cheated on me with his assistant, of all people, which is totally cliché. I fell for all the times he said there was nothing going on between them."

"Oh honey," I whispered. They'd been together barely over a year. She'd thought he was the one. The pain in her voice was only minimal to the fury making it shake.

"Then," she continued, slamming down the pot of coffee. "Because my day couldn't get any better, my boss at the salon told me she was closing up shop."

"What?"

"Yeah. There's a ton of construction in the area and it won't be done for another year. She's basically losing all her clients to the hassle of it, so she decided not to fight it anymore." She heaved a heavy, shaky breath. "So, in the last thirty-six hours, I humiliated myself walking into Kurt's office to see him, the surprise to end all surprises, making out with *Tiffany* of all people, the blonde, big-boobed, bimbo he probably hired based on her substantial cup size alone, and then I showed up at the salon to be told I had to find a new place to rent a chair or I wouldn't be working for the foreseeable future." She spun, still glaring at me, but this time I didn't take it personally. This would be enough to send anyone into a rage. "Since I suddenly found myself without a boyfriend and jobless, I decided, what the hell. You're here alone. I could use a break. So I hopped a flight and flew down."

"Gabby—"

"Happy now?"

"No." I shook my head. "Of course I'm not happy about any of that."

"It's fine. It'll be fine. My mom will give me more shit about acting before I think, saying I'm too emotional and not level-headed enough, but whatever." She shrugged and poured a hefty amount of sugar into her mug. "Seeing as how I helped Garrett rent this home and found it for him before he ever moved here, I figure it's half mine so I could be here."

"Of course you can be here. But can you at least come here and give me a hug and say hello to me like a normal person?" My lips twitched. While protective, she wasn't overly affectionate. Her blowing me off at the door wasn't really all that surprising if she was mad at me or hurting herself as the case appeared to be.

Her lip curled at the suggestion and I chuckled, dropping my hands to my hips.

"Okay, so we're not ready for hugs yet. Anything you want to do while you're here? I have some work to get done this week, but it's flexible."

"I think the only thing I want to know is if you're really here for Garrett this time. As in staying."

I sighed.

I figured she'd hit me with that eventually.

"Yeah. Gabby. I'm here for him. For *us*." To emphasize, I brushed my hand over my stomach. There was a fullness there I hadn't noticed even a couple days ago. Mostly I thickened at my hips, but there was a tiny bloat only I could probably notice. "I head back to Chicago next week and I need to talk to my boss about something, but yeah, I'll be moving back here. Permanently."

Her lips pushed out, dark eyes that looked nothing like Garrett's narrowed on me. She was gorgeous. Always had been. Even while she inspected me, ferreting out whether or not I was being truthful she was still one of the most beautiful women I knew.

"And you'll be okay, you know."

Her chin trembled and she set down her coffee mug.

With a slight lift of her chin, she stretched out her arms. "Come here, bitch. And give me a hug."

"THINGS OKAY?" Garrett asked. "Gabby didn't hurt you, did she?"

"No." I laughed and dug through clothes in my suitcases. I'd brought *way* too much stuff for a few weeks here and hadn't bothered unpacking a thing. But I was leaving in less than a week and I'd be back so I was trying to go through what could stay, what I could still fit into when I returned, or someday again. Garrett hadn't offered me space in his closet, but I didn't figure he'd mind.

"She's sleeping and upset. Apparently she lost her job and then Kurt all in one swoop. Came down here to get away."

"Fuck. I never liked that piece of shit."

"You wouldn't like anyone your sister liked."

"Not true." He laughed. "It'll just have to be a special kind of guy for me to like, and Kurt was too basic for her. Too much of an ego with shiny hair. Never trust a guy with so much gel in his hair it doesn't move in the wind."

"Is that a rule?" I asked, laughing at his description. He wasn't wrong. I hadn't met Kurt but I'd seen pictures.

"Should be. How is she then?"

"Tired. Upset. But I'm glad she's here. I like the company."

"I'm glad you're not alone, too. Hold on a sec." He must've covered his phone because muffled voices came through and then he was back. "Hey, listen, guys want to go grab some lunch before we need to get to the arena. Braxton found a juice bar he's forcing us to try so I need to get going okay?"

"Of course it's fine. And don't worry about us, okay? Gabby and I will be here, cheering you on tonight, but focus on the game. Don't worry about us."

"Two of the three most important women in my life? Of course I'll worry."

"I love you," I whispered. "You're so good to me. To us." Words came so easily for him, harder for me. I wasn't a heart and flowers kind of girl who needed flowers and I certainly wasn't good at giving them. Every time Garrett told me, and then showed me how much he cared I wanted to cry.

Happy tears.

Thankful ones. Because I'd almost ruined us and he kept giving me more chances.

My voice shook as I said, "Head in the game, Garrett. Gabby and I will be just fine. But we miss you and love you."

"You too, honey. I'll call you tomorrow."

I glanced around his room, at the messed up covers on his bed I hadn't yet made for the day and the enormous mess I had scattered all over it. "I'll be here."

"Yeah, you will."

His tone turned to gravel, letting me know he was thinking the same thing I was.

I would be here for him when he returned. And soon, it'd be for always.

"Before I forget. I left something for you in the cupboard by the fridge. Use it to your heart's content."

"What is it?"

"Go find out and have fun. But use it or I'll be pissed."

"Aye-aye bossy pants."

He chuckled, and that rumble drifted through the

phone, straight to my chest. Where my heart warmed and squeezed and other parts of me heated.

"Garrett," I said his name on a breath. There was nothing else to say. He was just so damn good to me.

"Yeah." He cleared his throat. "I gotta get off the phone, get rid of my erection now that you've got me all turned on with those sounds you make. Love you, Lizzie. Call you tomorrow."

BY THE TIME I unpacked all my clothes and spent a few hours working, I returned downstairs to find Gabby sitting on the couch, blanket over her lap, a glass of red wine in her hand and a Styrofoam container holding a massive pile of tortilla chips on the coffee table in front of her.

"You ordered Mexican food?" I asked. And she hadn't told me?

I wasn't sure if I should be offended. Mostly hurt. What kind of *friend* ordered Mexican and didn't let their friend place an order?

"Chips and queso and a few bottles of wine delivered via Door Dash. I didn't know if you were sleeping and I didn't want to wake you. There's more in the kitchen."

"Oh. Thanks."

It was a déjà vu to last week when Garrett ordered for me, but a girl could never have too much chips and queso. The smell of the spicy cheese drew me toward the kitchen.

"Um," I mumbled, as I took in the island. There were *five* bowls of queso. Five. Even for me, that was excessive. And the wine?

"Hey Gabby?" I leaned back around a wall and she turned, face me over her shoulder. "A case of wine?"

She grinned and took a sip of the glass in her hand. "Twenty percent discount if you ordered twelve."

"Right." Because that made sense.

How long was she planning on staying, though? "You know I can't drink, right?" I called out, moving back to the bowls of cheese. I grabbed one and a roll of paper towels from beneath the sink. While Garrett was gone, I considered helping to start decorate his home. Simple things, like a paper towel holder. Or a soap holder. Toothbrush holder. The idea of bracing my toothbrush on the edge of the sink near where his beard clippings fell made my stomach turn.

Men. They didn't think of all the small things.

Like hand towels.

"Duh," Gabby said, as I settled on my knees between a chair and the coffee table. Without hesitating, I dove in, groaning as that first taste of cheese fired up my senses.

"Garrett and I had this last week but I swear, if there was one food I could eat for the rest of my life it'd be Mexican."

She snorted. "That's not a food group."

"Should be," I mumbled over a mouthful of chips and cheese. "But if I had to narrow it down, it'd be cheese. All kinds."

"I hear that. As long as I can drink wine."

"You okay?"

"I will be." She shrugged. "You find out what Garrett left you yet?"

"What?"

"The kitchen cupboard. He texted me."

I'd totally forgotten. I pushed off the floor, shoving down my jogger sweats that had ridden up to my calves, and glared at her. "He called you?"

"Texted. Told me to make sure you use it."

"Did you peek?" What in the hell had he left for me?

She gave me a wicked look. "Would I do that?"

I huffed. "Of course you would."

"He said I can use it, too!" she called out. For the first time since she arrived at his doorstep she had a smile on her face so I hurried to the kitchen, opened the cupboard he'd told me about and then picked my jaw up off the floor.

"He left us his credit card." I waved it in the air, gawked at it like it was an alien life form I'd never seen before.

"Yeah. That's what those little plastic rectangles usually are called."

"Why?"

"He told me to take you shopping. Buy maternity clothes or whatever you need. Said he needs shit for his house. Basically, my favorite knocked up bitch, we're going shopping."

Oh, hell yeah we were.

25

LIZZIE

"I don't know if I've ever been so exhausted."

Gabby collapsed on the couch, piles and piles of shopping bags surrounding her, some falling onto her lap as she kicked off her shoes.

"That's probably because you bought out four complete stores."

I dropped my two shopping bags near the bottom of the stairs. This girl took her brother's assignment seriously. I was pretty certain she'd bought an entire wardrobe, including shoes and accessories, all while I struggled to find anything cute or worth purchasing. Who knew there'd be such a lack of maternity clothes and the few stores we'd found exclusively for expecting women, had clothes that were for when I was so much further along. It was infuriating. All I managed to purchase were a couple pairs of jeans in a size up, three longer T-shirts that would leave room for some growth in the stomach, and the stupid paper towel holder I'd wanted to get for Garrett's kitchen counter.

Every other time I picked something else, I became paralyzed with indecision. Would he like it? Did he want my help? Did he want to do it together? Was buying too much for his house too soon?

Ugh. I was giving myself a migraine.

"Do you want your smoothie?" I held up the drink carrier. We'd stopped at Smoothie King on the way home from our mall extravaganza because I was desperate for something in my stomach before I got nauseous again.

This morning I threw up, but I chalked it up to being up late last night to watch Vegas beat Anaheim. Garrett called earlier this morning before his team had to catch their plane up to San Francisco, encouraging me to do as much damage as possible to his credit card balance.

Gabrielle took that as her life's sole mission.

"I'm too tired to drink anything," she muttered from where she was plopped on the couch. Waving her hand, she eyed the smoothie. "But maybe I could drink some of it before I pass out."

"You're a piece of work," I told her, laughing as I pulled the cup out of the carrier and handed it to her. "I'm going to go upstairs and take a nap. You're all right down here?"

"Fine. I suppose I'll have to model all my new clothes by myself then."

It wasn't possible for a woman to sound so put out, and I shook my head. "Give me an hour or two and then I can watch."

Her head fell to the back of the couch, black hair pulled up in some fancy bun with braids that would have taken me days to figure out but she made it look effortless.

"You're a good friend, Lizzie."

"Thanks, but I'm pretty sure you should be saying that to your brother. He's the one who bought out Nordstrom's on your behalf today."

She closed her eyes and sighed. "Every girl needs some retail therapy in her life."

I grabbed my bags from the bottom of the stairs. "Did it help?"

She turned her head in my direction, barely managing to open her eyes. "No, not really."

"You'll be okay, you know that though, right?"

"Of course I will be. But that's because I'm awesome. I just need some time to lick my wounds and figure out what to do next."

I stopped on the stairs, hand curled around the banister. Watching Gabby get sleepy was making me even more tired. And when she yawned, I had to fight my own. "I don't think Garrett will care if you stay here while you do that."

"I know. He's the best." One eye peeked open again. "You are, too. Thanks for loving him."

"It's my pleasure," I replied, and at her soft, sleepy smile, I focused on the trek upstairs. I barely managed to reach the bedroom, slip off my shoes and tug my jeans down my hips to the floor before I trudged to the bed.

Pregnancy tired was a whole new level of tired I wasn't prepared for.

Lord, help me and a woman on a mission to see how large her brother's credit limit was.

As soon as I hit the bed, face-planting into it, I grabbed Garrett's pillow, inhaled the musky scent of him, hugged it to me and in seconds I was asleep.

"Hey. Wake up."

I was being shaken, and a familiar voice was whispering in my ears. Opening my eyes, I stared right into Gabby's face. "What is your problem?" I groaned, shoving hair from my eyes. My limbs were heavy from sleep.

I had to be out only minutes. Exhaustion made it seem

like a brick was settled on my chest, cementing me into the mattress.

"You need to wake up."

"Why?" I rolled over and closed my eyes.

"Because you've been asleep for like hours and you've missed three calls from your mom and some texts from Garrett."

"What? What time is it?" I shoved myself to sitting, hugging Garrett's pillow to my lap before realizing how deranged that was. What woman needed her man's pillow to feel better? Or sleep better?

"It's almost five. And I figured you'd need some food or something. Doesn't that thing inside of you need to eat?"

"That thing," I snorted, "is a baby and it's the size of a lemon or something like that." As I spoke, my stomach rolled. Maybe Gabby had a point.

It'd be nice if at some point, I started to get a hold of this pregnancy shtick better than the daddy or the aunt.

"I need food," I groaned and covered my mouth. I tripped over the covers on my way to the bathroom but made it to the toilet. As I leaned over it, I gagged, unable to throw up—was that a good sign or bad sign?—Gabby ran water behind me and then held a warm, wet washcloth to my forehead.

"It's okay. I'm sorry. I didn't mean to make you puke."

I choked out a laugh. Despite the urge to still throw up, nothing was happening. "Can you go get some crackers next to the bed? One or two might help."

"Sure." She placed the cloth into my hand and I sat back, knees to my chest, and rested my forehead against them.

At her footsteps returning, I reached out, plucked a cracker from her hand and munched on it. "Thanks."

"Is there anything else you need?"

"Yeah, to stop feeling like I'm going to throw up at random times throughout the day."

She laughed and took a seat next to me. Other than Garrett taking care of me, I'd done so much of this alone. Was it weird Gabby and I were hanging out in a bathroom while I tried not to vomit? Sure.

Did I like it?

"Thanks," I said again, and lifted my head enough to let it fall to her shoulder. "I'm glad you're here."

"At least someone's happy to see me." I squeezed her knee and ate another cracker. "Garrett always said you deserved better than Kurt. Said he was too basic for you, too distant."

"Yeah, well he was hot and the sex was out of this world amazing." After a moment, she snickered. "Probably not the best qualities to base a long-term relationship on, huh?"

"Nope." I popped the P and blew out a breath. "I think I'm going to be okay, but do you know what sounds really amazing to me right now?" At her raised eyebrows, an expectant look on her face, I said, "Olive Garden salad and breadsticks."

"Ohhh." She stood and brushed her hands down the thighs of her jeans. "I haven't eaten there since college."

"Sounds good, though, right?"

"Oh yeah. I could eat a laundry basket of those breadsticks. Do you want to go out or should we see if they could deliver?"

The laundry basket aspect made them seem slightly less appealing, but I understood her more general point.

"Delivery." The thought of getting dressed again to go out made me tired thinking about it. "I don't know if I can handle another marathon excursion with you."

Garrett's fridge and pantry were still overflowing with all

the food we bought last week, but the idea of cooking seemed way too difficult.

She stuck out her tongue and pointed to my nightstand back in the bedroom. "I brought up your phone in case you want to call your parents back or Garrett."

I climbed to my feet and thanked her. "Wouldn't he be on the plane by now?"

"They've probably landed already. Weren't they leaving this morning?"

Right. Because I'd slept for three hours, not one like I'd hope to do and I'd lost track of time while we were shopping.

Most likely Garrett and his team were having dinner somewhere or getting ready to. A lot of times when he was on the road, groups of guys would go find restaurants if mealtimes didn't come close to the end of practices in the visiting team rooms.

"Is there anything else you want from there? I'll order everything while you call your parents back."

"Give me a few minutes and I'll look."

After Gabby left, I used the bathroom and brushed my teeth to get the sleepy taste of my smoothie and lunch out of my mouth. After washing my face and applying moisturizer and feeling more awake as well as refreshed, I grabbed my phone and pulled up Olive Garden's menu. The longer I looked, the more gross I felt. Everything sounded like it'd sit in my stomach like a lead balloon which wouldn't help me feel any better. So help me, if pregnancy ruined my love affair with carbs, mainly pasta, I was never going to go through it again.

Soup didn't turn my stomach though. I texted Gabby a request for their chicken and gnocchi and told her I'd be downstairs in a bit.

I pulled up my mom's number on FaceTime and settled back into bed. Her face, so similar to mine with well-aged wrinkles came into view, the phone screen wobbling as she hurried to sit next to my dad. I didn't see him yet, but he was there. I might have been closing in on thirty in a few years but they always had to talk to me together like I was a freshman in college and homesick.

"Hey Mom."

"Hello beautiful. How are you feeling?"

She settled back on the couch and as predicted, my dad's arm slid behind her on the couch and then his face came into view. "Hey Dad."

"Princess." He blew me a kiss. "How's it going out there?"

"It's good. Great actually and I'm doing better. Most days, anyway."

"I'm glad," my mom said, smile wobbling. "You're almost through the worst of it, sweetie."

"Thanks, Mom." I ran my fingers through my hair. "You called earlier? I was sleeping."

"Good. You should be doing that as much as possible. Mostly I just wanted to see how everything was going with Garrett. We hadn't heard from you."

My dad tucked in so I could see his full face. "Your mom was worried."

Of course she was. "It's what she does best," I teased and Mom smiled.

"Just you wait. You'll understand that mama bear worry in a few months and you'll never give me a hard time again."

She was probably right, and in truth, my parents had always been pretty laidback. As long as I made good decisions, with only the occasional teenage or college-age screw up, I'd grown up with a lot of freedom. More so than most of my friends whose parents were way stricter.

"So, tell me. What are you thinking after being there a week now?"

It came to me in a flash. I didn't need to think, I didn't even need to consider, and I certainly didn't need to create a pros and cons list. "When I get back to Chicago, I'm going to give my notice and quit."

"Your notice," she said, brows lifting on her forehead in surprise. "I thought, I thought Shawna was okay with you working remotely."

"Yeah. And I think I could, but I'm not sure I want to."

"Why's that?" my dad asked. He'd give me time to think it through, question me to make sure I was making the right decision for myself.

"If I work remotely, I'll be doing it while I'm trying to get settled here, and even then, I'm still milling around the idea of starting my own business. I need something flexible, I guess, so I'm not even sure opening my firm is something I should do anymore, but I could get a job here easily I think." Even if it wasn't to the status I was used to, or the money, financial planning companies were a dime a dozen. I just needed to find one whose philosophy I agreed with. "Besides that, I want to be here getting settled, enjoying the rest of the season with Garrett. The off-season before the baby comes. We've had so little time together, really together, I think it'd be good for us."

My mom's chin trembled and she blinked harshly. "That does make sense," she whispered and brushed beneath her eyes.

"Aw, Mom." I laugh-cried right along with her. "Don't cry."

"I'm not."

My dad laughed. I arched a brow.

"Okay, so I'm crying." She giggled. "Only because I'm

happy for you, I really am, I'm just sad we're going to be grandparents and you'll be far away, and I never thought you'd leave Chicago so I'm just all... I'm all happy and sad at the same time."

Damn her. Now she had me crying. My dad, normally so stoic and reserved with his emotions, curled her into his chest and I swear even he had a tear in his eye. "Whatever you think is best for you, you know we'll support that."

"I know." I had the best parents in the world. Still madly in love with each other after thirty-five years and crazy about me. "Anyway, I'm going to give notice and then spend the time packing up everything I don't want to bring with me. Will you help me get the condo ready to list and sell?"

"Of course. Anything you need. Just answer me one question honestly."

"What's that?"

"Are you happy?"

I couldn't hide my immediate smile and didn't want to. "More than I've ever been."

"Get your ass down here!" Gabby shouted. "Food's coming and I'm bored and alone."

I laughed and my mom's brows furrowed. "Gabby's there?"

"Yeah. She surprised me so I wasn't alone this week."

"Wonderful. Tell her we said hello."

"I will. Love you both."

We ended the call and I was still smiling as their faces faded. I was sad to see them. But I was definitely happy.

In addition to planning for a future with Garrett, I had salty, buttery breadsticks and an OG salad coming. What else could a girl need?

26

LIZZIE

"Their defense really needs to pick up the pace," Gabby said, sitting on the edge of her seat in Garrett's living room.

Their game in Seattle was nearing the end of the second period and Vegas was down by one, two to three.

She was right. I wasn't the hockey pro like Gabby, primed to love the game from the time she could walk since Garrett started so young, but she had a point. Dominick Masters and Alix Halvrick both looked slow, unable to clear the puck from behind the net. Masters had already been in the sin bin for a total of five minutes, out early one time due to a goal. He looked pissed, shoving the other team into the boards with a fury that scared me and made me thankful Garrett was in the goalie box and on his team and not one of Dominick's victims.

Fortunately, he was coming home tonight, ending their week-long tour of Anaheim, San Francisco, and now Seattle. I missed him like crazy. We'd talked every day, sometimes more than once, but I hadn't yet filled him in on what I shared with my parents earlier in the week.

I wanted to tell him my decisions face to face, but I was already creating plans for how I would transfer clients to other members of my financial firm. Shawna could handle most of the back-end work, but before I gave my notice, I wanted my boss to know I had a plan to take care of everyone.

Leaving might not be as simple as that, there were companies I worked with who would want more time, who would be upset, and I planned to stay as long as possible for them to ensure smooth transitions. So far, I hadn't one single regret at my choice, but I was still antsy to talk to Garrett about it.

Watching the game on the television was almost better to me than watching it live. Live, the puck moved so fast, it was easy to lose it flying across the ice, but on TV, the game moved slower, where you had a better bird's-eye crew. Although I missed the noises, the slash of ice, the energy. But this way I got to watch Garrett save shot after shot, forty so far in the game, and well above average.

"Come on," I murmured, bouncing my feet on the floor next to Gabby. There were thirty seconds left in the period and the puck had been in front of Garrett for the last two minutes. Sticks were slapped, men shoved, forty seconds ago another fight broke out. "I didn't realize these teams were such rivals," I muttered.

"Seattle's new. From what I've heard, the teams are testing their mettle even though they were able to score several great players in the expansion draft. Miles Sutter, the center, was traded from Dallas. He's been in the league forever and is incredible."

She spoke without dragging her eyes off the screen.

"Seems to me it's Seattle testing Vegas's mettle tonight."

"They should. Vegas is leading the division right now

by three points without much time left in the regular season. Seattle wants to make the playoffs. It's no wonder why they're out for blood. It's only been done once before."

"Got it. Seems like you pay attention up there."

I was teasing her, but she slid her eyes in my direction and huffed. "Hard not to. It's all that's on the news. And the only good thing about Kurt was he played hockey as a kid. He got season tickets to Seattle's game this year so I was *close* to becoming a fan."

"And cheer against your brother?"

"Never." Her gaze slid back to said brother right as he slapped the puck away. "Come on, Vegas!"

She shouted so loud I jumped from my seat, watched as the timer ticked down. Ten seconds left and the center for Seattle whipped the puck across the ice. There were too many people in front of the goal, too crowded. Garrett couldn't get a clear view as Seattle and Vegas battled it out right in front of the crease and as the time reached three, Seattle grabbed the puck, made a wicked slap shot right at Garrett as the timer ran out, the buzzer hit zero, he stretched, flew out a leg, reached out, and the puck landed easily in his glove.

"Yes!" Gabby shouted.

A rush of breath left me and I collapsed back to the couch.

"He's so damn amazing," I said, reaching for my water. As I did, something wet and warm made me pause.

"Oh shit."

"What is it?" Gabby asked.

I looked down to my lap.

"I think I just peed my pants." I laughed and stood, shaking my head. "I heard it happened, but not this early."

"Maybe we should buy you stock in diapers." She giggled and took a sip of her water.

"I'll be back."

I headed toward the bathroom, still laughing at Gabby. I wasn't nearly far along enough to worry about needing adult diapers but I made a mental list to check into that. Did new moms wear them? Did massively pregnant women wear them? I knew my bladder would be overworked, and I'd feel the need to pee a hundred times a day, a common complaint I heard about in expecting mother groups online I'd been browsing.

In the bathroom, I pulled down my black leggings, relief hitting me as I gave my swollen stomach room and as I sat down, fear rushed through me.

That wasn't pee.

It was blood.

~

"You're okay. You're okay." Gabby patted my hand in the emergency room waiting room. As soon as I'd realized what was happening, I screamed for her. So much for joking about diapers. She ran to her room and grabbed me overnight pads she used during her period and a fresh pair of underwear from mine. Shaking like a leaf, and panicking, it was Gabby who helped get me resituated as I sat on the toilet, fear racing through me.

What do I do? What do I do?

I couldn't think. If I were in Chicago, I'd call my midwives. But I was states away, time zones and it was almost midnight there.

Gabby left me there at some point, and I heard her on the phone and as soon as she returned, she had my purse, my phone, and a pair of shoes. "Okay, Mom said to get to the hospital. She said to breathe. Bring some water. She said bleeding is totally normal. It doesn't mean anything's wrong."

I'd stared up at her with tear-soaked eyes. "What if there *is* something wrong?"

Miscarriages were common. But I was past the first trimester. My head spun and I barely remembered Gabby setting me in the Range Rover, driving us to the nearest hospital and as we got there, it was Gabby who signed us in, brought me forms to fill out, filled most of them out as I handed over insurance and ID, mumbling answers. It was Gabby who did everything, holding my hand. She asked me what midwife's clinics I'd visited and as I told her, she called them, left a message on their after-hours voice mail just in case she could help.

I did nothing except stare at the patterned navy and gold worn carpet in the waiting room, anticipating the worst-case scenario.

What would I do if I lost the baby? What would Garrett do? All the plans I'd made, all the excitement I had... what would happen now if they weren't necessary?

"Oh no," I groaned, and covered my mouth with my hand. I was going to throw up.

"Stay here," Gabby said, eyes wide as I leaned forward. I couldn't breathe. It stuck in my chest, in my throat, but every time I tried, my chest squeezed painfully against my ribs.

No room. There was no room.

In a flash, Gabby was back and there a kidney-shaped green plastic bucket in my lap.

"The front desk attendant said you can use this if you need to throw up." She wrapped her arm around my shoulders and tugged me close to her. "Breathe, Lizzie. In through your nose. Out through your mouth. Follow my count."

I shoved my face into her neck. "I'm so glad you're here."

"I know. And I'm staying. You'll be okay, but you have to breathe, okay? Right now, your only job is to think of the baby, he or she needs you calm, okay?"

As she spoke, she ran her hand gently across the top of my back, from shoulder to shoulder. I closed my eyes, focused on her words as she helped me breathe and once I could finally suck in a breath without my chest wanting to explode, I nodded.

"Thank you."

"You're welcome. Now, I need you to stay calm. We could be here for hours."

I flinched at that, but she was right. The emergency room was close to the Strip and there were a non-surprisingly large number of drunk people. Frat bros who looked like they were partying on spring break, a few with blood dripping from their temples with cut up knuckles. More glittery and sparkly tight and short dresses I'd ever seen, with drunken young females, mascara staining their cheeks. Two had their ankles propped up on chairs in front of them, an ice pack covering it. Then there were the typical elderly people, a few who appeared homeless.

"This really sucks." I dropped my head back, my hand falling to my abdomen.

I hadn't felt that warm sensation in my lap since we'd been here, but I was too scared to go to the bathroom to see if I was still bleeding. If I wasn't, I would still be worried. If I was, I'd panic.

Gabby was right. There was nothing I could do but wait, even though we'd already been here an hour and waiting longer to find out what was going on seemed like a nightmare.

"I'm scared," I whispered, my voice ragged.

She squeezed my hand. "I know. Do you want to call Garrett? He should know."

I shook my head. "I can't. I'll cry and worry him and he's so far away he can't do anything."

"No, but they're coming back tonight."

I knew that. Earlier, I'd been counting down the hours. I was supposed to leave in two days. Tomorrow was going to be a day where he and I could hang out and relax, where I could tell him what I was planning. He could spend time with his sister before his next home game and before he left town again, this time to Colorado.

"I can't." My throat clogged at the thought. What would I say? It was possible they could be in the air, or at least on the way to the airport and if he got that message from me while he was stuck in an airplane thirty thousand feet in the air, he'd have a heart attack.

"You call," I said. "I can't, but you're right. He should know." Risks be damned. It'd be worse if he returned home in four hours and we still weren't there. Or to hear the worst when it was over. A shiver of terror rolled down my spine, shooting out to my limbs at the thought.

What if I was losing our baby and he wasn't here?

He'd never get over the guilt of not being there for me.

"You sure?" she asked, but she was already typing in his name in her contacts.

"Yeah."

"Okay. I'm going to step outside. I'll be right back, though, okay?"

She looked at me like a wounded animal, ready to flee. I didn't blame her. Nothing made sense in my head. Not now.

I'd had everything I wanted in the palm of my hands and now...?

Now it could go *poof* without me being able to do anything to stop it.

I dropped my gaze back to my lap while Gabby walked away, closed my eyes, and while I wasn't the most religious person, I had been raised in a home where we went to church sporadically. I knew the basics and believed them to be true in an abstract sort of way. So for the first time since I had to for my confirmation classes, I closed my eyes and prayed.

My phone rang in my hand, startling me and I fumbled it, before recognizing the phone on the screen. "Hello?"

"Is this Lizzie Winston?"

"It is. Yes, thanks for calling." The caller was groggy, but I still recognized my midwife's voice.

"Hey sweetie. I hear you're having a little scare, huh?"

"Yeah." My throat threatened to close. "I'm bleeding."

"Okay. I know you're in Las Vegas visiting. Have you gone to the hospital?"

"Yeah. I'm here now waiting."

"Good. That's good. Do you have any pain anywhere else? In your stomach? Lower back?"

I didn't and told her so and then, because I was me, said, "Only from these plastic chairs I think."

Her soft laugh echoed. "Good. That's really good. You're thirteen-ish, close to fourteen weeks from looking at your chart. Have you had any spotting yet before this?"

"No. Nothing."

Silence as she typed something and the hairs on my arms stood on end. "There's not a whole lot I can tell you, obviously, but you're in the best place. Typically, this is simply nothing. There's no need to be worried although I know it's scary. It can be common for women to bleed, even for days like a regular menstrual cycle when pregnant, and everything right now is sensitive, swollen, and growing. There can be lots of reasons for the bleeding that don't mean anything is wrong, so I want you to remember that, okay? Right now, the most important thing for you is to stay calm. Watch your heart rate and stress."

"I will. Or try."

"Good. I'm going to let you go, so you can rest while you're in the waiting room because we both know that's easy. Now, can you tell me the name of the hospital you're at? That way I can give them a call first thing in the morning to see what they have to say and then I'll touch base with you after. When are you planning on flying home?"

"Sunday," I told her and gave her the name of the hospital.

"Okay. I want you to be prepared, sweetie. It might not be best for you to fly. Are you somewhere where you can stay a few days longer if necessary? And keep in mind, I'm only looking out for you, worst case... or bad case."

I'd stay here forever. The very idea of getting on a plane made me want to cling to the kidney-shaped puke bucket in my lap. "Yeah... yes, I can stay here."

"Good. That's good." Her voice lightened, still caring and soothing. This was why I loved the practice I found in Chicago. They weren't medicinal... they were compassionate. It was the same feeling I had when I talked to Serenity. The last thing I felt from the first obstetrician. "Okay," she said more cheerfully. "I'm going to let you go. Call me if you need anything. Anytime. We have actually a new mom getting ready to deliver, so I'll be up for hours. Sound good?"

"Yes. Thank you. I appreciate the call."

As I spoke it, Gabby appeared in front of me, phone in

her hand. Her brows pushed in when she saw me on the phone.

We hung up and as soon as I did, Gabby gave her phone a little shake. "Voice mail. I told him what was going on, but not to worry, I'm taking good care of you."

"Midwife," I said, doing the same to my own phone. "She said the same thing."

"Good." She faked a smile.

"Yep." I returned one of my own.

Absolutely nothing to be concerned about.

Right? *Please God. Make the words true.*

THE ROOM WAS STARK WHITE. We were secluded from other emergency room patients by blue curtains pulled shut that did nothing to mute the shouts from a gunshot victim or the whimpers from one of the women in the short glittery dresses with a broken ankle.

I tried hard to focus on the doctor, worn and weary at this late of an hour, and a man who didn't look that much older than me.

Another prayer was sent up. *God. Please don't let this be his first night in the ER.*

He rolled the fetal rate Doppler over my stomach. The gel was cold, but my skin was burning. It was taking him forever, and while he'd said similar condolences as my midwife did on the phone while a nurse drew blood and he came in and introduced myself, nothing would settle me until I picked up that telltale *whoosh whoosh whoosh* sound.

"There it is," he said, right as it happened.

"Oh my goodness," Gabby cried. She squeezed my hand

so tight I worried about broken fingers and as tears bloomed in my eyes, the same thing was doing in hers. "Is that her?"

"Her?" I asked, grinning at her.

"The baby. But it's a her. I can feel it."

She grinned at me. Tried to loosen the mood, but the worry lined her eyes. "But it's okay?" she asked the doctor.

"Everything sounds good." He handed me a handful of paper towels for my stomach and cleaned off the Doppler. "We're going to get an ultrasound machine in here to make sure and then wait for your blood tests. Could be awhile, though, okay?"

I nodded. "Sure."

His hand settled on my ankle and gave a gentle, comforting squeeze. "Things look good. This might be nothing but a blip, so stay hopeful, okay?"

"I've heard that phrase a lot today and I have to tell you, it's not really helping."

He rewarded me with a grin I'd call handsome and sincere, if I was in the right frame of mind. "I get that, too." His glance slid between the two of us. "I'll be back as soon as the nurses have the ultrasound tech and machine."

"Thanks, doc," Gabby said.

He nodded in response and left the curtained area. He was barely gone before I turned to her and waggled my eyebrows playfully. "He's cute."

She rolled her eyes. "Shut up."

"Well he is."

"I am not going to flirt with a doctor right now."

Stranger things had happened.

We sat, worried. My attempts at changing the subject fell flat quickly after. We were worried.

Scared.

And mostly, I needed Garrett.

27

GARRETT

We heard the heartbeat. Everything seems okay. But we're still at the hospital. Don't worry.

I stared at the text from my sister as soon as the plane landed. I got her first text after takeoff. Fuck.

Lizzie was in the hospital. Scared. Worried. And I wasn't there. My greatest nightmare. That I wouldn't be the dad I wanted to be. The partner I wanted to be. All because of my goddamn job.

It was so reminiscent of my own dad. Deployed. On training missions. My head spun and I almost cracked the armrest when Gabby's first voice mail came through right as the plane was backing from our departure gate.

"Hey Garrett, it's me. Listen, I don't want you to worry..." because nothing good ever started with that phrase. *"But Lizzie and I are at Desert Springs Hospital. She's... well, um... she's had some bleeding."*

And my heart stopped. Right then and there. My future flashed in front of my eyes and it wasn't pretty. In fact, it was downright ugly. If Lizzie lost the baby, would she stay? Still, I powered through. Forced myself to listen to the voice mail. We were headed home. I'd be there soon.

"She wants you here, but she's upset and worried, obviously. So, you know, when you get in, don't go home. Just come here. I'll update you as I know more, but please, don't worry. I've been on my phone. Every site says this can be normal, there might not be anything wrong. The baby might be okay. And shit... that's not helpful, so I'm sorry, but I'm upset too, but I don't want you to be. So just... you know... call when you land or get this or whatever. I'll tell you all I can. Love you, bro. To the stars and back, just like Dad."

She hiccupped and hung up, and that was the last thing I heard. *Just like Dad.*

I'd never been afraid to fly but I gripped the armrests and scowled out the window that entire almost three-hour flight like my livelihood depending on me not letting go.

The baby might be okay.

Might wasn't enough. Maybe was not the answer I needed and as much as I wanted to tell someone, anyone, there were few guys on the plane who had kids, fewer who were sitting close enough to me without making a spectacle of myself. If I opened my mouth now, I had no idea what would come out of my mouth.

Yeah, we had a great run on the coast. Yeah, I liked my new team.

But if Lizzie lost this baby and left for Chicago, never to return because of it?

Then I had nothing.

Shit.

I needed her to know how much I loved her. How much I wanted her, with or without a baby. Now. Or any time.

All I needed was her.

Thoughts raced through my mind the entire ride and I swore I didn't breathe until I saw that text from Gabby.

I hadn't even deplaned before the phone was to my ear.

"Tell me," I demanded. And I must have demanded it loudly because several heads swiveled in my direction.

"We're good, Garrett," Gabby said, her voice tired and tight. "Lizzie's sleeping though. But she's okay. They're keeping her here—"

"I'm on my way."

"Good. That's good. But everything has come back normal. She's good. I promise. It was so busy in the ER they moved us up to a room on the maternity floor. We're still waiting for an ultrasound tech."

"What's the room number?"

I needed these guys to move. Maybe if I knew them more, I would have told everyone, shoved my way off the plane because they wouldn't have cared, but for now, I kept my mouth shut.

"Four eighteen."

"I'll be there in thirty."

As soon as she told me what hospital they were at, I Google mapped it. I didn't even know where I was going. Where they were.

If I'd left her in Chicago, she'd be more comfortable. She'd have her parents. Friends.

"Fuck," I groaned, and scrubbed a hand through my hair.

"She's *safe* and sleeping, Garrett, but she wants you, so be safe, but get here."

"Damn I'm glad you came."

"Yeah." She huffed but it was cold, calculated and my sister was too full of life to be either of those. Something I'd think about in more detail later. "Such a great idea I had."

"Gabby—"

"Nope. Not me. Not now. I'm here until you get here and then I'll go back to your place. I need sleep and a shower and you probably do too, but..."

I didn't give two shits about sleep or a shower. Not until I saw Gabby. But even as I thought it, I was already loosening the tie at my throat and popping buttons. Dressing up for plane rides didn't bother me even if some of the guys changed clothes once we were boarded.

But now everything felt like it was choking me.

"Love you, G. See you soon."

"You too, sis."

"You okay?" It was Alix, the guy in front of me the entire flight. His noise canceling headphones draped over his neck, suit similar to mine.

"No." I couldn't even lie. Even while I hated myself for the truth.

"Yo!" Alix screamed, cupping his mouth with his hands. "Garrett has bad news. Needs to go. Let him off first."

"Really it's no..."

"You're family," he stated in a way that broke no argument. "Go. Need company? A friend?"

I was shaking my head, but it was Joey who stepped out in the aisle, and yeah—I needed that.

A Taylor. Might not be Jude, but Joey knew me enough.

"Let's go," he said, not knowing anything, just that I needed something. "I'm driving."

And thank fuck for that because I was sure if I'd had to drive, my Suburban would have ended up in the fountain outside Caesar's Palace.

"All right," I mumbled. "Thanks."

"You've been family as long as I've known you, and now you're a teammate. A brother. Might be now that I'm giving to you, but I'm pretty damn sure there'll be a time you give to me."

And fuck if all that wasn't the truth.

"Hospital," I choked out. "Lizzie's in the hospital. Bleeding."

"Fuck." He glanced behind me. "Max. Grab Garrett's shit off the plane. He and I are headed to the hospital."

"Which one?" someone called, and I thought it was Masters but there was no way he cared.

Joey glanced up at me.

"Desert Springs," I rasped out. This was too much. Yeah, the guys in Chicago would have done this, hell I would have done this for a new guy, but to be the recipient.

Well, fuck. That was something.

"Desert Springs. Off the Strip. We're headed there."

Murmurs followed us as Joey led me off the plane. "They'll be there, you know. One needs help. We all fall in."

"I know." I just hadn't expected my chest to hurt so much because of it.

But that might have been my fear.

Lizzie was hospitalized. Bleeding. I hadn't only not been there to help her through it, I wasn't sure she knew how much I needed her, how much I loved her—with or without our child.

Fuck.

It was Joey who guided me to the elevator, led me down the hall to the floor's receptionist. My heart leaped into my throat as I took in the words *Maternity*. They'd moved her to the maternity floor. When she could be losing our baby? What kind of sick, twisted cruelty was that?

"Come on," Joey said. His hand settled between my shoulder blades as we walked down the hall. I'd texted Gabby when we arrived and she was near the end of the hallway, pacing back and forth across the double door opening.

She stopped when she saw us and then ran toward me. I barely had time to catch her before she threw herself at me, arms around my shoulders. My arms wrapped her up as she sobbed into my chest. "You're here. Thank God you're here."

"What's wrong?"

"Nothing." She shook her head, swiped her tears against my shirt. They soaked through my dress shirt and she pulled back. "I told Lizzie I'd wait out here for you, but the ultrasound tech just got here. *Fucking* finally. It's been hours. But they keep checking the baby's heartbeat and it seems to be okay."

"Good. That's good."

I unpeeled her from my body where she still clung to me, fingers gripping my shirt, and handed her to Joey as gently as I could.

"I got her," he said, and wrapped his arm around her, bringing her to his side. "Go do what you need to do."

I took off, jogging the short distance to Lizzie's room, inhaled a deep breath to try to settle my racing heart and the fear burning my veins. I needed to be strong for her. For whatever we were about to find.

I opened the door and didn't give one shit about the woman to her right, the machine with a small screen on a tray. My focus was entirely zoomed in on Lizzie, a scratchy blue hospital gown over her. Her legs covered by a thin white blanket and her stomach exposed.

"You're here," she whispered, chin shaking and lips

pressed together. Her hand reached out for mine and I grabbed hold of her immediately.

She was freezing, her body shaking, and I could barely choke out a sound, much less speak.

"I'm here." It came out garbled, strained. "You okay?"

She nodded, but fear had drained the color from her face and darkened her eyes.

The tech moved closer, into my peripheral, but I didn't care she was there. I leaned down, pressed my forehead to Lizzie's and whispered in her ear. "I'm so damn sorry I wasn't here for you. So fucking sorry."

Her hand was at my neck, fingers in my hair. Nails dug into my flesh and I relished the pain. Deserved it.

"I'm not mad. And they say so far, everything's okay. Mostly. We're just waiting for the doctor to come back before we do the ultrasound."

"What do you mean, mostly?" I twisted, glaring at the tech.

"You'll have to ask the doctor."

"Garrett." Lizzie's hand slid to my cheek, turned me back to her. I was half bent over her bed, one hand bracing myself by her opposite shoulder. My arms shook with restraint and exhaustion. "I've heard the heartbeat, everything's good. My hormone levels are just higher than they should be, so they're being cautious."

"Hormone levels?" I should have done more reading on the plane. At home. I'd had a week to read the book I downloaded, but even in the parts I did read, I couldn't recall a mention of that. Or what it meant.

Movement caught my attention and I spun, expecting to see Gabby or Joey but instead it was a guy old enough to be Lizzie's grandpa, gray hair from what he had left, wearing scrubs and a stethoscope draped around his neck.

"Hi. You must be the father. I'm Dr. Drake." He held out his hand and I shook it, firmly.

"Garrett Dubiak."

"I know." He grinned and it vanished quickly. "Big hockey fan myself, played for Harvard. But that's not why we're here." He smiled warmly at Lizzie and then at his tech. "Since you're the main player tonight, let's get on with this, huh?"

Any other moment, I might have appreciated his small joke. Tonight I was too tense. Too scared. Too racked with anxiety to give him any more attention.

He glanced at me quickly while he tore a pair of gloves from a box on the counter. "Usually, I let the techs do their job and take a look at the digital pictures, but I have some time in between a couple moms about to deliver and I know you've had a long night, so I figured I'd sit in. Get you checked out, okay?"

Lizzie nodded.

"Thank you," I gritted out. I didn't know if the special treatment was because he knew me, or if he was truly that generous.

Didn't give a shit either.

He took a stand on one side of the monitor, gestured for the tech to go ahead and she turned to Lizzie, holding up a bottle of something. "This will be cold on your stomach, so take a deep breath. It warms quickly."

She got to work, plopped some clear goopy shit on Lizzie's stomach. She hissed, and I reached for her hand, hating that she'd be cold and miserable and scared and shit. I needed to get my act together. And quick.

As soon as it was done, the tech held a device in her hand. Looked a lot like how we heard the heartbeat the other day, but as she moved it, grainy, fuzzy images appeared on the screen.

"Holy shit," I said. There were black spaces, white lines and dots and a whirring noise that sounded like distant traffic on a busy road.

"There we are," the tech said, and on the screen, not only did I hear that louder sound of the heartbeat, there was another one, slower.

"What's that? The slow sound?"

"That's Lizzie's heart. The faster one is the baby," the doctor said, and he gestured to a tiny white blob that looked more like a miniature gummy bear. "And there's your baby..." He grinned at both of us as the tech continued wiggling the wand and then....

No fucking way.

Lizzie gasped at the same time I swore I saw something else... something else moving.

"There's the other one."

Lizzie's hand squeezed mine in a bone-crushing grip. "What?" she breathed, her jaw hitting her chest. "What'd you say?"

"Right here." The doctor pointed to a second gummy bear. "Baby B, we'll call this one. Baby A is to the right."

As he pointed them out, the tech started typing, so the words the doctor spoke appeared right above the tiny, blurry blobs.

"Sometimes, one baby can hide behind the other, making it harder to find another heartbeat. If you haven't had ultrasounds early on, this can happen."

"Twins?" Holy freaking shit. I'd thought I was seeing double. But there they were. Curled into large lima bean shapes, little limbs sticking out. And as he zoomed in, their faces came into the picture. Well, their skulls. Eye sockets.

Creepy little things, really, but so freaking beautiful. "You're kidding, right?"

We were just getting used to the idea of one. And...

I peeled my eyes off the screen and back to Lizzie.

"Twins." She smiled at me, color still gone from her face but her eyes back to their lustrous gleam. Although that could have been from the tears giving her eyes a sheen. "We're having twins."

"Fuck," I breathed out and she laughed, tugged on the hand she was holding until I almost fell on top of her.

"Twins. Two of them." I kissed her, slid my tongue into her mouth and didn't give a single fuck we had an audience until the doctor cleared his throat.

When I pulled back, the color returned to Lizzie's cheeks, flushed pink, and I grazed her cheekbone with my thumb. "I love you."

"Me too." She smiled, and it was so beautiful. Almost as beautiful as the family she was preparing to give me.

"So," the doctor said, "I assumed this was the case once we saw your hCG levels, hormones," he clarified, looking at me. "But we had to make sure. Based on everything we've seen initially, both babies look completely healthy, but I'll still take a look at the digital images as soon as I can." He focused on the tech. "You'll get those to me?"

"Yes, sir," she replied, and was still moving the wand, clicking still images and smiled at us. "Would you like some pictures printed?"

"Yes."

"Please," Lizzie said the same time I did. "So, the bleeding?"

The doctor shrugged. "Probably nothing. I'm told you're only spotting now, which is a great sign. It's possible you overdid it in the last day or two." He cleared his throat and continued. "Sex can sometimes cause it, too. Everything down there is swelling and sensitive and stretching at an alarming rate, especially now that we know there are two in there. I'm going to suggest, since it's late and since you don't have a local provider that we keep you here overnight to be on the safe side. And for the next week or two, I'd abstain from intercourse, give your body a chance to strengthen up that little cocoon you're building."

At both of our nods, an embarrassment little smirk on Lizzie's lips from the mention of sex, he continued. "When do you return to Chicago?"

"I was supposed to go back Sunday, but when I called my midwife earlier, she suggested I wait a few days."

"Excellent. I agree. Flying isn't a risk, but better safe than sorry. You left her name and number on your intake forms?"

"I did."

"Good. I'll give her a call first thing tomorrow, send her the ultrasound files so she has them so she can take a look as well. Anything else you need from me?" As he asked, his pager on his hip lit up. He pressed the button to silence it without losing focus on us. "Questions?"

"No." I shook my head. "I think we're good. Surprised and I might still faint, but I'm good. You?" I asked Lizzie.

She was laughing at my fainting comment, but I wasn't entirely joking. My knees were wobbly as the tech continued to click picture after picture. Babies.

Two freaking kids.

Heaven help me.

"I'm good," Lizzie said. "Thank you."

The doctor nodded, snapped off his gloves. "Good. Then try to get some rest. You need it now more than ever."

He left, the tech finished up and finally, Lizzie and I were alone. Our world rocked again but at least I hadn't missed this one.

I grabbed a chair and pulled it up so I could sit. With one hand still holding hers, I brushed hair off her forehead with my other. "How are you? This is... incredible."

"I'm great." She laughed, still cried. Happy tears, I brushed away with my thumb. "How are you? This is wild."

"It's the best thing that ever happened to me outside of meeting you."

"Twins," she breathed and picked up the string of four pictures the midwife printed out. "What in the hell are we going to do?"

We stared at the pictures, a thousand more images just as grainy flashed in my mind. Youth hockey games. Laughter. Messes. Bath times where water ended up all over the floor. Piggyback rides. Sleepless nights. Bottles and boxes of diapers. I saw my future clear as the pictures in Lizzie's hand and I leaned into her, brushed my lips over her cheek and whispered, "We're going to have one hell of a family. One hell of a damn good life."

28

GARRETT

Lizzie and I spent who knew how long staring at the photos. Laughing. Kissing. There were things I needed to say to her. Things I wanted to hear.

The last thing I wanted was for her to leave for Chicago. Even if she was gone for only a few weeks, I didn't want that. But she was exhausted, and the more we talked, the more her sentences were punctuated with yawns. It wasn't going to happen then. We had more time to talk once she slept.

"Go to sleep," I finally told her, when her eyelids were dropping. "I'm going to go find Gabby, see if she's still here."

"You'll be back?"

"Yes." I stood from the chair, crouched over her and slid my thumb over her eyebrows. The gesture soothed her, was something Mom used to do to Gabby and me when we were little kids to help us sleep. No idea why I thought of it then, but it worked and her lips tipped up at the corners. "I'll be here when you wake up. I promise."

"Good," she said, eyes closed, head turned toward me.

She was hanging on to awareness by a thread, so I

brushed my lips over hers, whispering, "Love you, Lizzie. See you soon."

"You too," she mumbled and turned away from me. It took seconds until her lips parted and her breaths came in a deep, even pattern.

I left the room, scrubbed my hands over my face. I had nothing with me. Which meant I'd be sleeping in my suit pants and dress shirt. The couch was built for a guy half my size. I'd be miserable, and I needed the rest after our game earlier but it'd be worth any misery I'd face.

Heading down the hall, I grabbed my phone from my pocket. I pulled up Gabby's number and texted her, only to see I'd missed several texts from her.

Shit. I'd been in Lizzie's room for an hour.

Gabby was freaking out. The last text she sent me told me she and Joey were still in the waiting room on the floor, so I headed that way, hurrying my steps.

They needed to get home, but there was no way Gabby would leave without knowing things were okay.

Twins. We were having twins. Everything wasn't just fine, it was better than I could have humanly expected it to be.

Shit. A grin stretched my lips and I stepped into the waiting room, only to immediately freeze when I saw it packed.

"Holy shit," I muttered, as every single eye in the room turned toward me.

Men stood. Women covered their mouths with a hand.

My team.

All of them. Every single damn man on that plane and some of their wives were here. Hell, even Dominick was there, in a corner, somehow still an island in a sea of people, but he was there, standing as everyone else did.

For me. No. For *us.*

"Holy fuck," I said. I crossed my arms. Shoved them to my hips. Dropped them to my sides before bringing them back to my hips. "I can't believe you're all here."

Joey stood first, Gabby next. "We're a team. Family. Where else would we be?"

Fuck. My head fell and I squeezed my eyes closed. I hadn't expected this. Or the rush of emotion to batter into my chest. Coaches. Teammates. I'd been there three months and was still getting to know them.

I shook my head and inhaled a deep, shaky breath to settle myself.

"Is everything all right?" Gabby asked. Her hand hit my arm, making me jump.

"Yeah." I cleared my throat, tried a smile to everyone else as I nodded. "Doctor says she's fine. It's..."

Twins.

I could barely believe it myself, much less say the word.

"So, what's going on?"

I grinned down at Gabby, who looked as exhausted as Lizzie had been.

I palmed the back of her head with my hand and shoved her against me. "Twins," I whispered and before she could truly understand, I stood in front of my team. My brothers. Guys who had sat here for an hour after a week-long road trip all because they wanted to be here for me, rumpled, exhausted, sore... but here.

"Lizzie and I are having twins. But everything looks good."

Whoas and *fucks* and *holy shit* and gasps from women and hollers from men broke out in a round robin cacophony of noise in the waiting room until men were slapping my shoulders. Joey was hugging me, slapping my back. Gabby was yanked into the women's arms telling her she was going to be an aunt to twins and everyone was so damn happy, I could have dropped to my knees and thanked God for looking out for us, for giving us this family who would be there every step of the way.

"That's amazing," Alix said, pulling me in for a quick handshake and hug.

"Thanks. And thanks for being there for me earlier."

He threw out an arm. "It's what we do. She is okay?"

"Yeah. She's good. Sleeping, but the doctor said everything should be fine. And the babies look good."

"That is great news."

It was. It was the best news.

SUNLIGHT PEEKED through the curtains the next time I opened my eyes. Not that it was much different than the last time I had them open. I barely slept. I switched from the chair to the couch and back to the chair to trying to sleep on the couch with my feet on the chair. Nothing was comfortable and every bone in my body screamed in painful agony, like it was my body that'd been slammed into the boards a half-dozen times the night before. Instead, I kept watching Lizzie. She slept peacefully, barely waking when nurses came in to check vitals and the babies' heart rates. Strong. Fast. Well over 150 beats per minute, which the nurse told me was perfect.

My babies were perfect.

I scrubbed a hand over my mouth and yawned and as I did, Lizzie's eyes fluttered opened as she faced me. "Hey," she said, and I blurted out the first word I'd been thinking all night while I couldn't sleep, while I imagined her leaving me even for a few weeks.

"Stay."

She blinked, and shit, I was an idiot. She'd just woken up, for Christ's sake. "What?"

I pulled the chair toward her bed and sat on it, bracing my elbows at the edge of her bed while I took one of her hands in both of mine.

"Stay. Don't leave. Not now. I couldn't handle it if something happened and I wasn't there for you."

Three quick blinks. A tightening of her hand in mine. A small, quiet laugh that cleared the sleep from her eyes and her other hand pressed to my cheek.

"I'm not going anywhere."

"No." She didn't understand. I didn't mean I didn't want her to leave *me*. "That's not what I meant. I mean, don't go back to Chicago."

Her sleep grin stretched wide. "I know what you meant. And I was going to tell you this when you came home, or today, which, I guess it is today, but what I'm trying to say is, I've already decided, Garrett. I'm not going back to Chicago. Not any time soon."

"You're not?"

"No. I have it all planned and plan on giving my boss notice on Monday."

Holy shit. She *did* understand. "You're staying here. With me."

"Yeah." She grinned again and I barked out a laugh. "Holy crap. I've been thinking all night long of how to convince you and you beat me to it."

"I'm here. With you. I love you. There's no need to go back just to return and I don't like the idea of traveling now anyway and yesterday I talked to my parents. They said they'd help with moving and packing and all that stuff."

Holy shit. She was doing it. She was truly leaving the life she'd always known behind for me. For us.

I barked out a laugh and then crouched over her. I kissed her senseless until her fingers dug into my hands and she pulled back. "I can't remember the last time I brushed my teeth."

Like I cared. I kissed her cheek. Lizzie turned her face away before I could reach her mouth again and chuckled, pressing her hand to my face and pushing me back.

But no way was I leaving her. Not ever. After seven years of friendship and sometimes extra benefits and a handful of miscommunications and fights along the way—I finally *had* her... all of her.

"Marry me," I said, and it wasn't exactly a question. Her eyes widened and I repeated it. "Marry me, Lizzie. I'll get you a ring later but say yes now anyway. I want you having my name and us being a family before our babies get here. Please... marry me."

She laughed. She might have called me a dumb oaf, but I was waiting for her answer, so I said nothing.

"Lizzie..."

"Oh I didn't realize that required a response."

"Marry me." We'd fumbled along the way, missed a few shots at the goal, but there was no hesitation. No point in waiting another minute to start my forever. Marrying Lizzie and having babies with her would be the greatest win of my career.

"Name the day, Dubiak, and I'm yours."

Today worked for me.

EPILOGUE
LIZZIE

"Ready?"

I took one last look at my dress. Off-the-shoulder cap sleeves, with a sweetheart bodice and an empire waistband that barely hid my growing belly beneath. It wasn't the wedding dress of my dreams, but my marriage would be, so the dress was perfect anyway.

I smiled at my mom, holding my bouquet of white roses sprinkled with purple forget-me-nots, the closest I could find to something blue... both for good luck and to symbolize the boys I was carrying.

Yes. Boys. Two of them.

Fortunately, I had months to get used to the idea of raising twin boys—moments to prepare to become Garrett's wife.

Not that I needed the time.

"I'm ready."

"You're stunning," she said, walking into the simple back room at the Botanical Garden. I'd been fortunate to snag an opening on a Tuesday night for our wedding ceremony.

Sure, not the ideal day of the week to get married, but I'd wanted it this day.

Tomorrow, Vegas would head to the Stanley Cup Finals last round of playoffs against Boston and I wanted to join Garrett at the games with his name on my back, our new name on our marriage certificate, and his wedding band on my finger.

Plus, all our family was in town for the playoffs. Jude, Katie, their daughter along with the rest of the Taylor clan made the trip. Jude wanted to watch Boston get their asses beat by Garrett's team, Katie wanted to be with me when the team headed to Boston for games three and four and after if necessary.

So, everyone I loved was here. Had planned it. I didn't see the point in scheduling our wedding in the off-season.

We'd take a honeymoon then at some point, although that depended on my ability to travel and if I could still fit into an airplane seat.

Based on the size of my stomach these days, I was leaning toward a short road trip to San Diego.

"Thank you. Kelsey did an incredible job on my hair and makeup." She was the daughter of Garrett's goaltending coach and had insisted on doing my look. My hair was elegantly knotted at the top of my neck, a veil tucked into it with matching forget-me-not flowers and miniature roses. My makeup was dewy. Hopefully semi-permanent because my emotions were a roller coaster lately.

"That dress is gorgeous on you too," I told her.

It was gold, with similar cap sleeves as I was wearing but my mom's dress fit her like a glove, showing off her incredible figure even edging close to sixty. Her hair was done similar to mine as well.

"This old thing?" She swung in a circle, laughing. "I had it in my closet."

Liar. I'd let her. Mom knew how to lighten the mood even while we both fought tears.

"Let's do this," I said and took the flowers from my mom. Our small family crowd was already seated in rows of white chairs our wedding planner had handled. Because we were getting married in the center of beautiful, tropical gardens, there were very few other flowers or decorations. Sure, we could afford an expensive affair, but it wasn't either of our personalities.

We were basic, and simply ready to be husband and wife. After all, we'd waited long enough for this.

My mom walked me through the halls, empty but for the string quartet music filtering from the ceremony area beyond rows and hedges of sculptures and flowers and trees. As we reached where I'd walk down the aisle, my mom stopped me. I gasped, seeing my dad in a gray suit, white shirt, black tie— the same outfit I knew I'd see Garrett in any minute, but dang. My dad was a handsome man and wore it well.

"My girls," he said, coming to us with arms open and tears swelling.

Maybe hormones weren't to blame for all the tears I came by so easily lately. Happy tears were in my family's DNA.

"Ready honey?"

I settled one hand on my stomach, grinned up at him, and slid my arm through his. "You bet I am."

He kissed my temple, opened the door and as we stepped through, I only had eyes for Garrett.

Standing proud and tall at the altar, grinning at me like I was his world.

Which was a good thing—since he was mine.

It'd taken us years to get here, many ups and downs, but I'd never been so ready. With my arm slipped into my dad's hold, I took my first step toward Garrett, the rest of my life, the rest of my forever, and I couldn't wait to get started.

THANK YOU for reading Game Changer! Want more Las Vegas Vipers? Dream Maker, Joey Taylor's story, is releasing in March, but you can Pre-Order TODAY! Click here: https://amzn.to/3IAGR1j

Never miss a release and be the first to know about upcoming books and sales! Subscribe to my newsletter here: https://bit.ly/3nC4exd

ABOUT THE AUTHOR

Stacey Lynn likes her coffee with a dash of sugar, her heroes with a side of bossy, and her wine a deep shade of red.

The author of over thirty romance novels, many of which have been best-selling titles on Amazon, AppleBooks, and Barnes & Noble, she loves being able to turn her vivid imagination into a career that brings entertainment and joy to her readers. Focused on sports romance and emotional, small-town romance, she also loves stretching herself in different genres.

Born in Texas and raised in the Midwest, she now makes her home in North Carolina and loves all things Southern. Together with her ultimate tall, dark, and handsome hero, she has four children. Her life is a chaotic mess that fights with her Type-A, list-making, neurotically organized preferences and she wouldn't have it any other way.

Subscribe to her newsletter so you can stay up to date on all her new releases. www.staceylynnbooks.com

OTHER BOOKS BY STACEY LYNN

Las Vegas Vipers ~hockey romance

Game Changer

Dream Maker – March 2022

Ice Kings Series ~hockey romance

Playing With Fire

Playing To Win

Scoring Off The Ice

Hooked One Her

Hard Checked

Fighting Dirty

The Rough Riders Series ~football romance

Dirty Player

Filthy Player

Wicked Player

Cocky Player

Love and Lies Duet ~angsty slow burn, romance

All the Ugly Things

All the Beautiful Things

Love and Honor Duet ~angsty, romantic suspense

Twisted Hearts

Unraveled Love

Love In The Heartland ~small town romance

Captivated By You

This Time Around

Long Road Home

Before We Fell

Crazy Love Series ~West Coast romance

Fake Wife

Knocked Up

28 Dates

Weekend Fling

The Fireside Series ~small town romance

His to Love

His to Protect

His to Cherish

His to Seduce

Tangled Love Series ~erotic romance

Entice

Embrace

Enflame

The Luminous Series ~BDSM romance

Dominate Me

Crave Me

Long For Me

Just One Series ~rockstar romance

Just One Song

Just One Week

Just One Regret

Just One Moment

The Nordic Lords Series ~MC romance

Point of Return

Point of Redemption

Point of Freedom

Point of Surrender

Standalones

Remembering Us – Available in Kindle Unlimited

Don't Lie To Me – billionaire romance

Try Me – A Don't Lie To Me Novella